Mina's Joint

D1468626

Keisha Ervin

Compilation and Introduction copyright © 2004 by
Triple Crown Publications
2959 Stelzer Rd., Suite C
Columbus, Ohio 43219
www.TripleCrownPublications.com

Library of Congress Control Number: 2005936179
ISBN: 0-9767894-5-0
Cover Design/Graphics: www.MarionDesigns.com
Author: Keisha Ervin
Associate Editor: Maxine Thompson
Typesetting: Holscher Type and Design
Editor-in-Chief: Mia McPherson
Consulting: Vickie M. Stringer

Printed in the United States of America

Dedication

To all the people who believe in love like I do,
I dedicate this book to you.

Acknowledgements

Dear Lord,

What a year and a half this has been! Friends have come and gone, people have talked behind my back and smiled in my face, relationships have failed, family has been regained and through it all you were there. Lord you have blessed me with far more than I could have ever envisioned for myself. Sometimes I wake up and wonder is this really my life. Yes sometimes I have moments of sadness, loneliness, and defeat but when these feelings occur, I think of you. Your love, strength, and guidance has continued to pull me through. No matter what I do in this life, I know that with you by my side I can do anything.

Dear Kyrese aka Sexual Chocolate,

Hey Momma's baby! I know that I've said this before but Kyrese you are truly the love of my life. I pray that you grow up to be the beautiful, intelligent, funny, confident man that I

v

see in you and when you grow up I hope that you know that all of this was done for you!!!

Dear Momma aka Ms.Pat,
We argue, aggravate, love, and support one another. You have stuck by my side through thick and thin. I don't know what I'd do with out you. And even though I don't say it much anymore, know that I do LOVE YOU!!!

Dear Dad,
What's up Daddy? Thank you for being so hard on me and for encouraging me to do my best. I love you.

Dear Keon aka Poe Boy,
Hey big brother! Keon I love you more then you will ever know. I pray that one day you and I can become closer then what we are.

Dear Poe, Ervin, and Blackshear family,
Thank you all for your constant love and support of me and my work!!!

Dear Miesha,
What would I do without you? I pray that I never know. You are the greatest hair stylist in St. Louis and an even greater sister. Thank you so much for taking care of Kyrese when I have book signings or either when I just want to go out. What can I say…you're simply the best!!!!

Dear Alocia aka LOL,
Can you believe that we have been friend for fourteen years! Damn time flies! It seem like we were just in fourth grade on the play ground making up dances. Alocia you have

so much potential and soon you'll find your niche in this world. You are one of m closest friends and I pray that we can have fourteen more years of friendship and laughter.

Dear Monique aka Merleen,
You are one of the brightest, intelligent, funniest women I know. For a while there our friendship was lost but God brings people in and out of your life for a reason. You have gone beyond the call of duty as a friend to me. Trust when I say that you are making your mother proud!

Dear TuShonda aka T Weezie,
We've dust the dirt off our shoulders, shut up all the haters, and laughed the whole way through. Over the past year and half TuShonda you have become the big sister I never had. Your writing inspires me to step my game up and your heart makes me want to be a better person.

Dear Janea aka Granny Panties,
Girl we weathered the storm together during our days at Shop N Save and came out victorious! Janea you have beat the odds and the example you're setting for your girls is inspirational. Keep on doing the damn thing ma!!!

Dear Vickie,
Can you believe that we are on out third book together? It seems like it was yesterday when I got signed. Thanks for pushing me so hard on the Chyna Black project because that extra little umph really helped the book to be what it is today. Thank You!!!

Dear TCP Family,
Thank you all for working so hard on my novels and for

getting my work to the masses. Know that all of your hard work doesn't go unnoticed. Thank you so much from the bottom of my heart.

Dear Girlfriendz Book Club,

I never knew that I would meet a group of ladies that were smart, beautiful, funny, and kind. Anica, Sherry, Dallas, Neisha, Nikki, Tam, Corless, Mona, and Angie you all have supported me and my work to the fullest and the only thing I can say is thank you!!!

Special Shout Out To:

Cynthia Parker(my editor), Danielle (my friend),Kevin Ervin, Barbara Whitaker Tammy, Mia, Ms. Marie, Kelly, Miss Danielle. Cassandra Spencer, K'Wan, Tracy, T.N, Brenda Hampton, Bonnie, Stacy, Marcus, Debra, Anthony Talton, the other Sherry, Micaela Pascal, Kim warlock, Sylvia, Ashley Stuckey, Ms. Monalisa, Millie 28, and Reydee!!!

To All the Readers,

Without you all supporting and believing in my work I wouldn't be here! I love you all so much. I pray that I can continue to give you all stories that you want to read. Hit me up at keisha_ervin2002@yahoo.com for any questions or comments.

Sincerely,
Keisha R. Ervin aka Fat Momma

P.S: To all the haters out there I have only one thing to say
Shut Up Bitch!!!

Mina's Joint

Chapter One

CD Select

I wish he could see me sitting here. I wish he knew the pain behind my smile. I try so hard not to cry but each day becomes harder. This thing is coming to an end no matter how hard I try to fight it. Somehow I knew this day would come. I only wish that, for once, I was wrong. Why can't he be the man that I deserve? Mina mused, thinking of her feelings for her fiancé, Andrew. Crossing her right leg over her left, she brushed her hand through her shoulder-length hair and sighed.

Delicious, a stylist, wiggled his fingers in front of her face. "Earth to Mina!"

"What, Delicious, damn?!" Aggravated that he'd stopped her ruminations, Mina snapped. She didn't mean to snap at him, but she couldn't help it. Heavy feelings had been weighing on her chest for months and she had a serious decision to make.

"Fall back, lil' Momma; did we get the new supply of Motions in today?"

1

"*Motions*?" Mina looked confused.

"Hellooo. What's got your thong in a bunch today?" Delicious scrunched up his face and went into the storage room.

Absently, Mina shook her head. "I have to go to another boring-ass political party with Andrew tonight."

"Girl, you better get wit' it. A man like Andrew only comes around once. Please believe me." Delicious snapped his fingers in a sweeping arc.

"You got to be kidding me." Mina waved her hand in dismissal.

"Excuse me, Mina." Jodie the receptionist interrupted their conversation. "Tiffany just called. She said she won't be in today."

"Great. That's just great. What else is going to happen today?" Defeated, Mina threw her hands up in the air. "It's Friday − one of our busiest days! How she gon' call off today, of all days!"

"I swear that girl call off more than I bend over," Delicious said, coming out the back.

"I rebuke you Satan in the name of Jesus," Jodie, a devoted Christian, prayed while making an imaginary cross across her chest.

"Eww, you are so nasty." Mo, Mina's best friend, rolled her eyes as she got her nails done.

"You know her and Antonio are having problems," Mina reasoned.

"You're running a business, sweetie! I'm having problems with my man, too, but you doing the damn thing! You're about to marry the mayor's son. You need to fire her ass." Delicious twisted up his lip. Opening a container of Vaseline he began to base one of his clients' heads for a perm.

"Nigga you was trippin' too when you were going through

your changes with Dominic," Neosha, a nail technician, point-ed out as she buffed Mo's nails.

Holding a pair of scissors straight up in the air, with his other hand on his hip, Delicious looked over at Neosha and said, "Are you trying to get cut with these scissors today?"

"I'm just saying…" Neosha flashed a broad grin.

"I thought we were girls, Nee. I thought we were better than that. You know that man broke my heart." Delicious put down the scissors, balled up his fists, rubbed his eyes, and pre-tended to cry.

"Yeah, right. Your dramatic ass just needed an excuse to go to Mexico for a week." Janiya, another stylist, joined in and laughed.

"Mina, she lying. I wasn't in Mexico, I was laying at home sick with the flu." Delicious licked his right index finger and held it up to God in mock seriousness.

"Delicious, quit lying cuz I already know." Mina couldn't help but smile at Delicious' antics.

"Well, I guess the gig is up." Delicious stuck his tongue out at Neosha, then threw back his head and let out a deep belly laugh.

"Tasha, sweetie I'm ready," Janiya called out to one of her clients, who was sitting in the front of the shop.

"I feel so sorry for that lil' girl." Delicious shook his head as the young girl walked to the back of the shop.

All eyes fell on Tasha as she walked to Janiya's station from the front waiting room. Tasha looked to be about thirteen years old. Every Saturday at eleven, her mother, Patrice, would drop her off to get her hair done and by the way she pouted, she hated it. Tasha would rather be out on the bas-ketball court shooting hoops with the fellas, not in a hair salon getting her hair done every weekend.

"Why you say that?" Mina whispered.

Delicious put his hand over his mouth and spoke in a conspiratorial tone. "You can't tell? That child is an O.B.D."

"Don't you mean O.D.B, like Old Dirty Bastard?"

"No, honey, I mean O.B.D.—Obvious Baby Dyke," he whispered back.

"Delicious, now you know that ain't right. Don't be talking about that lil' girl." Mina tried her hardest not to laugh.

"You know I'm right, girl," Delicious teased. "Look at her. That girl's pants sagging lower then Nelly's on the MTV Music Awards."

"You going to hell for that," Neosha cracked up laughing.

This was a typical afternoon at the salon for Mina Matthews. Clients were everywhere. The sound of dryers humming and the scent of Sebastian hairspray filled the room. Mina's Joint Salon and Spa was one of the hottest salons in the St. Louis area. The pink and white exterior and interior stood out amongst all the other salons. Mina's salon was designed with a touch of elegance and sophistication.

With four rooms built for styling hair, facials/massages, storage and Mina's office, everyone had enough room to do their own thing and not be crowded. With the day beginning to wind down Mina prepared to leave the shop for yet another boring political soiree with her fiancé, Andrew. Andrew's father, Mayor Andrew Wellington, was nearing the end of his four-year term as Mayor of St. Louis, Missouri. Mayor Wellington was now in the running for Governor against Carol Leverly. The two had been campaigning furiously for months and Mina and Andrew were required to attend every social event given.

Mina dreaded going to the stuffy political events because she always felt out of place. She was a girl that grew up in Pagedale, one of the grimiest sections of St. Louis. She wasn't born with a silver spoon in her mouth like her fiancé. Mina grew up in the hood amongst killers and thieves. She never dreamt that one day she would be engaged to a fine, wealthy socialite like Andrew.

The two dated for six months, became a couple for another six and after a year of being together, they were engaged. At first, everything was great between them. Mina was dazzled by the glitz and glamour of being engaged to the Mayor's son, but after awhile, the excitement of it all died quickly. Being around stuck up socialites who discussed nothing but politics and wealth bored Mina to death.

Since Mayor Wellington was running for Governor, any bad publicity could be damaging to his career. Andrew forbade Mina to visit Pagedale or any other crime ridden section of St. Louis. The only time she was allowed to visit was to see her family. Mina missed the sounds of bass booming from old school Cutlasses and new school Escalades. She missed sitting on the porch gossiping with the girls. Mina was only twenty-six years old. She deserved to have a life but all of the publicity and attention she got from the media made up for that.

In the beginning, Andrew loved Mina's outspokenness and ghetto fabulousness, but that quickly turned into her just being loud and ghetto. Mina knew deep down in her soul that she was not in love with Andrew but she felt obligated to him because he provided her with a better life. A better life that included the start-up money for Mina's Joint. To Mina's surprise, after only being in business for a couple of months, she and Andrew were in the process of opening their second salon.

"Ya'll crazy, but I gotta get out of here so I can go home and get dressed. Make sure the shop is clean and that ya'll lock up," Mina said, heading out.

"A'ight," Neosha replied.

* * *

Standing in front of a full-length mirror, Mina did a quick

survey of her physique. The fitted, one strap, black Stella McCartney dress that hit her right above the knee was a sure show stopper. Large wavy curls flowed over her shoulders and framed her round face perfectly. Delicious had outdone himself. Mina looked like a 1950s sexpot. The silver strapped Swarovski encrusted Jimmy Choo shoes made her legs look full and firm. Hearing the doorbell, she grabbed her Ferragamo purse and headed for the door.

"Hey, baby."

"Hey, there, sweetie." Andrew slowly eyed her from head to toe.

"You like?" she asked, her hand on her hip, posing.

"Um, honey. I don't mean to be rude but this is a cocktail party not a night at the club with Mo."

"What's wrong with my dress? You said to wear a nice black dress, this is a nice black cocktail dress, so what's the problem?"

"Turn around."

Doing a perfect spin, she gave him a good view of her frame. Andrew stopped her once she got to her backside. In a cold voice, he said, "See, look at your butt. It's sticking all out and that dress is entirely too tight around your hips. You have to learn to conduct yourself in the right manner, sweetheart. You know that in the next four years I will be running for mayor so you have to make a good impression at all times."

"Whatever," she quipped with an attitude.

"Watch your, mouth Mina. You know I don't like when you talk to me like that." Seeing the disappointment on her face, Andrew stroked her cheek. "Look. Don't be mad, sweetheart." He kissed her forehead.

"I'm not." Mina eased up and gave him a light kiss on the lips.

"Okay, then let's go. The driver is waiting for us. But, oh

I'm going to let this mishap slide this one time. If it happens again, I won't be so nice." Andrew's tone was serious, then he walked away.

Mina was used to Andrew making smart, threatening remarks to her, but the shit was starting to get old. Staring at his back she tried to shoot daggers with her eyes. Mina wondered if she could live the rest of her life with Andrew. As soon as they walked through the doors of the Wellingtons' mansion, Mina felt uptight. The Victorian style furnishing, crème walls and Da Vinci paintings gave the home a dull, boring appeal.Taking her by the hand, Andrew led Mina over to his mother, Pearl Wellington.

"Hello, there, Mother."

"Hi, sweetheart. You look handsome," she said. As usual she had a drink in her hand.

"Thank you, Mother."

"Mina," Mrs. Wellington spoke flatly.

"Hello, Mrs. Wellington," Mina replied back dryly.

It was common knowledge that there was no love lost between the two. The only reason they hadn't clawed each other's eyes out was their mutual respect for Andrew. Everything about Mrs. Wellington, the former Miss Black Universe, from her beauty queen hair, to her plastered on makeup, to her tailored-made suits made Mina sick. The Wellingtons, especially Mrs. Wellington, wanted her to be something that she just was not, which was fake.

"Well, don't you look festive," she replied with a sarcastic tone.

"I know, don't I?" Mina shot back with a roll of the eye.

"Now, now, ladies. Withdraw your claws, there will be no fighting tonight."

"I was only stating that Mina's dress is very provocative for it to be a plus size dress."

"Look a here, old lady," Mina began.

"Mina dear, come on, we have to go mingle," Andrew interrupted, pulling her away from his mother. "You didn't have to argue with her, Mina. Learn some self restraint," he snarled.

"That old bitty started it, Andrew."

"You know how she is."

"I don't give a fuck! She is not about to talk to down to me."

"I'm not about to argue with you. People are beginning to stare. I see my father over there standing with Congressman Davis. I need to go and talk to him, you stay here."

Hurt and embarrassed, Mina stood by herself in the corner, nursing a drink, thinking of the day she met Andrew. The day couldn't be any clearer in her mind. It was a cold November afternoon and she was getting off of work.

"Beverly, I got to get out of here before I miss my bus," Mina said to her manager as she grabbed her purse and book bag.

"I thought I asked you to stay an extra hour."

"You did and I thought I told you no. I do have a life outside of the mailroom."

"But we need you, Mina," Beverly said sternly.

"I don't know what to tell you," Mina replied as she ran to catch the elevator. Checking her watch, she hoped that she could it make out of Graybar in time to catch the bus. Her job in the mailroom was in Clayton and if Mina missed her bus she would have to wait another thirty minutes before the next one came. Seeing the bus nearing the bus stop she cursed Beverly for making her late. Racing down the street, she stopped at the end of the block. The light was green but Mina didn't care. She had to catch that bus.

Running across the street, she opted not to look both ways,

which nearly cost her her life. Hearing a car coming toward her come to a screeching halt, Mina looked at the car which was barely two inches away from running her over. Looking into the driver's eyes, Mina thanked God that she hadn't been run over. Staring back into her eyes, Andrew saw the most beautiful creature God had ever made. Andrew leaped out of his brand new Jaguar, then hurried over to a shaken Mina.

"Are you okay, ma'am?" he asked, sincerely worried.

"Yeah, yeah, I'm just a little shaken up." Mina held her chest as it heaved up and down.

"You really should look both ways when you cross the street."

"I know, I'm sorry." She shook her head, trying to regain her composure. *Beep! Beep!* The car behind Andrew blew. "I'm sorry but I have to go. Are you sure you're all right?" he said as he scurried to get back into his car.

"Yeah, I'm okay," she answered as she watched her bus ride by. "Stop! Wait, come back!" She hollered out as she waved her hands in the air to signal the bus driver but to no avail.

"Damn! Fuck! What am I going to do now?" She stomped her feet. *Beep! Beep! Beep!* The car behind Andrew blew again.

"Come on, asshole! Move your car you're holding up traffic!" the guy yelled.

"Miss, do you need a ride?" Andrew asked.

"Thank you, but I don't know you."

"You can get to know me. Come on, hop in before I have to kill this guy," Andrew pointed. With no time to contemplate an answer, Mina walked around the car and got in.

"I do have a can of mace if you try any slick shit," she warned.

"Trust me, you won't need it." He smiled.

9

Before she knew it an hour had dragged by and Andrew still hadn't returned to her side. Searching through the crowd of people she looked for him. Fed up, she decided that she was ready to go home. Reaching the spiral stairway, she prepared to go up when she was stopped by Mayor Wellington.

"Mina, darling, you look wonderful," he said, eyeing her hungrily.

"Thank you, Mayor Wellington," she replied, uncomfortably staring at the fifty-two-year old, caramel-skinned, two hundred pound, salt and pepper-haired man.

"Call me Dad. After all, we are going to be family, right?"

"Yeah, we are."

"It's yes, we are. Not yeah, we are."

"Ah huh," She smiled half-heartedly.

"Where were you headed?" he asked, rubbing her hand with a lustful hint in his eye. Feeling sick to her stomach, Mina eased her hand away.

"I'm looking for Andrew. We seemed to have lost each other."

"The last time I saw him he was talking to Christi and Congressman Davis. I think I saw them heading upstairs together."

Mina had no idea that Christi was there, too. Christi Orten was a very close friend to the Wellington family. She and Andrew had grown up together and even dated a while in high school. Christi was the daughter of Donald Orten, the factory king. The Ortens came from a long line of money and stature.Christi was everything that Andrew needed in a wife. She was wealthy, blonde, blue-eyed and an heiress. It made no sense to Mina why he didn't choose Christi. Playing it cool on the outside, Mina asked, "How's the campaign going?"

"Even though we're in the early stages, it's looking quite well for me. Carol Leverly doesn't stand a chance," Mayor

Wellington boasted. "You know that the wedding is fast approaching. We're going to have to get our families together before the rehearsal dinner. How about you bring your mother and that grandmother of yours over for tea one day this week?"

"That would be nice," Mina lied.

She knew good and well that her family and Andrew's family would not get along. Her family was from the heart of the city and spoke whatever was on their minds, especially her mother, Rita, but Nana Marie was the core of the Matthews circle. She treated Mina as if she were her own, and Mina loved her dearly.

"Well, if you'll excuse me I'm going to get my fiancé."

"Nice talking to you, Mina." The Mayor flashed her a sinister smile. Even though Mina kept her poker face on, she could tell he knew she was pissed. If everything went accordingly, Mina would be out the picture and Christi would be painted back in, in no time.

I'm gonna kill that muthafucker, Mina hissed under her breath. It would be a relief if she did find Andrew cheating on her with Christi, but the thought of him trying to play her had her at the boiling point. Taking the steps two at a time, she checked every bedroom only to find them all empty. Just as she was about to give up, she heard muffled noises coming from a near by bathroom. Knocking on the door she yelled, "Andrew, is that you?"

"Yes, sweetheart. It's me," he stuttered, unlocking the door and peeping his head out.

"Where have you been? I have been looking all over for you."

"I've been uh…discussing business with Congressman Davis," Andrew said as he opened the door a little farther. Shocked, she saw the young blonde Congressman seated on the toilet behind Andrew.

"Mina, darling, it's wonderful to see you again," he said, easing up, visibly flustered.

"Hello, Congressman. What are you two doing in the bathroom together?"

"We were discussing business. Nothing you would want to worry your pretty lil' head with," Andrew assured her.

"Mina, I thought you wouldn't be here tonight," she heard a female voice say from behind. Turning around, she came face to face Christi Orten.

"Why wouldn't I be here?"

"I know how these functions make you a little uncomfortable seeing as though you weren't raised like me and Andrew."

"What did you say?" Mina said with a roll of the neck.

"Don't take offense. You've come a long way."

"Are you trying to get knocked out?!"

"If you'll excuse me, Andrew, I will talk to you later," Congressman Davis said as he left the bathroom.

"And what was that shit about?" Mina turned, focusing her attention back to Andrew.

"I told you we were just talking."

"Mina, have some faith in your man," Christi added.

"Okay, who was talking to you, White Chocolate?"

"And this is who you want to be your wife?" Christi shot as she turned and walked away.

"Oh, no. That bitch didn't," Mina said, ready to attack but before she could Andrew pulled her back into the bathroom and locked the door.

"What the fuck is going on, Andrew?!"

"I love it when you're feisty," he growled as he began rubbing her thighs.

"What? Andrew, I'm not playing with you! What the fuck

were you doing in here with a man?"

"Sweetheart, calm down. We only came in here to discuss business."

"What kind of business?"

"You know that his father is one of our biggest campaign contributors."

"Okay and?"

"It really doesn't matter what we were discussing. You're just overwhelmed with the wedding and all dear," he said, nibbling on her ear.

"I am a little overwhelmed."

Andrew was a good-looking, brown-skinned, thirty-one year old brotha. He was six feet tall and had an athletic build. He kept his hair cut in a close fade and the one dimple in his right cheek made her heart melt every time.

"You are so freaking sexy," he growled.

Hungrily kissing her neck, he raised her dress up over her hips. When he found that she had no panties on, he smiled. With a grunt of surrender, he grasped both of her legs and eased her on the cool countertop.

"Andrew, somebody might hear us."

"I don't care who hears us," he said, sliding a condom on.

Gliding his way inside of her, Andrew grabbed a handful of Mina's ass and pumped away.

"Ughh, Mina, you feel so good," he grunted.

As she stared up at the ceiling, Mina wished that Andrew would hurry up. She didn't understand how his little bitty dick-ass thought that he was putting it down. To help stroke his ego some, she threw out an occasional "ooh," and "ahh," to make him feel good. Mina missed having a big dick nigga up inside of her rocking her world. Three minutes later, Andrew pulled off the condom and came on her thigh. Every time he did this, Mina felt degraded, but she never spoke up for herself. Andrew was going to be her husband and he was the owner of Mina's Joint. To Mina, she had no choice but to put up with Andrew and his egotistical ways.

Chapter Two

Play

The next day at the salon, Mina sat chatting with her staff.

"Mina, honey, your hair is still slamming," Delicious remarked, looking in the mirror. Delicious was a tall, dark, handsome man with platinum blonde waves and gray contacts. Today he wore a pink tube top, low-rise jeans, and heels. As usual, Delicious thought he was the shit.

"Thank you, Delicious. I even got a couple of new clients for you Saturday night."

"See, that's what I'm talkin' about! Even when my girl is partying, she is still networking."

"Hey, I gotta make sure that my peoples are straight or else I won't eat." Mina sat in a salon chair picking at her fingernail and tapping her foot.

"So how was the cocktail party at the Wellingtons'?" Tiffany, a massage therapist, asked.

"Boring, as usual."

"I don't understand you Miss Mina. I wish I had a man as

fine as Andrew. Honey he could slap it up, rip it and turn me around anytime," Delicious declared.

"You better watch him, girl. Delicious gon' steal yo' man," Janiya teased.

"Shit, I wish Andrew did swing that way. Maybe it would be easier for me to drop his tired ass."

"Girl, you are crazy." Delicious laughed.

"Hey, everybody!" Mo spoke, coming into the shop.

Speaking back Mina replied, "What's up, girl?"

"We still on for lunch, right?"

"Yeah, but I got to finish up some paperwork first."

"A'ight, I'll wait. What's up, Delicious? You know I want my hair done Friday morning, right?"

"Excuse me, Miss Mo, but the correct way to ask is, *'Delicious, the most beautiful man in the world, will you please do me the pleasure of styling my nappy wig?'*"

"See. I was trying to be nice but now I see I have to get ghetto. Nigga, have yo' ass here at seven o'clock on the dot to flat iron my long, silky mane."

"Oh, no, bitch. No you didn't. Have we forgotten that you are the same muthafucker that needed your hair hot combed, relaxed, Super I might add, and blow dried straight last week? Don't make me go there, honey, 'cause I will!" Delicious put down his flat iron ready for war.

"You ain't even have to say all that, Delicious, you know I was just playing," she said embarrassed.

"Girl, please. Everybody knows yo' shit is rough. You just betta have yo' ass in my chair on time Friday," he laughed.

"Thank you, Delicious. Mina, I'm getting ready to run down to *Rag-O-Rama* right quick. I'll be back.

"A'ight, girl."

Sitting at her custom made mahogany desk, Mina tried to focus on the numbers in front of her, but her eyes kept on darting over to the childhood picture of her and Mo. Mina and Mo met when they were eleven years old on Mina's first day of school. She and her family just moved to the Normandy school district area. Mina dreaded the first day of school. Up until then, she didn't have any friends in the neighborhood but that quickly changed when Mo singled her out.

Everybody was outside during recess playing and doing their own thing. Mina was standing over to the side watching a group of girls dancing and singing. She was amazed to see eleven-year-old girls blowing like Whitney. Before she moved to Pagedale, she was bussed to an all white school in the county. She was so happy to finally be around children who looked and talked like her.

Staring at them in amazement, she watched as Mo ran the show. Even when they were little, Mo was something else. She was taller than most of the girls in their class and she had smoldering black eyes with long thick eyelashes. Mo had large heart shaped lips and she talked with her hands on what would be her hips.

Mina never saw a girl like her before. She was in total awe. Mo was everything that Mina wished she could be. For her to only be eleven she had more confidence and style than your average woman. Mina was on the short side and still had her baby fat. Yes, her face was pretty, but the size of her body always overshadowed that. Snapping her from her daze, Mo had yelled, "Ay, girl, you wit' the braids."

Looking behind her, Mina made sure that she was the one being spoken to.

"Me?" she asked shyly.

"Yeah, you, come over here."

Slowly moving her feet, Mina edged her way over to the group of girls.

"You know how to sing?"

"Yeah."

"Sing then."

"Sing what?" Mina asked, feeling suffocated.

"Sing *Michel'le*'s song '*Something in My Heart*.'"

"Okay," Mina gulped.

Staring around at the crowd of girls, she realized that all eyes were on her. She cleared her throat and wondered, *What if I crack? Will they laugh at me?*

"Come on, girl. We ain't got all day, the bell about to ring," Mo had become agitated.

Taking a deep breath, Mina closed her eyes and sang, "*You take my love and I'm willing…There's no limit to the love I'm givin'…The love I'm givin'…Ohh…Hi, yeah…*"

"Stop, stop, stop that's enough! Girl you can sang! Who taught you how to sing like that, yo' Momma?" Mo asked in shock.

"Ah uh. I just sing like that I guess."

"Well, from now on you're hanging with me. My name is Monsieur."

"Mon, what?"

"Monsieur. It's French but everybody calls me Mo. What's your name?"

"Mina."

"That's a cute name. You wanna be my new best friend?"

"Yeah," Mina replied, excitedly.

"You have to pinky swear that we will be BFFs for life." Mina and Mo

extended their pinky fingers and smiled.

"That big bitch can't sing!" a young boy by the name of Dro yelled, laughing.

"Shut up, Dro! Don't mind him he stupid!" Mo stuck up for her new friend.

"I know you hear me!" Dro continued.

"Just ignore him."

"Well, fuck yo' fat ass then!"

"Leave her alone, man," Dro's cousin, Victor, ordered. Turning around, Mina got a good look at the boy, Victor. He was handsome and possessed a confidence about himself that rivaled that of a twenty-year old. Looking into his eyes, it was love at first sight for Mina.

"Who are they?" Mina asked.

"Two trouble makers that you don't want to mess with. Victor's pretty cool, but his cousin Dro is an asshole."

Fifteen years went by and Victor moved away. Throughout the years, Mina always wondered what happened to him. Suddenly Jodi buzzed Mina, interrupting her reverie. Mina buzzed back. "What's up, Jodi?"

"I just wanted to let you know that Mo is outside waiting for you."

"Okay, thanks, Jodi."

Checking her makeup in the mirror, Mina fingered her hair. She was becoming bored with the long shoulder-length hair that Andrew required her to grow. She wanted desperately to have her short funky hairdo back, but politicians' wives had to have long hair, Andrew explained. Despite the fact that Mina hated her hair, she still looked good. Her caramel complexion, hazel eyes, high cheekbones and Angelina Jolie lips gave her a sexy but sweet look. Mina stood about 5'8" without heels. Her perky 36 C breasts, flat stomach, size fourteen waist, round hips, and Serena Williams ass made up her look. She often was mistaken for the fashion designer Meesa.

"I'll be back in about an hour and half," Mina yelled over her shoulder as she left.

"It's about time you brought your slow ass outside," Mo said, bumping Young Buck's "Shorty, Wanna Ride Wit Me."

"Shut up, Mo."

"It's a'ight, though, I been peepin' ol' boy across the street."

Staring in the same direction as Mo, Mina spotted the finest man that she ever laid eyes upon. The unknown male was walking out of the Foot Locker located across the street from the shop. Locking eyes, they gazed at one another. His eyes alone caused her lower lip to tremble. Something about him told her to look the other way but she couldn't take her eyes off of him. Strolling over to his motorcycle, a 2004 Hayabusa 1300, Mina's eyes skimmed over his well-toned physique.

He stood about 6'2", had olive-colored skin and small brown eyes. His low cut Caesar and goatee showed off his Latino features. His broad shoulders and carved out arms were visible because he had on a black wife beater. Gazing over his arms, Mina saw about five or six different tattoos on each arm. The man's army fatigue shorts and all black Chuck Taylors looked quite nice on him. To Mina he was absolutely breathtaking. Getting on his bike, he winked his eye at her as he placed his helmet over his head. Licking her lips Mina smiled back as she watched him ride away.

"Are you done drooling because I'm hungry?"

"Don't hate. He looks familiar doesn't he," Mina responded as she got into Mo's 2005 BMW 645i convertible.

"Yeah, I've seen him from somewhere."

As they sat at the very popular soul food restaurant, Sweetie Pie's, located off of West Florissant, Mina gazed over the photos of famous sixties soul singers. Singers such as Marvin Gaye, The Dramatics, Jackie Wilson and Aretha Franklin all were showcased on the brightly colored blue walls. Mina listened to each of these artists on a daily basis because they all sang of love and the pain it sometimes brings.

Thinking of pain, Mina brought up the subject of Andrew.

"Shit, as much money as that nigga got you betta make yourself love him."

"How can I marry him when I don't even want to be in the same room as him?"

"Have you told your mother this?"

"Hell, naw, I ain't tryin to get cut. Rita would have a fit. She has it in her mind that Andrew is this perfect guy. Whatever I say is just going to go in one ear and out the other."

"Well, you know what I say, you ain't got to love him to be with him. Just love

that money honey."

"Are you serious?" Mina laughed.

"Sweetie, you don't have to love him. He loves you and that's all that matters. Remember at one point in time, you did care about Andrew. Just go back to that happy place and everything will be a'ight. Girl, haven't I taught you anything?" Mo replied as she bit into a piece of catfish.

"I guess you're right."

"You know I am. Now eat your food before I eat it for you."

"Enough about me. What's been up with you? Besides your drama with Quan," Mina asked, eating a fork full of collard greens before Mo ate it. The girl was that greedy.

"You know I just did a photo shoot for that new magazine, *Mic Check Magazine*, right?"

Nodding her head, Mina agreed.

"Well, while I'm on the set getting my make-up done, this guy approaches me and hands me two tickets to the magazine's launch party for next Saturday. Come to find out, the owner/Editor-in-Chief lives here in St. Louis."

"Who was the guy?"

"I don't know, but the brotha was fine and I gots to see him again."

"Quan gon' fuck you up."

"Fuck Quan. He ain't my muthafuckin husband. Me and that nigga have been together for eight fucking years and I have yet to see a ring. I ain't his baby momma, his fiancé, or wife so we don't have any ties to each other. When he makes me his wife, that's when I will be faithful. Until then there a whole hell of a lot of men out there who have my attention."

"You are crazy," Mina laughed.

"Girl, that's real. Quan ain't shit wit his cheatin' ass. I'm doing me. Fuck him."

"So I guess that means you want me to bring out my inner hoe that night?"

"Exactly."

"I don't know, Mo. You know I can't be out kicking it at the club all night wit you. The Wellingtons would have a fit if they found out that I was in a night club, let alone one on the Ill Side."

"Girl, fuck them. You ain't marrying the Wellingtons, you're marrying Andrew. Shit, the rest of them muthafuckers can kiss yo' ass," Mo declared, tooting up her nose.

"But still."

"But still my ass. Just because you're going to be the mayor's daughter-in-law doesn't mean that you have to forget who you are and where you came from. Now loosen the fuck up, bitch, you're turning into one of them."

"Fuck you, hoe." Mina let out a good-natured laugh.

* * *

Sunday afternoon, on the way over to her mother's house, Mina thought back on her relationship. The past year and half had been a chaotic one for her. Once Mina learned that Andrew was the son of the mayor, she couldn't believe her luck. He was everything that she wished for—distinguished, smart, sexy and aggressive that was until aggressiveness turned into abuse. Four months into their relationship, Andrew moved Mina out of her parents' home and into a house in the Delmar Loop. After hearing her dreams of opening up a full service salon, he ordered that she quit her job at Graybar.

Three months later her salon was open and business was booming. Mina had everything. A loving man who adored and worshiped her, money in the bank, platinum credit cards, a brand new CLK 55, designer clothes and a $200,000 house. When Andrew asked for her hand in marriage and presented her with a flawless four carat, square cut diamond ring, Mina couldn't have asked for more. There she was, a girl from the hood who wasn't a size 2, who had found her prince charming — or so she thought. Andrew swept her off her feet in a matter of months and changed her life drastically. To Mina she had met the man of her dreams.

She never even realized that she had set herself up to be controlled by a man. Everything she had was in Andrews' name. At any given moment or time it could all be taken away. Andrew loved the power he had over Mina. Whatever he told her to do, she did it without question. He even had her parents in his pocket. Her father, Ed, was an electrician so Mayor Wellington got him a contract to work on a new hotel being built in Chesterfield, Missouri. Her parents couldn't have been more grateful.

The first time Andrew hit Mina was a day that would be forever etched in her mind. It was a couple weeks into their engagement and Andrew had came home angry. He had a long, hard day in court. All he wanted was to come to a home cooked meal and a supportive fiancé. Placing his briefcase on the floor he called out for Mina.

"Mina! Honey I'm home."

"I'm in the sitting room," she yelled. When Andew entered the sitting room he found Mina, Mo and Delicious on the floor eating popcorn and drinking soda while watching "A Walk to Remember" with Mandy Moore for the umpteenth time.

"Hey, Andrew," Mo said.

"Hey Andrew, you look nice today," Delicious spoke and gave a broad grin.

"Hi," he spoke, aggravated with their presence. "Mina, can I talk to you?"

"Yes, sweetie." She kissed his cheek.

"What are they doing here?"

"We're watching a movie."

"Do you know how hard my day was?"

"No, what happened?"

"It doesn't even matter because you don't care anyway!" Andrew's voice grew louder with each word.

His raised voice frightened her. "I do, baby. What's wrong with you?"

"I don't want to talk about it Mina! Leave me alone," he barked as he went upstairs. Standing still Mina looked around the room trying to figure out what just happened. Shaking her head she went back into the sitting room. Delicious and Mo already had their shoes and coats on by the time she got back.

"Where are ya'll going? You don't have to leave."

"Yes, we do. You and yo' man need some alone time," Delicious remarked.

"Right. Sounds like he needs some pussy. Go tend to yo' boo," Mo added.

"Shut up, lil nasty. I'll talk to ya'll later." Mina walked them to the door. Heading up the steps she found Andrew in the bedroom, undressing. "What was that all about?" she asked, massaging his shoulders.

"I don't want to talk about it," he said, walking away.

24

"You don't want me to touch you now?" Mina said, hurt.

"Just leave me alone! Can you *not* comprehend that? Oh, I forgot if it doesn't have anything to do with food then you wouldn't understand!"

"What?"

"Have you taken a look in the mirror lately, Mina? You're fat!"

"Fat?" Mina felt even more crushed now.

"You heard me! I come home from a hard day at work to find your overweight behind, that gold digging and fag-ass friend of yours lounging around on my floor like ya'll don't have anything else to do! When I come home, I want to come home to a clean house with dinner on the table! And from now on you ask me when you can have company!" he yelled, startling her.

"Look, I don't know who you think you're yelling at but you need to check yourself!"

"Who do you think you're talking to?!"

"I'm talking to you!"

"Didn't I tell you to watch your mouth!" he snatched her by the neck.

"What are you doing?! Let me go," she begged, barely able to breathe. Andrew aggressively pushed her head up against the wall and continued to choke her.

"When I tell you to do something you do it! You hear me!" he yelled putting his finger in her face.

"Let me go!"

"Shut up!" he slapped her.

"Muthafucker!" Mina hit him back just as hard.

"Oh, so you want to fight back!" He grabbed her neck again, this time tightening his grip. "Don't you ever lay your hand on me, bitch! I own you! You do as I say!"

Staring into his eyes, Mina saw a man with eyes like the

25

devil. His face was red and wrinkled with anger. Sweat poured from his head. He no longer looked like the man she loved. Seeing that her face was turning blue, Andrew let go. He had a look of alarm on his face. Dazed, Mina held her throat, then collapsed to the floor, gasping for breath. Andrew became paranoid with fear, watching her in so much pain. He feared that Mina would leave him.

"Baby, I'm sorry. I didn't mean it. You have to believe me," he begged.

"Leave me alone," she cried, scooting away from him.

"Come here, baby. I would never hurt you. I was just a little upset and I got carried away," he apologized now, holding her in his arms. "I promise it will never happen again. Do you believe me?" He held her face and looked into her eyes.

"I don't know," she cried.

"I love you, Mina. You are my life," Andrew kissed her tear-stained face. "Promise me that you won't leave me. I couldn't live if I didn't have you in my life. You know that right?"

"Yes." Mina nodded. She looked into Andrew's eyes and saw the man that she loved had returned.

"Good, because I love you. I would die if I didn't have you." Pulling up to her parents' house Mina tried erasing the horrible day from her mind.

"Momma!?" she yelled as she entered the house.

"I'm in the kitchen."

Walking into the Matthews' kitchen, everything was still the same. The walls were still painted bright yellow and the childhood familiarities, a wooden fork, spoon and cross were still nailed to the wall. The white and yellow curtains on the window were made out of old sheets but to the naked eye you would have never known. The same fake plastic fruit sat in the center of the table and right next to the refrigerator was the washer and dryer.

"It smells good in here. What you cooking?"

"I'm fixing macaroni and cheese, fried chicken, cabbage and corn bread. You staying for Sunday dinner?" Her mother smiled as she kissed her on the cheek.

"Yeah, I'm staying for dinner."

"Good, 'cause yo' Auntie Bernice and Uncle Chester are coming over. And yo' cousin Nay and her kids are coming over too."

"Huh, I knew I should've stayed at home." Mina rolled her eyes.

"Oh, now wait a minute. Don't be getting all high and mighty 'cause you marrying the mayor's son, them is still your family," Rita pointed the big heavy spoon in her daughter's face checking her.

"Don't nobody think they better than nobody, Momma. It's just that Nay be getting on my nerves sometimes."

"Shit, you get on my nerves all the time, but I love you anyway," Rita joked.

"Oh, so you got jokes, Ma," Mina laughed.

"Please believe me." Rita smirked doing the chickenhead dance.

"Oh, my God. It's time for me to go. Where is Nana Marie?"

"Upstairs with your father playing that damn game."

"Last time I came over here they were playing that video game."

"I swear it's like they hooked. I think them PlayStation and Game Cube people be putting some kind of mind control device in them games I swear they do."

"What's up, big sis?" Michael, Mina's fine younger brother whom everybody called Smokey, said, hugging her.

"Eww, nigga, you stink. Get off of me. You smell like sweat

mixed with weed."

"Shut up. I just got done hooping at the park."

"I done told you about smoking that shit, Smokey!" Rita yelled.

"A'ight, Momma, dang. Ya'll trippin' up in here. I'm getting ready to hit the shower now."

"Wait on me. I gotta say hi to Nana and Daddy."

"Ya'll hurry up so you can help me with this chicken," Rita yelled over her shoulder.

"Yes, ma'am," they both yelled as they rounded the steps.

Peeking her head through the crack of the door, she watched as her grandmother kicked her father's butt playing "Def Jam Vendetta." Mina couldn't help but laugh at the sight. There her seventy-three-year-old grandmother was sitting in her recliner with a joystick in hand, pretending to be Ghostface Killa. Her father Ed sat beside her on the edge of the quilted bed totally entranced in the game. Neither had noticed Mina standing there.

"That don't make no sense. The last time I was over here ya'll were in the same position," Mina finally said with her hand on her hip.

"Mina!" Nana Marie shrilled in delight.

"Nana!" she yelled as she ran over to hug her grandmother.

"Child, I ain't seen you in a month of Sundays."

"I know, I'm sorry. The shop has been keeping me busy and I've been trying to plan this wedding."

"Mina, you ain't got to explain nothing to me. I'm just an old lady who misses her grandbaby."

"There you go trying to make me feel bad."

"Well, you should," Nana Marie said playfully, hitting Mina on the arm.

"I know you got some suga for yo ol' man." Her dad

smiled with a cigar sticking out the side of his mouth.

"Hey, Daddy." She hugged him.

"Hey Fat Momma, yo' daddy missed you. You need to come by more often to see us."

"I am, I promise." Mina winced, hearing the nickname that her father had given her as a child.

Ding, Dong, Ding, Dong!

"Mina, get the door for me!" Rita yelled from the kitchen.

"Yes ma'am," she said as she raced down the steps.

Opening the door she found her cousin Nay and her three kids. Nay was the same age as Mina, but Nay already had three kids and was pregnant with her fourth. Her kids ranged from the age of six, four and two-and-a-half. The oldest, Jimmy Jr., was by her high school sweetheart named Jimmy. Jimmy was now serving time in the state penitentiary for aggravated assault after he caught Nay in bed with his best friend Craig.

Nay's second child, Jamie, by Craig, was the baddest little girl the world had seen to date. After Nay and Craig broke up, she began to date a married man by the name of Eric. After only messing around a month she became pregnant with her third child, Jasmine. She and Eric continued to mess around and now she was pregnant again and Eric was still with his wife whom he'd said he'd leave after Jasmine was born.

"What's up, cousin?! I ain't know you was gon' be here," Nay said louder than she needed to.

"Hey, Nay," Mina said through clenched teeth.

"Jimmy Jr., bring yo' ass in here," Nay yelled out the door to her son.

"Here I come! I had to get Jasmine!"

"Oh, well, hurry up!"

"Momma." Jamie tugged on her mother's shirt.

"What?!"

"Mina is big like you said on the phone the other day."

"Girl, shut up! Didn't nobody ask you nothing! You gon' have to excuse her, Mina, 'cause she don't know no better. Is my Momma and Daddy here yet?"

"No." *I wish your ass would leave,* Mina said under her breath.

"Is them my great grandbabies?" Nana Marie asked as she entered the living room.

"Nana Marie!" they all yelled.

"Come give Nana some suga. Ooh, I missed you. Ya'll want a peppermint 'cause yo' breath a little tart?"

"Yes," Jasmine said the loudest.

"Okay, then let's go in the kitchen and get some," she said, taking all of them by the hand. Just as Mina was about to escape into the kitchen with Nana Marie and the kids Nay stopped her.

"Mina, come here let me holla at you." Nay patted the seat next to her on the plastic covered couch. Sitting down next to her, Mina inhaled a deep breath and exhaled because she knew whatever was about to come out of Nay's mouth was going to be something that she didn't want to hear. "Girl, you know I've been seeing Eric for about three and half years now?"

"Yeah, I know."

"Girl, you know that I loves me some Eric." Mina nodded and agreed, ready to kill herself. "Girl, why I just find out that this muthafucker got another baby on the way by this girl that live in Northwoods."

"What?"

"Yes, he's cheating on me and his wife. How he gon' do us like that?" Looking at her as if she had lost her mind, Mina tried to keep her composure.

"Nay, I don't know what to tell you."

"I know you don't because you got a good man. Why don't

you hook yo' cousin up with one of yo' man's politician friends? You know them muthafuckers got benefits."

Ding, Dong, Ding, Dong!

Thank you, Jesus. Nay I'm gon' talk to you later." Mina hopped up to get the door.

"Okay, girl, but you be thinking about which one of them fine brothas you gon' hook me up with. Shit it ain't even gotta be a brotha. I'm willing to put a little cream in my coffee, you feel me," Nay laughed.

"I feel you, girl," Mina pretended to laugh with her while opening the door. "Aunt Bernice, Uncle Chester!" Mina yelled happy to see them.

"Mina, girl, where have you been?" her Aunt asked.

"At that dog gon' shop and I've been planning the wedding."

"When is the wedding?" Uncle Chester questioned.

"The wedding is August first."

"That's right around the corner. I'm gonna have to dust off my good suit."

"Not the brown one, Uncle Chester, with the light blue ruffles on the chest and the brown cummerbund."

"Yes, sir! That there is my lucky suit."

"Ain't nothing lucky about that suit man," Aunt Bernice replied.

"Oh, yes, it is. I wore it to our prom and that suit got them panties off that night didn't it!"

"Chester you ought to be ashamed yo' self," Aunt Bernice blushed.

"Ya'll are too freaky for me," Mina teased.

"Oh, hush child, is Nay here yet?" Aunt Bernice asked.

"Don't you hear your grandkids making all that noise? They're in the kitchen."

"Granny, Granny," the kids yelled when they saw their

grandmother and grandfather.

Mina missed being around her family. It was the only place that she felt truly loved. Family was a big thing to her, but the Wellingtons had different views on family, especially hers. They never said it, but Mina sensed that Andrew and his parents looked down on her family because they weren't rich. But Mina looked at it as they might not have been rich money wise but they were rich in love.

Thirty minutes later, after everybody had arrived, the Matthews clan sat around the large, wooden dining room table, holding hands as Mina's father said grace. Afterwards they passed plates, cups, forks and knives to one another and they all stood to fix their plates. Trying not to be greedy, Mina placed small portions of food on her plates, buffet-style. Her mother must have noticed what she was doing because Rita stopped her.

"What are you doing?"

"I'm fixing my plate."

"You better quit tryin' to be cute and eat."

"I have to be able to fit into my dress, Ma."

"Mina, just face it you gon' be fat."

Looking around at her family Mina knew that her mother was right. Everyone in her family was overweight, except for Smokey. Piling her plate with macaroni and cheese, Mina sat back down in her seat at the table and stuffed her mouth with a piece of Jiffy cornbread.

"Fat Momma, I was thinking the other day that I want to start me up a business," Uncle Chester said.

"That's good, Uncle Chester," she replied.

"But you know that yo' ol' unc here can't get a loan to save my life. So I was thinking that that there fiancé of yours could give me the start up money." Damn near choking on a piece of chicken, Mina hurried and grabbed a cup of water to calm herself down. "So what you think baby girl?" Uncle Chester asked with a piece of cornbread hanging from his lip.

"Um... Uncle Chester, I don't..."

"Chester, don't be sittin' up there asking that girl nothing like that." Aunt Bernice slapped his hand.

"What? This here is about business."

"That still don't make it right," Nana Marie spoke. And when Nana Marie spoke everybody listened.

"All right, Momma," Uncle Chester said gloomily.

"Now enough about money and carrying on. Mina, how are the wedding plans going?" Nana Marie asked.

"It's going great," she lied. "I forgot to tell you that Mrs. Wellington invited us over for tea Wednesday. She wants to meet you, Momma and Aunt Bernice."

"Oh, really? Miss Thang want to get to know her in-laws now." Rita rolled her eyes.

"Right, Mina has been planning this wedding for damn near a year and that witch ain't bothered to get to know us all this time. Why she want to meet us now?" Aunt Bernice hissed.

"I don't know, maybe because the wedding is three months away," Mina tried reasoning.

"Maybe but I still don't like the chick," Rita stated.

"Me either, but you know yo' Auntie gon' have to pull out the rabbit coat for this one," Aunt Bernice smiled.

"Ooh, Bernice, we could dress alike. I'm gon' wear my faux fur Wednesday, girl." Rita sounded excited.

"Girl, we gon' be sharp." Aunt Bernice high-fived Rita. Shaking her head, Mina hoped that somehow the universe would skip Wednesday.

Chapter Three

Skip

Unfortunately for Mina, Wednesday came quicker than usual. She dreaded the day all week and even went as far as to back out of the meeting with the two families, but Mrs. Wellington wasn't having it. She insisted on meeting Mina's mother. Riding over to her mother's house that afternoon, she prayed that her mother and aunt did not have on their out-of-season furs. But lo and behold, as soon as her mother stepped out the door, Mina's worst fear was a reality.

It was the beginning of May and eighty-three degrees outside. Her mother and aunt glided down the steps decked out from head to toe in designer fakes. Rita sashayed toward the car in a long sleeved, black, fake Fendi top with a huge gold 'F' on the chest, black and gold Fendi logo pants, black chunky boots and her infamous black fox wrap. Now, mind you, Rita was a size eighteen and the outfit that she got from Frison's Flea Market was a size fourteen. How she squeezed herself into a size fourteen outfit, the world would never know. The night before, Janiya styled her hair in a French roll, with Shirley temple curls and finger waves in the front.

Aunt Bernice was an even hotter mess. Aunt Bernice was 5'11" without heels and weighed two hundred pounds and she dared to wear a denim cat suit like J.Lo. She got that thing from the Rainbow on Page in Overland Plaza. Now Aunt Bernice had more butt than a lil' bit and it looked like a camel's hump. Since she was so tall the hem hit her about five inches above the ankle, giving the outfit a capris effect. Aunt Bernice was flooding worse than the forty days and forty nights that Noah talked about in the Bible. What do they say? Just because they make it in your size doesn't mean you should wear it.

The white and tan rabbit coat that Aunt Bernice got from Wilson's hugged her body tight and the tan stiletto heels caused her already swollen crusty feet to puff up even more. With her swoop bangs, crinkled ponytail, red lipstick with black lip liner, white eyeliner around the rim of her eyelids and fake eyelashes, Aunt Bernice was ready to rock and roll.

Nana Marie was the only who came out of the house looking like she had some sense. Somebody had told her daughters they were still sixteen. Nana Marie knew better though. She was tastefully dressed in a pale pink Ann Taylor suit jacket, skirt, white sheer stockings, pale pink Nine West one inch heels and a white clutch purse. Her pale pink wide-brimmed hat was tilted to the side showcasing her salt and pepper side bun. Nana Marie was simply beautiful.

"Hey, girl, let's go rock this bitch," Rita yelled as she put on her seatbelt.

"Momma, watch your mouth in front of Nana," Mina scolded.

"Last time I checked, baby girl, I was grown."

"All that cussing ain't necessary, Rita," Nana Marie replied with her hands in her lap holding her purse.

"A'ight, Momma, dang you always gotta spoil all the fun."

The ride to the Wellingtons' mansion in Jefferson, Missouri was a long but eventful one for Mina. Her mom and Aunt argued the entire time about the intro of Tupac's CD, "Makaveli" while Nana Marie ordered that they listen to Gospel 1600. The debate was over whether or not the male voice in the intro said *Suge shot me*. Rita swore up and down that the male voice said *Suge shot me* but Bernice thought otherwise. By the time they pulled up to the mansion, Mina needed three aspirins to soothe her pounding headache.

"So this is it?" Aunt Bernice spoke with her nose tooted up.

"I frankly don't see what all the fuss is about. It look like a regular ol' house to me," Rita hated.

"Now let me tell you two one thing," Nana Marie said, staring her daughters down. "Don't go in these people's house embarrassing me."

"What you gon' do, Momma, whoop us?" Rita challenged.

"Don't let the old age fool you. I will still put you over my knee and spank yo' behind," she smiled. Mina didn't care whether or not her mother and Aunt behaved or not. She was tired of pleasing the Wellingtons anyway.

"Nice to see you again, Mina," the maid spoke as she opened the door.

"Hi, Rosario. Rosario, this is my mother, Rita, my Aunt Bernice and my grandmother Nana Marie."

"Nice to meet you all. Follow me, please. Mrs. Wellington is expecting you. She's outside by the pool."

"What's up with all the antique furniture? It look a funeral home up in here," Aunt Bernice whispered as they followed Rosario through the house.

"Girl, don't it. It look like we up in A.L. Beal," Rita

responded.

"Mrs. Wellington, your guests have arrived."

"Mina, darling," Mrs. Wellington said properly with wide open arms. Mina didn't know whether to hug her or run. Opting not to run, she hugged her soon-to-be mother-in- law. "And this must be your beautiful mother, Rita, that I have heard so much about." Mrs. Wellington eyed Rita up and down.

"Yes, it is I," Rita imitated Mrs. Wellington's proper tone. "Pearl, is it okay that I call you Pearl?"

"Why sure."

"Okay, Pearl. This is my sister Bernice."

"Nice to meet you, Bernice. I must say that you look absolutely ravishing on this fine, HOT, sunny day," Mrs. Wellington said, trying to stifle a laugh.

"Thank you, girl," Aunt Bernice smiled, knowing none the wiser.

"And who is this charming young lady?"

"This is my grandmother Marie but everybody calls her Nana Marie," Mina replied.

"I am so happy to be meeting the matriarch of your family. How are you, dear?"

"I'm doing well and you?"

"Oh, I'm doing just fine. Why don't you all have a seat? Cook has prepared us a wonderful lunch."

"Good 'cause a sista is starving. I had to skip dinner and breakfast this morning just to get into my skinny pants," Rita explained.

"Momma," Mina said a little embarrassed.

"What? I'm sure Pearl has had to do the same thing on occasion, right, Pearl?" Rita asked.

"Well, umm… I'm not sure I have."

"Oh, girl, quit frontin' we all have but anyway this is a nice backyard ya'll have. Chile, we gon' have to have a barbeque back here."

"Right cook up some rib tips, pork steaks, neck bones and snoots, girl, it'll be on!" Bernice added.

"Snoots, what are those?" Mrs. Wellington asked.

"Girl, you don't know what snoots are?"

"No."

"Come on Pearl, I can tell behind that fake accent that you from the south. I know yo' folks have barbequed some snoots before."

"Snoots are the meat from a pig's nose," Mina said, hoping that the conversation would end.

"Oh, my word! Christi, darling, you're here, thank God!" Mrs. Wellington said as Christi walked onto the patio.

"I wouldn't have missed this for the world." Christi smiled deviously.

"Rita, Bernice, Nana Marie, this is Christi, a good friend of the family," Mrs. Wellington hugged Christi.

"Hello, everyone," Christi spoke gleefully.

"Hi," Rita spoke dryly.

"Nice to meet you, Christi," Nana Marie returned her greeting.

"Mina, how are you?" Christi smiled.

"I'm good," Mina rolled her eyes.

"Lunch is served," Cook said as she rolled out a table filled with cucumber sandwiches, fruit, cookies, pies, tea and coffee.

"This looks absolutely wonderful, Cook. You did remember to add my special ingredient to my tea didn't you?" Mrs. Wellington questioned.

"Yes, ma'am."

"Wonderful!" Mrs. Wellington said as she gulped down the first cup. "Ooh, that hit the spot, another cup please." Staring down at their plate of cucumber sandwiches and fruit, Rita and Bernice looked dissatisfied.

"Where's the real food?" Rita asked.

"That's what I want to know. Shit I could've stopped at Burger King if I would've known this," Bernice added upset.

"Momma this is what they serve at tea parties."

"Well, remind me to never come to a tea party when I'm hungry."

"Lest we know who'll be doing all the cooking for the wedding," Bernice laughed high fiving her sister.

"I wanted to talk to you about that Rita," Mrs. Wellington said, tipsy from her spiked tea. "It normally is custom for the bride's parents to pay for the wedding but since we are so, how shall I say... a little more fortunate, Mr. Wellington and I have agreed to pay for the wedding for you all."

"What you think? We can't pay for our daughter to have a nice wedding?"

"I'm not saying that."

Christi cleared her throat. "What Mrs. Wellington is trying to say is that she and Mr. Wellington only want the best for Andrew and Mina. And if that means them footing the bill for a fabulous wedding, then that is what they're willing to do."

"Who asked you and why are you here?" Rita shot. "Look, thanks, but no thanks. Mina's father and I will throw our baby girl the finest wedding this town has ever seen. Even if that means we have to max out every credit card, we have to do it."

"I would think that you would be a little more grateful that we offered to do this. I mean let's be real here, if it wasn't for my husband getting your husband a city contract you would-n't even have a roof over your head," Mrs. Wellington slurred.

"Oh, no, she didn't!" Bernice threw her napkin down.

"If I didn't love my daughter and your son, I would bust yo' ass right now!" Rita yelled.

"I ain't got no ties to her bougie ass, I'll do it," Bernice went to grab for Mrs. Wellington's neck knocking over her best china.

"Auntie!" Mina yelled, grabbing her Aunt's hand.

"Nah, let her go, Mina," Rita yelled.

"Cook! Call security!" Christi screamed.

"Bernice and Rita, ya'll stop all that foolishness," Nana Marie reprimanded her grown daughters.

"Ah uh, Momma, you heard her. She got this coming!" Rita shouted.

"I want them out of here!" Mrs. Wellington said with her cup of tea still in hand.

"I'm sorry, Mina, but your mother and aunt must go," Cook said.

"Momma, Aunt Bernice, let's go!"

"You ain't said nothing but a word!" Aunt Bernice said as she and Rita left out.

"Come on, Nana." Mina helped her grandmother up.

"I just have one thing to say before I go.Mrs. Wellington, I came into your house today with an open mind and an open heart but that was quickly changed when you made derogatory remarks about my family. Now I don't care how much money and fame you have, if you don't have love and compassion for the next man then you have nothing. Now come on, Mina. I think my blood pressure don' went up."

"Spoken from a poor person," Christi whispered under her breath. Halfway to the door, Mina was stopped by Mrs. Wellington.

"Mina, can I talk to you?"

"What is it now, Mrs. Wellington? Haven't you done enough?"

"I'm sorry for what I said but it's true. Our families are just too different. I really think that you should reconsider marrying my son. Now I love my son and I want the best for him.

But the two of you marrying is just not a good idea and I know deep down inside, you feel the same way too. Will you please just go home tonight and think about what I've said," Mrs. Wellington asked trying one more time to stop the wedding before it happened.

"Yeah, I will," Mina said as she and Nana Marie walked to the car.

"Thank God, they're gone," Christi said.

"Why my son wants to marry a piece of trash like that I'll never know," Mrs. Wellington said.

* * *

After a long exhausting week at the salon, Mina decided to spend the night at home alone. A long hot bubble bath was the only thing on her mind. Placing her things down, Mina checked her voicemail and learned that she had two new messages. The first one was from a telemarketer, trying to sell homeowner's insurance. The second was from Andrew's assistant.

"Hi, Mina. This is Carrie, Mr. Wellington's assistant. Mr. Wellington just wanted me to let you know that next Saturday you and he will be having dinner with the Carters. You will be having dinner at Zinnia at 8:00. The car will be there at 7:15. Have a good night."

Rolling her eyes, Mina deleted the message and continued to strip down. It seemed like the only time she and Andrew talked were when they were at a social event. He claimed that he was just too busy during the week to call her. Sometimes it felt like she was in a relationship with Carrie and not Andrew. While the hot water ran, Mina placed lavender bath beads and bubble bath into the water. Once the water hit the middle of the tub, Mina turned the faucet off and eased her way in.

Over the week she had thought a lot about what Mrs. Wellington said and she agreed that not marrying Andrew was the best thing to do. But Andrew wouldn't dare agree to that. For some reason he loved her and wasn't willing to give her up. And the fact remained if she left Andrew, her shop and everything else she had would be taken away.

Pulling her hair up into a ponytail she wrapped a pink scrunchie around it to keep it from getting wet. Leaning her head back, Mina closed her eyes and let the soft tranquil sounds of Sade take her away. The words from the song "Kiss of Life" brought back memories of the mystery man on the sports bike. The way his eyes stayed glued to hers had her shook. Never before in her life had she met a man that made her feel the way the mystery man did.

His demanding eyes held more intensity and desire than Andrew's ever did. Mina could almost feel her tongue run across his soft pink lips. Sliding her hand down her wet body, she found her inner being and toyed with it. Her breasts were nice and ripe as she visualized how his cut muscles flexed as he walked and how his tattoos danced across his arms.

Mina moaned as she pretended that her hand was his. Biting down on her lip she rotated her index finger across her clit. Just as she was about to cum, the sound of her phone ringing startled her. Searching the room for the mystery man, she quickly remembered that she was alone. Looking down at her breasts, she saw that her nipples were hard and the inside of her pussy was still tingling. When she heard the phone ring, she reached for the cordless phone on the wall. "Hello?"

"What took you so long to answer the phone?" Mo questioned.

"I was taking a bath—something that some of us take time out to do," Mina joked.

"Bitch, please, I take baths," Mo shot back.

"Yeah, on Sundays so you can wash all your sins away," Mina joked.

"Ha ha, funny, bitch," Mo laughed, too. "But look I didn't call you to discuss my personal hygiene. I called to see what you were wearing tonight?"

"Ah, damn, that party is tonight isn't it?"

"Yeah, don't tell me you forgot?"

"Mo, I don't feel like going out. Besides I ain't got nothing to wear."

"Don't be trying to back out on me now. You're going. I will be there to pick you up in an hour so be ready." Mo hung up not waiting for a reply.

After bathing and getting dressed, Mina was ready to go. It took the girls about twenty minutes to get to the East side of St. Louis and to Club Rio. The line reached all the way to the parking lot but Mina knew that she would not be standing in it. Driving Mina's CLK55 the girls got out and strutted across the gravel-filled parking lot and into the club. Both of their outfits left little to the imagination.

Mina had on a pale pink Valentino shirt dress with a pair of Seven jeans. The pink Prada heels and clutch purse made the outfit complete. Mo wore a yellow Versace halter dress with silver Jimmy Choo heels. Mina and Mo both looked fresh to death. Making their first trip around the club the girls surveyed the crowd. For it to be an industry party the atmosphere was crunk. Taking a seat directly in front of the dance floor, Mina sat.

"I'm getting ready to go get a drink, you want one?" Mo asked.

"Yeah, get me a Long Island Iced Tea."

"A'ight, I'll be back," Mo yelled over the loud music.

Upstairs in the VIP area, Victor and his business partner/cousin/best friend Alejandro aka Dro stood surveying the crowd. The club was packed. Strobe lights and photos of the magazine cover filled the walls. In the center of the room was the dance floor and around it sat tables and chairs. Victor couldn't have been happier. All of his dreams were coming true.

"A playa sure to cut something tonight. It's some fine honeys up in here," Dro said, amped.

"Yeah, it is, but ain't none of these bitches got shit on mommy sitting by the dance floor," Victor declared.

"Who, ol' girl with the pink on?"

"Yeah, her. The one with the big booty and the tight waist that I was telling you about from the other day."

"Her? She cute and all but she a little bit on the thick side dog," Dro said looking at Victor like he was crazy.

"You know who that is don't you?"

"Nah who is it?"

"That's Mina and Mo from elementary school."

"Word! Mo looking kinda good, but Mina still on the thick side."

"I know, but it's something about her man. I ain't seen a chick that fine in a long time." "Well, what you waiting on, nigga? You betta go down there and get on her before some other nigga do."

"I am. I'm just taking my time," Victor said as he eyed Mina from afar.

Slowly sipping on her drink, Mina kept looking around to see if anybody was staring at her. Every time she looked around she saw people minding their own business, doing their thing but she still felt like she was being watched.

"Girl, what is wrong with you?"

"Nothing. I just feel like somebody is watching me."

"Everybody is watching us, Mina. We're the finest women up in here. Even that dorky looking brotha over there on the wall thinks so. He's been staring at me all night with his funny looking ass."

"Whatever, Mo," Mina said, waving her off.

"I'm getting ready to hit the dance floor. Meet me out there when you get done."

"A'ight."

With her legs crossed, Mina sat self-consciously gazing around the club. She hated going to clubs, men never paid her any attention. It seemed like they only paid attention to the petite girls with skimpy outfits on. She took another sip of her drink and bobbed her head to the sound of Tha Hole 9's "So Heavy".

"Ay, Ma. My boy wanna holla at you," Dro said, taking Mo's seat next to Mina.

"Excuse me. Do I know you?" Mina asked with an attitude.

"Fall back, shorty, I'm just relaying a message for my boy."

"And who is your boy?"

"I'm surprised that you don't know who I am."

"And why should I?"

"Because me and boy run this city."

"Oh, really," Mina said laughing.

"Yeah."

"Well, tell your boy that if he's a real man he'll come holla at me himself."

"A'ight then shorty, I will." Dro stood up and left.

Rolling her eyes, Mina checked her watch and decided that she was ready to go home. One thing that she didn't have time for was some bum broke-ass nigga trying to holla at her all night. Finishing the last of her drink she got up and prepared to find Mo. Across the room Dro and Victor stood watching her.

"Yo', dog, I can't stand her."

"What happened? She didn't remember who you were?"

"Nah, she sittin' up there, acting all snotty and shit."

"Word?"

"Yeah, she act like her shit don't stink or something, stuck up-ass broad. I never have liked her."

"So she really didn't know who you were?"

"Nah."

"Yo' I gotta go see what's good wit' mommy."

"Don't say I ain't warn you," Dro shouted after him.

Shaking his head, Dro fired up another blunt. To him, Victor always seemed to pick the wrong women to fall for and something about Mina screamed "Snake Bitch."

"Girl, you shoulda came out there and danced wit me."

"How are you ladies doing tonight?" a waitress asked.

"We're doing fine," Mo responded.

"I've been told by the owner that you two are welcomed to anything that you want tonight on him."

"Oh, really," Mina grinned.

"Well, in that case I want a bottle of Cristal," Mo replied.

"Anything else?"

"No, but thank you and tell the owner I said thank you, too," Mina said.

"See, girl I told you we were gonna have fun." Mo danced in her seat.

"It just feels like something ain't right."

"Quit trippin', girl, just relax and enjoy yourself." After about a half an hour, the girls were tipsy and kicking it.

"I want another bottle of Cris," Mo shouted over the loud music.

"Yeah, the bottle is almost gone."

"You see the waitress anywhere?" Mo asked, looking around.

"There she is."

"Is that that sexy muthafucker from the other day?" Mo questioned as both of their eyes locked on Mina's mystery man.

"What's up, ladies?" he said as he approached the girls' table

"Everything's going great now that you're here." Mo grinned from ear to ear while pinching Mina's arm. Taking a seat next to Mina, Victor stared at her as if she were an angel.

"Do you remember me?" Now that they were face-to-face Mina realized that her mystery man was Victor, her childhood sweetheart.

"Yeah, I remember you. Good to see you again." Mina extended her perfectly manicured hand as she seductively gazed into his eyes.

"Good to see you," Victor replied. He could feel his dick harden from the touch of her soft hand.

"You're on the cover of my magazine this month aren't you, Mo?"

"So you own *Mic Check Magazine*?"

"Yeah, me and my cousin Dro are co-owners."

"Gon' boo do yo' thang?" Mo flashed a winning smile.

"Let me guess, you own this club, too?" Mina questioned.

"I do and a couple of others."

"What's up, Victor?" said the dorky guy that had been eyeing Mo all night.

"What's up, man?"

"You know I had to come through to support you."

"Thanks for coming out."

"I'm getting ready to get out of here though. I'm gon' holla at you later." The guy eyed Mo lustfully. Mo just ignored him as she rolled her eyes.

"A'ight then, man." Turning his attention to Mo, Victor said, "I think my man wanted to holla at you."

"Who was that? He had been staring at me all night?" Mo asked.

"That was Isaac Bruce from the St. Louis Rams," Victor

48

explained.

"HOT DAMN!" Mo shot up, searching the crowd for him, almost knocking her drink over. "Is he gone? Do ya'll see him?"

"He's gone, you gold digger." Mina chuckled.

"Goddamn! I could've hit the jackpot!" Mo pouted. Doubling over in laughter, Mina couldn't get over how silly her friend was.

"See, you should never judge a book by its cover," Mina replied.

"Oh, shut up."

"It's good seeing you. I haven't seen you since you were in the fifth grade," Victor said speaking to Mina.

"What happened to you?" Mo asked.

"My family and I moved, but me and Dro moved back here about a year ago."

"If you two love birds will excuse me, I'm getting ready to hit the dance floor again."

"A'ight." Mina gazed back into Victor's eyes.

"You own that shop across the street from the Foot Locker?"

"I bet you own that, too," Mina said, trying to be funny.

"As a matter of fact, I do."

"Yeah, that's my shop. I'm in the process of opening up another one in the city," she replied, feeling stupid.

"I keep my eye on all the businesses on that block and your shop is poppin' Ma."

"Thanks. It's funny because before the other week I had never seen you," Mina replied dropping her napkin.

Dropping her napkin on purpose, Mina bent over to pick it up. She made sure Victor got a good view of her round plump ass.

Smiling to himself, Victor knew exactly what her slick ass

was up to. She needed a man like Victor. Somebody that was going put her ass in check and beat the pussy up right. If he could have, Victor would've broke her ass off right there in the club, in front of everybody. He wanted to fuck her in the worst way.

"Trust me, I've been around. But check it. Now that the small talk is out of the way, let's cut the bullshit, Ma. What's really good wit you?"

Shocked at his bluntness, Mina sat, stunned and speechless.

"I don't mean to be rude, but when I see something I want, I go after it." He licked his bottom lip in a suggestive manner.

"First of all, how do you know that I want you?"

"Come on, Ma. Be for real. You were feelin' me when we were kids, you got to be feelin' me now. A nigga grown up, lookin' good, smellin' good," Victor joked, running his hands over his face and watch.

"Whatever." Mina waved him off.

"But, nah, for real,it's written all over your face."

"Oh, really?"

"You know that your eyes show everything you're feeling."

"But eyes can be deceiving."

"Nah, your eyes never lie. They're like a window to your soul."

"What are my eyes saying now?"

"They're telling me that you're unhappy and you're searching for something."

Shuffling around in her seat, Mina looked down at her hands to try and hide the uneasiness she felt.

"I guess I was right?"

"No, you weren't. As a matter of fact I'm engaged." She flashed her five-carat ring.

"What's that supposed to mean?" he said, ignoring her

ring like it was cubic zirconium.

"It means that I am happy and I shouldn't even be having this conversation with you."

"Quit lying."

"Why can't you respect the fact that I'm just not feeling you like that."

"Yeah, a'ight. Whatever. I bet I'll have you saying you love me."

Knowing that he was telling the truth, Mina laughed.

"I gotta burn out so give me yo' number."

"Listen, Victor, you're a nice guy. We had a thing when we were younger, but I'm engaged. Besides there are plenty of skinny, available women in here. Go and holla at one of them."

"Are you done?" Staring him in his eyes, Mina said nothing. "I don't give a fuck about your size. I think you're beautiful and ever since you walked in here my eyes have been on you and only you. So you can quit wit all that slick shit you talking."

"Excuse me," Mina said, ready to go off, but intrigued as well.

"Look, I'ma holla at you Friday so have your cell phone on."

"Are you crazy or something? How do you even know if I have a cell phone and how can you call me if you don't have the number?"

Standing up Victor leaned over and whispered into her ear, "Tonight while you're playing wit your clit, I want you to scream my name while you're cumming."

Mina could feel her cheeks turning red as his breath tickled her ear. Biting down on her bottom lip, she watched as he disappeared through the crowd. As she tried steadying her heartbeat his words still lingered in her mind. She couldn't understand how he knew her so well. The way he got into her mind intrigued and scared her all at the same time.

Chapter Four

Now Playing

Friday, May 10, 2005, Mina was having yet another boring dinner date at a Restaurant called Choice's with Andrew and his friends. The Italian restaurant locatedin downtown St. Louis only catered to the rich and famous. In the corner of the room a string quartet played soft classical music. Playing with her food she tried to pretend like she was following along with the conversation they were having.

"Well, I personally feel like Carol Leverly is making a fool out of herself. Her campaign strategy is all wrong," Joseph Carter commented.

Andrew nodded. "My friend, I agree."

"Does she really think that targeting the black communities will assure their vote?"

"Right, I mean everybody knows that you can't depend on them. The only thing that you can depend on them for is to show up for two dollar Tuesdays down at the Spot." Andrew laughed.

Dropping her fork, Mina sat appalled at Andrew's smart remark.

"Doesn't she know that focusing on the Casinos and industrial businesses are the way to go." Joseph grabbed his napkin and dabbed the corners of his mouth.

"Exactly what does she expect to accomplish by promising more funding to inner city schools? No disrespect, Mina, but half those kids won't even graduate, so really what is the point?" Eleanor Carter's nostrils narrowed in disdain.

"Mina, you have been fairly quiet this evening, what do you have to say on the subject?" Joseph asked.

"I don't think that you all really want to hear what I have to say."

"We do."

"Are you sure that you want my opinion?"

"Please, be as frank as possible," said Eleanor.

"Well, honestly, I feel that Carol Leverly is doing a great job. I think that targeting inner city schools, promising funding, better homes and jobs for us minorities," she paused with and emphasized the word minority as she glanced at Andrew, is what is needed right now. If I had to vote today, right here and now, she would most definitely have my vote." She ended on a strong note.

Astonished at Mina's thoughts, they all sat speechless. For a moment no one spoke. Finally breaking the silence, Andrew said, "You all will have to excuse Mina. She doesn't know the game of politics like we do."

"Andrew my boy, you have to admit that the girl has spunk." Joseph laughed, then took a sip of water from his glass.

Disgusted with their blatant disrespect for her and her thoughts, she sat back in her chair with her arms folded across her chest. As they continued to talk nonsense, Mina's mind wandered back to Victor. She kept her cell phone on all week like he asked her and yet he still hadn't called. Checking herself, she remembered that he didn't have her number in the first place, but the memory of his face was etched in her memory.

He looked so different from when they were young. Mina could still remember how he used to stick up for her. One day in particular she was on her way home from school when Dro and another boy began to torment her. Rain was pouring from the sky and Mina had her science project in hand when they approached her.

"Mina!" Dro yelled into her ear, scaring her half to death.

"Leave me alone, Dro."

"I'm trying to be nice to you, girl."

"What do you want?"

"I wanted to walk you home since it was raining. Give me your project, I'll hold it." Thinking he was being sincere, she obliged and continued to walk.

"Those are some nice pants you got on," the other boy said, giggling a bit.

"Thanks," she smiled, looking down over her all-yellow Cross Color jeans.

"Syke," Dro laughed as he dropped her science project while the other boy pushed her down onto the ground. The next thing Mina knew she was diving face forward into a puddle of mud. Not able to stop herself from falling, her body hit the pavement and her face was drenched with mud.

"Ha ha!" The two boys cracked up, laughing.

"What the fuck is yo' problem, dog?" Standing up, Mina wiped her face and saw Victor.

"What? We just fucking wit her."

"Touch her again and I'm gon' fuck you up," he warned, pushing Dro.

"My bad. Sorry. Come on, man." Watching as they walked off, Mina began to pick up her belongings.

"I'm sorry. My cousin can be an asshole sometimes."

"I can't stand him. Look at my science project. It's ruined."

"Come here. You got some grass on your cheek." Victor took her by the arms. Standing perfectly still Mina watched as he removed the grass from her face. Gliding his thumb across her cheek they gazed into each other's eyes.

"Thank you."

"You're welcome," he said, totally mesmerized by her. "Can I kiss you right now?"

"I might be bad at it," she answered nervously.

"That's not possible." Leaning in, Victor took her delicate face into the palm of his hands and gently placed his lips onto hers. Lightly, they both kissed one another. As Mina's lips pursed up against Victor's, her left leg went weak. "See I told you." Blushing some, she looked the other way. Suddenly her cell phone began to ring, bringing her back to reality.

"Honey, I asked you to turn your cell phone off tonight. You know how I find that to be rude," Andrew said sternly.

"Yes, you did, sweetie, but I am expecting an important call so if you'll excuse me," she said, not waiting for them to reply.

"Hello?"

"Speak to Mina."

Hearing Victor's sexy voice brought an instant smile to her face.

"So tell me, how did you get my number?"

"I told you I get around. I got friends in high places. I always find out what I need to know."

"Is that right?"

"Nah, for real I got it from Mo."

"I'm going to kill her."

"So what's up wit you? What you doing?"

"I'm having dinner with my fiancé and his friends," she said dryly.

"You don't sound like you're having a good time."

"I'm not."

"See I told you that ring don't mean shit."

"Just because I'm not enjoying myself doesn't mean that I'm not enjoying my life with him."

"If that nigga really made you happy you wouldn't be on the phone wit me right now. I'm telling you, if you was wit a nigga like me, no matter where you was at or who you were wit you would always enjoy yourself."

"What's up with the nigga shit? Aren't you Latino?"

"I'm half Black and Puerto Rican."

"Oh," she uttered, feeling stupid again.

"But anyway if you quit playing hard to get I promise I can make you happy."

"That's what they all say in the beginning."

"I'm telling you, shorty, I'm gonna make you mine."

Biting down on her lip, Mina closed her eyes and pretended as if Victor were right there with her.

"So how was your day?" he asked.

"It was cool."

"I bet it got a lot better since I called, right?"

"Something like that," she admitted.

"Don't front, Ma, you know you was waiting on me to call."

Blushing, Mina didn't say a word.

"But, uh, I gotta go so I'ma holla at you later, a'ight."

"Okay," she whispered, wishing the conversation weren't ending so soon. Hanging up, she opened her eyes and continued to smile.

"What the hell is your problem?"

Startled, Mina jumped back as Andrew got in her face.

"Don't ever in your pathetic little life disrespect me like that again," he spoke in a harsh tone.

"Pathetic? Who are you talking to?"

"You! When I tell you to do something you do it, do you hear me?"

"Nigga, please. You don't run me."

"There you go with that ghetto talk."

"Whatever. This ghetto girl is getting sick and tired of yo' sorry ass," Mina snapped as she tried to walk away.

Grabbing her by the arm, Andrew warned through a clinched jaw, "If you ever, and I mean ever, talk to me like that again, your ass will be back in the hood so fast it will make your head spin, you project bitch." He held her arm tightly.

"Let me go."

"Not until you beg for my forgiveness."

"Fuck you, Andrew," she yelled as she yanked her arm away. Standing outside of the restaurant, she hailed down a cab and headed to her parents' house.

***

"Mina, honey, is that you?" Nana Marie said as she entered the house.

"Yeah, it's me, Nana. Why are you up so late and in the dark?"

"Chile, you know I gotta watch Forensic Files."

Slipping off her shoes, Mina rubbed her feet across the red and black shag carpet that her mother had put down in the Seventies. The red crushed velvet wallpaper matched the floor and the red Valentine's Day boxes that Mina and her father had given her mother over the years adorned the walls. The floor model television still had the aluminum foil wrapped around the tips of the antenna for reception, even though they had cable. The couch was wrapped in plastic preventing any stains.

"What you doing over here so late?"

"Andrew and I just got into a fight."

"Come talk to your Nana about it." Taking a seat on the plastic covered couch, Mina's butt made a farting sound. Rolling her eyes, she placed her head on her grandmother's lap and began telling her the story.

"Nana, I don't know what to do. I used to love Andrew, but now things have changed."

"You know, Mina, I've kept my mouth shut about this whole wedding thing but now I have to speak my piece. I know you're not happy. I can see it in your eyes. Now Andrew seems like a pretty good man but I know he ain't treating you right. Remember we love you and we are going to stick by any decision that you make it." Nana Marie stroked her hair. As Nana Marie continued to talk, tears streamed down Mina's face. "I love you, Mina, and I only want the best for you but you have to want the best for you too."

"I know," she sniffled.

"What's going on down here?" Rita asked, coming down the stairs and switching on the light. Her hair was filled with rollers and the pink robe that she wore was an old and tattered mess.

"Nothing. Mina's just doing a little soul searching, that's all." Rising up, Mina wiped her face so that her mother wouldn't see her crying.

"You all right, honey?"

"Yeah, I'm all right. I just miss ya'll—that's all," she lied.

"Did Andrew drop you off over here?"

"You know Andrew would never be caught dead in Pagedale."

"How are you getting home?You want me to drop you

off?"

"Nah, I'll probably catch a cab. Where's Smokey? I didn't see his car outside."

"Out with that fast-ass girlfriend of his, Sharnetta."

"Oh."

"You know what I was thinking would be fly for the wedding?"

"What, Momma?"

"If you have Lil Jon and The Eastside Boys 'Lovers & Friends' playing while you walk down the aisle."

"Okay, it's time for me to go," Mina said, easing off the couch.

"What? Will you at least think about?"

"I have to make a phone call, Momma."

* * *

Across town at Victor's crib he and Dro sat, getting blazed and discussing business.

"So what's the daily report?" Victor asked while inhaling.

"Everything is good, dog. Shit is moving as usual."

"What kind of profit did we make down in New York?"

"Business is booming, dog," Dro boasted.

"Good, but check it, did you the read the paper today?" Victor questioned.

"Nah, dog, you know I don't keep up wit that shit."

Didn't I tell you you gotta keep up with the media? You know that punk-ass nigga Wellington is coming after us. We have to be on point at all times. You trippin', dog. Don't get caught slippin'," Victor warned.

"I feel you."

"I don't think you do," Victor said with a menacing stare.

"Quit trippin', man, and finish telling me." Dro laughed to ease the tension.

Staring at him for a second longer, Victor picked up the

daily paper and threw it at him. The headline read as Dro skimmed over the cover page, "Mayor Wellington to End Drug Trafficking."

"Damn, cuz! Shit about to get hot for real."

"Now you see what I'm talkin' about. That nigga is straight up gunning for us."

"Since he couldn't get in on a profit, he gon' try to shut us down," Dro said more as a comment and not a question.

"Yep."

"Damn, that's fucked up."

"Ain't, it though?"

"Yo', let's just murk that nigga and get over wit."

"Dro, we can't handle this shit like we do on the streets. We on a whole 'nother level now, baby. I'm gon' think of something, trust me."

"Yeah, a'ight. I hear you talkin' but anyway, what's up wit you and ol' girl?"

"Who? Mina?"

"Yeah, nigga, who else?"

"I don't know, man. I can't quite figure baby girl out. I think she on some hard-to-get type shit."

"Yo', that shit is for the birds. I don't know what you see in that broad anyway." Dro lit a Black-N-Mild.

"Nigga, you know exactly what I see in her, mommy got a fat ass," Victor joked.

Ring...Ring...

"Ay, hold up let me get that," Victor replied as he got up to find his cell phone. "Who dis?"

"Mina."

"What's up, Ma?" Victor said with a smile.

"Nothing."

"So you finally decided to give a nigga chance."

"Nah, I'm at my parent's house now and I'm bored so I

decided to give you a call." She laughed while Victor savored the sound of her voice on the other end of the phone.

"Is that right?"

"Ay, dog I'm gon' holla at you later," Dro replied as he got up to leave.

"A'ight hit me on the hip later."

Shaking his head, Dro left the room disgusted. Once again, Victor was letting a broad get in between their pursuit of paper. To Dro nothing was more important than getting money. He would do just about anything and everything to get it. Despite what Victor said, Dro knew that he had plans of his own. If killing Mayor Wellington, or anyone else for that matter, kept them on top of the game then killing him was indeed what Dro would have to do.

"You know you need to go on and leave that nigga and come get wit me," Victor spoke deeply in to phone.

"I didn't call you to discuss him." Mina shook her head with the hope of getting Andrew out of her head.

"Why don't you come over and chill wit me tonight?"

"I don't think so."

"Come on, Ma, we're both adults. Ain't nothing gon' happen that we don't want to happen."

"I know that. Anyway, I'm over my mother's house."

"I remember where your mother stays. She lives on Ferguson. I'll have one of my cars come and pick you up."

"Maybe another night, Victor. Look, I gotta go, I'ma holla at you later." Mina felt overwhelmed as she hung up.

* * *

"This my shit!" Mo yelled, dancing to Lil Jon & The Eastside Boys' "Get Crunk" as she drove on the highway.

"Girl, you know my momma wants me to walk down the aisle to their song 'Lovers & Friends'," Mina said as the wind blew threw her hair.

"Hell, naw, Rita done lost her mind."

"Right."

"I'm hyped as hell! Let's go to Fairground Park."

"Bitch, is you crazy? I ain't trying to die. I want to live to see tomorrow."

"Come on Mina? It'll be fun. I heard they're having a basketball tournament down there this weekend."

"No," Mina shook her head.

"I'm telling you, it be a lot of sexy lil' daddies down there."

"You need to get your old ass somewhere and sit down. That don't mean nothing to me. No!"

"Please, do me this one favor."

"Bitch, I'm always doing you a favor."

"Come on Mina, please?" Mo said, pouting.

"All right, but we ain't gon' be out here all afternoon."

Everybody and their momma was at Fairground Park chillin' watching the tournament as Mina and Mo pulled up. Wanting to catch some attention, Mo whipped her Lexus 360 into a parking space like a pro. She caught everybody's attention, bumping Lil Webbie's "Bad Bitch". Wondering who it was making so much noise, Victor turned to see who it was. With a split Optimo Cigar in hand ready to be filled with purple haze, Victor and his boys stared in amazement as she and Mina got out. So far they were the finest chicks there.

Mina noticed him staring at her as she sashayed around the car and winked her eye. Happy to see her again, Victor smiled to himself. Putting up his hand, he signaled to the referee that his team was taking a break. Mina perched on top of the car like one of those girls in a car magazine as she waited for Victor's arrival. Not even a minute later, he was all in up in her face.

"What's up, baby girl? You got a man?"

"Nope. Don't want one, don't need one." She smirked,

playing his game.

"Is that right," he said in a slow drawl, letting her know he was high.

"Hey, tell yo' man over there in the red I said 'what's up'," Mo replied.

"Go tell him yourself. He won't bite."

"But I do." Mo laughed as she got up to go talk to Victor's friends leaving Victor and Mina alone.

"So what's up? Why you play me the other night?"

"How many times do I have to tell you that I'm engaged?"

"Fuck that nigga. You know you don't want to be wit him. Call him up right now and tell him you want to be with me," he said showing off his sexy smile.

"I don't think so. I can't just up and leave him like that."

"Why not?"

"'Cause he's pays my rent and all my bills."

"Okay, so move out, I'll get you your own place. As a matter of fact, just so he won't be mad, I'll do him the favor of paying both of ya'll rent. Look, I ain't trying to do this like Tony did Frank, but if you keep on playing hard to get I'm gon' have to take it there with your man sweetheart," Victor said seriously, referring to the movie "Scarface".

"Who said I was playing? I am hard to get and besides, me and you are just friends."

"Oh, so we're just friends?"

"Yeah."

"You and I both know that there is more going on here."

"You think it's that easy to take me away from him?"

"If it wasn't we wouldn't be having this conversation right now." He checked her. Liking his assertiveness, Mina folded her arms across her chest and continued to look him in the eyes. Victor swore if he looked at them too long, he would become lost in her hazel eyes. "Your eyes are beautiful, Ma."

"You just won't quit will you?" Mina blushed turning beet red.

"Come on Ma, quit frontin'. Let me take care of you." He whispered into her ear. Stepping in closer Victor stood in between her thighs, causing Mina's nipples to harden.

"You know people are watching," she whispered back, barely able to breathe.

"I don't give a fuck. I'm trying to get wit you. Quit fighting me and get rid of that nigga."

"Now why would I leave the man that I have waiting at home, for you? What you got to offer me that he can't?" Silencing him for a moment, Mina pushed him off of her and closed her legs. "That's what I thought. You can't replace him."

"I ain't trying to replace that nigga 'cause he ain't nothing to be replaced. I already got you and you don't even know it. Come on, Ma, you know that nigga ain't treating you right. I can tell you're not happy." He caressed her cheek. "Come on, Ma. I'm trying to wife you, Bamboo earrings, white Air Nike you," Victor joked.

"I can't stand you." She couldn't help but laugh, though. Knowing that if she gave into Victor she would be breaking all of the rules, Mina hopped off the hood of the car.

"Yo', Vic, we gotta get back. Times almost up," Dro announced.

"Tell the Ref here I come." Running behind Mina, he asked, "Where you going? You just got here."

"It's too much action going on for me, you dig, and plus you gotta get back to coaching your team."

"I got you," Victor grinned leaning down into her car window. "Let me get yo' phone number though?"

"I'm gon' be real wit you, Victor. I want to but I can't. Fucking around wit you, I might end up letting you get the best of me," Mina replied truthfully.

"I just want to get what's left of you, like your heart. 'Cause that nigga you wit' for damn sure ain't got it."

Never before had a man gotten to Mina the way Victor did. He knew how she felt before she even felt it. He had her mind and he could do whatever he wanted to do with it, which was a dangerous thing. Mina knew that she should drive away and put him out of her mind forever but something in her wanted to take it there one time.

She wanted Victor to put it on her in the worst way. Victor had her feeling things she never felt before. And for the first time in her life a man had Mina confused. Not knowing if he was gaming her or not, she told herself that if they did hook up it would be a one night thing so she gave in and wrote down her number.

"I'm gon' call you tonight so don't be on no bullshit," Victor said all up in her ear.

"A'ight."

Getting back into the car, Mina checked her makeup and blew the horn, indicating to Mo that she was ready to go. After flirting some more Mo hopped in and they drove off. Later that night Mina found herself sitting by the phone, awaiting Victor's phone call. As each minute passed by she became more and more irritated.

She didn't know if Andrew would be coming by, so every minute she had alone to talk to Victor was crucial. Pacing back and forth in a tank top, pajama bottoms and pink bunny slippers, Mina prayed to God for the phone to ring. Several times she picked up the phone and even checked to make sure she had a dial tone. Feeling stupid she hung the phone back up and got into bed.

"Fuck him," she exclaimed, eyeing the clock seeing that it was almost after midnight and he still hadn't called. "Nigga ain't gotta call me. Fuck his punk ass," she said turning off the lamp. Pissed off, she tossed and turned until drifting off to sleep. Not even twenty minutes into her dream the phone rang. Jumping up Mina turned on the light, checked the caller ID, cleared her throat, and picked up her cell phone.

"Hello?" she said in her sexiest tone.

"You sleep?"

"No," she answered with an attitude.

"What you doing?"

"Nothing."

"Yo' man there?"

"No."

"Come by and come see me then."

"Nigga, you crazy? I'm not coming to see you. It's going on one o'clock in the morning." She let out a nervous laugh in disbelief.

"Come on, Ma, quit bullshittin. I'm trying to see you tonight."

Good sense was ruled out as she felt the warmth from in between her thighs. Mina wanted to se him so she gave in and gave him her address. Jumping into the shower real quick, Mina freshened up. Something sexy, but not slutty, was the choice for the night so she slipped on a wife beater, a True Religion mini skirt, and on her feet she wore a pair of Roberto Cavalli heels. Approximately forty-five minutes later, Victor's driver was knocking on her door.

Sitting in the back of the Rolls Royce Phantom, Mina tried to contain her nervousness. She knew that Victor was doing the damn thing but she never knew that he was doing it this big. Fucking with Victor could cost her everything. Turning around and going home is what she should've been doing but her heart wouldn't allow her to.

It was pretty dark outside so Mina didn't know what part

of the city she was in. As the driver made a right onto a dirt road the palms of her hands began to sweat. Suddenly she saw a glimpse of light. Following the light, Mina saw a large mansion appear behind a cloud of trees.

Her mouth literally dropped as soon as she realized that the Mediterranean-style mansion was Victor's. Doing a quick estimation in her head she figured that the house had to be worth, at least, four million. With a disappearing edge pool, Jacuzzi, and exotic landscaping, it was like Victor had his own little tropical paradise right in the middle of Missouri.Once the driver opened the door and led her up the flight of steps to the double doors, Mina's nervousness doubled.

"Welcome, Miss Matthews. Mr. Gonzalez has been awaiting your arrival. I'm Julisa; allow me to escort you to the study."

As the maid led Mina down a long corridor she gazed around at all of the different antiques, sculptures and paintings. *Who would have known that a thug would appreciate art?* Mina thought. The walls were decorated with crown molding and the floors were marble. The dimly lit lights made the brown and gold interior feel warm and inviting. Victor had a gourmet granite kitchen, gas fire places and a guest cabaña in the back. Victor's house was the shit. The Wellingtons' mansion didn't have a thing on his.

Knock…Knock.

"Mr. Gonzalez, your guest has arrived."

"Thank you, Julisa. Damn, Ma, you look even better than I remembered," Victor smiled as he greeted Mina with a hug.

Thoughts of sunsets, ocean waves and hot summer nights with him filled her head as she inhaled his scent. Just the feeling of his arms wrapped around her made her feel safe and secure.

"I missed you," he spoke softly in her ear.

"You could've come to pick me up yourself instead of having some driver that I don't even know come and get me," she said as she pushed him in his chest playfully.

"I had some paperwork that I had to finish. I promise I will next time," he said smiling.

"How do you know that there will be a next time," she said her hand on her hip.

"Trust me, there will be," he said with a devilish grin.

"Anyway."

"You want something to drink?"

"Yeah, what you got."

"How about a glass of Chateau La Mondotte?"

"I don't know what that is but cool." Mina sat back on the edge of the couch.

"It's a very expensive, vintage wine."

"Oh, okay," she shrugged.

"You gonna learn to not wear short skirts around me," he said as he eyed her thighs.

"Is that right?" Mina blushed and crossed her legs to show a little more thigh.

"You sexy as hell, Ma." Victor handed her glass.

"You're not too bad yourself."

"I can't believe you're here."

"Me, either. Hey, I've never heard you speak Spanish. Say something in Spanish for me."

"A mi no me la das."

"And what does that mean?"

"It means you can't fool me."

Victor got all up in Mina's personal space as he stood in front of her. Putting himself in between her thighs, he spoke almost in a whisper, "I wanna kiss you." Slowly bending down without taking his eyes off of hers, he pushed her thong aside. Still watching her he applied pressure to her pussy with his tongue.

"Stop… *Gulp*. Victor we can't do this."She spoke between moans of pleasure which escaped out of her mouth.

Ignoring her, he continued to indulge in the sweetness that lay between her thighs.

"I thought… you said… you wanted to… ummm… kiss me." She sighed, almost out of breath.

"I am kissing you." Savoring her juices, he licked his lips.

As she watched his head sway from side to side, her lips trembled from excitement and pleasure. Not able to take anymore, she pushed his head back and stood up.

"I didn't come over here for this." Mina pulled down her skirt, shaking.

Grabbing her hand, Victor pulled her back into his arms.

"Let me take care of you." He nibbled on her ear while holding her tight.

"I'm engaged, Victor." Breathless, Mina jerked her ear away.

"Quit fighting me, Ma." He pushed her shirt and bra up and toyed with her nipples.

"I can't."

Taking one in his mouth he licked and probed.

"Vic…tor," Mina moaned.

Victor took turns teasing both of her nipples with his tongue while holding both of her breasts in his hand. As he bit and licked her breasts Mina tried to regain some type of composure. Pushing him away once again she pulled her shirt down and tried to breathe.

"Come here, Mina."

"Ah, uh. You stay over there."

"Mina, look at me."

Glancing over in his direction, she stood and listened.

"Why are you here?"

"I don't know."

"You know damn well why you're here. You want me. There ain't no hiding that shit."

"But, I can't do this, I'm engaged," she said, confused.

"Then go home, I ain't got time for this shit. My dick harder than a muthafucker. A nigga gonna end up getting blue balls fucking wit you."

Torn between what she knew was right which was to leave and what her heart was telling which was to stay, Mina grabbed her purse and headed for the door. Once she got there, though, the wetness between her legs had won her over so she stopped.

"Look. I don't want to leave like this."

Not really wanting to see her go, but wanting to make her suffer a little bit, Victor sat in his chair and said, "Ain't no hard feelings, shorty. I'll have my driver take you home since you don't wanna be here with me."

"But I do," she replied as she approached him.

Taking her by the hand, he led her onto his lap and whispered, "Then don't."

"Why you doing me like this, you know I gotta man." she asked as tears fell from her hazel eyes down onto her cheek.

Lifting her head up so that she could face him, he replied, "Trust me. Let me be your man."

Pushing her hair away from her face, Victor kissed away every tear that fell from her eyes. With a remote in his hand he pressed a single button turning the lights off, the fireplace on. The stereo was now bumping a Slow Jam mix tape. Destiny's Child's "T-Shirt" was playing in the background as he eased Mina's shirt over her head. As he kissed her collarbone the sound of rain falling outside intensified their encounter. Secure in his arms, Victor carried Mina over to the window and placed her on the window sill. Opening the window up he resumed kissing her body.

Overwhelmed with desire, Mina let a subtle moan escape her lips. Loving the way her skin felt against his, Victor caressed her back as raindrops fell from the sky. A trail of kisses was then planted from her neck to her navel. Stopping once he got to her hip bone, Victor picked Mina up to unzip her skirt. Watching as it fell to the floor he then sat her back down on the window sill. Skillfully he released the clasp on her bra and took it off. Now fully undressed Mina couldn't wait for her body to be satisfied.

Staring each other intensely in the eye, Victor grabbed her face and kissed her hungrily. Barely able to breathe she tore his one hundred and fifty dollar Purple label button up shirt off. Mina ran her hands over his chiseled chest as she released her lips from his and placed loving kisses onto his body. Each and every tattoo that adorned his chest was given her undivided attention. Leaning his head back, Victor enjoyed the feeling that her lips gave him.

Wanting to feel him inside of her, she unbuckled his pants and let them fall to his feet. Sticking her hand into the slit of his boxers she found that she was working with a well-endowed man. The feel of his thick hard dick in her hand caused Mina to go insane. She couldn't wait to feel Victor's big dick inside of her.

Without knowledge she almost begged for it. Stroking him from his shaft to his head, Mina licked his neck and listened to Victor's moans as they grew louder. His moans aroused her even more. Her heart was racing a mile a minute, but Mina's nervousness only drove her passion for Victor to a higher level. Not able to take it anymore, he wrapped each of her legs around him and entered her slowly. The sound of thunder and rain playing in the background made his first time going inside of her even better.

Massaging rain drops into her skin with his hands, Victor

felt complete for the first time in years. Picking Mina up while still stroking her, he placed her up against the wall. Victor turned her around and reentered with caution so he could feel all of her.

"Damn, you feel good," he groaned.

"Ooh…Victor."

"Mina."

"Ooh…Victor, I can't breathe."

"Ma, yo' pussy so tight. I'm gon' fuck the shit outta you," he moaned. He held her hands up to the wall with one hand and then slapped her ass while pumping hard. The tingling sensation made her crave his stroke even more.

"Victor, give it to me deeper."

With both of her hands in his, Victor leaned in so that his dick could reach her stomach. Digging in deep he hit all four corners until he found her spot. Suddenly her thighs started shaking and her lips began to tremble as she tried to hold on. Taking his hand around he began stimulating her clit while continuously hitting her spot.

"Ooh, baby, you're so deep," Mina screamed.

"You want it deeper?"

"Yes, baby, give it to me deep!"

Pushing in even deeper, Victor hit her spot with no remorse. He had Mina's entire body shaking.

"Baby, I'm about to bust," Victor grunted.

"Ooh, Victor, fuck me! Fuck me hard!" she pleaded.

Nearing an orgasm herself, Mina started throwing it back at him so that her orgasm would intensify. They both pumped hard against one another, then, in a paroxysm of pleasure, both climaxed at the same time.

"Ooh… Victor…ohh…I never came this hard before. Ooh, I love you… I love you." Mina cried out loud. She caught herself and wondered if she said that out loud.

"I love you, too."

Hearing him say it back, she realized that she had. Mina felt embarrassed and ashamed as she covered her breasts and private parts up with her hands. Never before in her life had she acted in such a way. Victor did something to her that no other man had been able to do. Make her feel free. It hadn't even been a good five minutes and she already longed for his touch.

Pushing the button on his desk, Victor turned the lights back on and the fire place off. Now with the lights back on Mina saw things more clearly. Thoughts of Andrew, the Wellingtons and the shop came flooding back. If anybody ever found out about her tryst with Victor, her career and relationship with Andrew would be over.

On one hand she wanted things between she and Andrew to end because she wasn't happy. On the other hand he believed in her dreams when most didn't and she felt she owed him for that. Searching the room she found her bra and skirt by the window. Over by the desk she found her shirt dangling from an African statue. While quickly putting her clothes back on Mina occasionally would glance over to Victor to see what his face was saying.

Even though they hadn't seen each other in years, some how she could read him like a book. He was right; the eyes are a window to the soul and his soul was clearly saying that he knew that she would leave and never return. No matter how much Mina's heart begged her to stay her head was demanding that she return home to life as she knew it.

"So what now?" Victor asked.

"I don't know," she replied as she stepped into her heels.

"You know I'm feeling you—right?"

"Yeah, I'm feeling you, too."

"But."

"But I can't do this. I shouldn't have done this. This whole thing was just a big mistake."

"So the way you were just calling my name was a mistake?" he said with a hint of desire in his eye.

Not able to lie she stood silent.

"Ma, just give me a chance to make you happy."

"Can you tell your driver to pull the car around?" She tried to avoid his eyes.

"I ain't got time for this bullshit! If you want to be with that man be with the nigga but don't try to play both sides of the fence, Ma!" Victor said as he walked out of the study, leaving Mina alone.

Standing there for a couple of minutes, Mina thought that Victor would return but he never did. She knew that she had hurt him but she was making the best decision for herself and he would just have to understand that.

"Excuse me, Miss, but your cab is waiting outside," the maid spoke.

"Cab?"

"Yes, ma'am, your cab is outside waiting."

Sucking her teeth, Mina snatched her purse off the desk but not before leaving Victor a note.

"Did he give you some cab fare for me?"

"No, ma'am, Mr. Gonzalez didn't say anything about cab fare."

Beyond pissed off, she stomped her way past the maid.

"Wait up, ma'am, I will see you to the door."

"If you don't mind, I will see my own way out," she said with an attitude.

As she left Victor's house, she vowed to never look, speak, or acknowledge him ever again. She did have to admit to herself that sending her back home in a cab and not the Phantom was funny. When she pulled up to her house and the cab driver told her the fee she didn't find it quite so funny anymore. The ride home from Victor's cost her fifty-seven dollars and eighty-nine cents.

Back on the other side of town, Victor had just gotten out of the shower. A cold shower was what he needed because his dick still hadn't gone down since Mina left. He knew that it was fucked up to send her home in a cab and to stick her with the fare but he had to teach baby girl a lesson. She was gonna have to learn the hard way that she was meant to be with him. To Victor, Mina needed a little tough love and a nigga like him was just the one to give it to her. Returning to the study so that he could grab some paperwork that he hadn't finished he ran across Mina's note.

You knew that I had a man from the start so don't start catching feelings on me now. The dick was good but don't ever call me again 'cause I ain't even feeling you like that.
Mina

Chapter Five

Repeat

The next day at the shop was a hard one for Mina. Even though the shop was full, the sun was shining, customers were smiling and money was flowing, she wasn't happy. The more she tried to keep her mind off of Victor the more she thought of him. It didn't help that everybody in the shop wanted to listen to Teedra Moses. Her song "Backstroke" evoked every thrust that Victor had given her the night before.

"Mina, you have a call on line one," Jodi buzzed.

"Thanks, Jodi." Mina buzzed back as she sat at her desk going over design plans for the new salon.

"Mina's Joint, this is Mina speaking."

"Where were you last night? I called you at least three times," Andrew questioned.

For a moment, Mina sucked in her breath. "I was with Mo." She was not prepared to lie. "What did you want?"

"I called you to apologize."

"Oh."

"I'm sorry, Mina, baby, I shouldn't have yelled at you like that."

"I'm sorry, too. I shouldn't have left like that either."

"How about I make it up to you by taking you out to a movie tonight?"

Not really wanting to, but knowing she should, she agreed and hung up. Deciding that she needed some fresh air she left her office and went into the salon.

"Why the long face Miss Mina?" Delicious questioned.

"I'm okay."

"She had a bad night but she'll be a'ight." Mo waved her off while sitting under the dryer reading a magazine.

"Shut up, Mo," Mina warned.

"Don't be getting mad at me. I ain't do nothing to you."

"Why ya'll gotta listen to Teedra? It is too early to be listening to all this sad shit."

"You know Teedra the truth." Tiffany looked at her like she was crazy.

"Ooh... Miss Thang you must've done something devious last night." Delicious smiled.

"She sure did." Mo grinned.

"I'm not playing wit you Mo. Don't put my business out there on front street."

"You putting yo' own business out there by walking around moping and shit. The bitch has been complaining for months how she ain't getting dicked down. Now she finally get her some good dick and don't know how to act."

"Miss Mina, you cheated on my future baby daddy, Andrew?" Delicious asked, excited.

"I'm not talking about this wit ya'll."

"Why not? Come on, Mina, please, tell us. I need to *feel* what you felt last night," he stressed.

"It doesn't even matter 'cause I won't be seeing him anymore."

"Hump, somebody spoke too soon." Mo giggled, eyeing the door.

The salon went quiet as Victor's presence filled the room.

"Good God, I'm about to faint," Delicious said as he fanned himself with a magazine.

Every woman in the shop's radar went off, including Delicious', as they sized him up. The man knew he could make a woman's heart melt with his face alone and he was there to see Mina. He was standing in the doorway for about a minute, just staring at her, and not one breath had been exhaled by a single client or stylist.

"What do you want?" Mina finally said.

"Come here. Let me holla at you."

"Who me?" Delicious asked.

"I ain't got nothing to say to you." Mina said as she rolled her eyes at Delicious.

"Yo', don't even try to play me. I know you don't want me to act a fool up in here?"

"Please don't, Poppi," Delicious pleaded.

"I said come here," Victor demanded.

Angry and embarrassed, she followed him outside, stomping her feet like a child. Mina was so caught up in Victor that she didn't even notice that Mo, the stylists and their clients were in the window eavesdropping.

"Don't be coming up in my muthafuckin establishment ordering me around!"

"I see you came."

"Whatever. What do you want?" she asked with her arms folded across her chest.

"What the fuck is this shit about?" he said, pulling out the note throwing it at her.

"It means exactly what it says."

"I don't wanna hear that shit! Fuck yo' man! You the one catching feelings. And, yeah, I'm feeling you, but don't even try to front like you ain't tell me that you loved me last night."

"I didn't mean to say that. Besides you told me you loved me, too." She smirked as she turned and looked back at the shop.

Turning her back to Victor as if she were about to leave she found that all eyes and ears in the shop were on her.She turned her head and looked at them as all if to say "Get the fuck out my mouth." Rolling her eyes at every last one of them, she turned back around and resumed her conversation with Victor.

"I know what the fuck I said. You ain't gotta remind me," he yelled.

"Look, I ain't got nothing to say to you. Last night was what it was. Let's just leave it at that."

"So, it's like that?"

"What, you ain't know?"

"Humph, a'ight then, shorty," he said as he walked across the street to his bike.Swallowing her pride, Mina gathered her heart up off the ground and headed back into the shop. As she turned around, she noticed all the stylists were running back to their stations. Each of their clients found their way to the lounge area or back under the dryers. She shook her head, let out a short laugh, then walked back into the shop. Glaring around at all of them, she swore that she could have heard a pin drop, it was so quiet. Everybody tried to act as if nothing had happened, but secretly, they all were staring at her out of the corners of their eyes.

"So, Miss Mina, how is the weather outside today?" Delicious asked.

"I'm sure you know how it feels outside."

"I mean, I just wanted to know 'cause suddenly it got a little *Hot In Herre.*"

"What ya'll nosey asses wanna know? Since everybody wanna be all up in my business, WHAT?" Mina questioned the whole the shop.

"I mean, I wasn't gonna say nothing but since you brought it up, who was that stallion that just walked up out of here? 'Cause baby boy so fine he make me wanna dance!" Delicious declared while turning his booty up in the air. "Hit it from the back, boy! Hit it from the back! Hit from the back, boy!" he sang.

"Lord, bless his soul." Jodie shook her head in disgust.

"That was my friend, Victor. He owns the Foot Locker across the street and Club Rio over on the Ill side, anything else?" Mina answered, not finding him funny.

"Miss Mina, now you know I'm just playing wit you," he said as put his arm around her shoulder. "Your business is your business and we all respect that."

"Thank you."

"But, baby, if things don't work out between you and Lil Pun tell Poppi that I am ready, willing and able to *drop down and get my eagle on girl,*" he sang while taking it to the floor again.

Wanting to hold back her laughter, but unable to, Mina busted out laughing. She joked around with Delicious for a while, then decided that she should busy herself with busy work and ordered more supplies for the salon. After talking to four of her suppliers, she rested her head back into her chair and dozed off. An hour and a half later she was awake and ready to head home. Busying herself worked and the nap did some good but as soon as she awoke reality hit her smack dab in the face.

Memories of Victor's face danced around in her head over and over again. She wanted to forget him, but couldn't.

Grabbing her purse she headed for the door. On the way out she noticed that everybody was gone and that it was past six o' clock. Hitting a button on the wall, the automatic blinds came down and the "open" sign now read "closed". Just as she was about to set the alarm she heard someone enter the salon.

"I'm sorry, we're closed," she yelled over her shoulder.

A minute passed, she didn't hear the person leave the shop so she became afraid. Looking around, she scanned the room to see if there was something she could protect herself with. For the first time in her life, Mina wished that she had a gun.

"The money is in the drawer. I haven't taken it to the bank yet so just take it and get out!"

"Mina."

Realizing whose voice it was speaking to her, she spun around. It was dark outside and the lights were off in the salon so she really couldn't see his face.

"What are you doing here?" she asked with an attitude.

"I ain't gonna let you walk away from me like that." Victor locked the door behind him.

"I told you I ain't got nothing else to say to you," she replied as he approached her.

"I ain't got nothing to say to you, either," he said as he took her into his arms and kissed her lips.

Dropping her purse to the floor, she held on to his face and kissed him back.

"Damn, I missed you," Victor whispered as he lifted her up.

"I missed you, too," she moaned.

Lifting her skirt, he reached for her thong to push it aside. He realized that she had on a pair of crotchless panties. He looked up and smiled in a conspiratorial way at her, then he unzipped his jeans and let them fall around his ankles. Gliding his way in he grabbed her waist and stroked. With their eyes focused on his dick, Mina held onto Victor's neck while letting out moans of ecstasy. She knew in her heart that she couldn't continue to play with Victor's feelings, but at that moment she had to have one more night of his good loving.

Mina's neck was so close to his mouth that Victor had no other choice but to lick and suck it. His hands gripped her waist as he relished the feeling her pussy gave him. He already made it up in his mind that no other chick's pussy could feel the same. He almost felt as if he acquired a drug habit messing with Mina. Her pussy was that addictive. Slowing down a bit, he made sure that every stroke spoke what he was feeling. Intently he gazed into her eyes while pumping slow and hard.

Staring back at him, Mina bit into her bottom lip and moaned in delight. She wanted to say something back with her body but her heart wouldn't allow her to. She pressed up against his chest and rubbed his back and kissed his ear. Kicking his shoes and pants off Victor took her over to the rug by the door, laid her down, and took his shirt off. Now on top of her, he pushed her shirt up and kissed her stomach.

"Yes!"

Pushing her bra up over her breasts, he began to nibble and suck her nipples while still stroking her.

"You want it deeper?"

"Yes!"

He grabbed her legs, held them in the air, then balanced himself on his knees and pumped faster.

"Ohh, Poppi, please, I can't take it," Mina begged.

"I like it when you call me, Poppi."

Victor spread her legs open and slowed it down for her. Taking his thumb, he played with her clit. The combination of his thumb and his dick drove Mina crazy.

"Ohh, Poppi! Poppi, it's yours!"

"Goddamn, Ma, yo' pussy drippin' wet. Is it drippin' wet,

baby?" Victor teased as he felt her nearing an orgasm.

"Yes! Ohh, yes! Yes... ahh, Victor! Ohh," she squealed as she was about to cum.

"Baby, I'm cumming," Victor grunted as he came inside of her.

Still cumming, Mina lay on the floor and held her legs because they were shaking uncontrollably. Panting, she tried to steady her breath, but found it hard to since Victor was standing above her naked. The sight of his dick alone caused her to cum again. Looking at her he put his clothes back on. Pulling her bra and shirt back down, she attempted to stand up but failed.

Victor reached his hand out to help her and lifted her up off the floor. Standing up, she tried to walk to her office, but she still felt weak and her leg went out on her. Almost falling Victor grabbed her before she hit the floor.

"You a'ight?"

"I'm fine." Mina pushed him away. "I can stand up on my own." Embarrassed, she got an attitude yet again.

Victor laughed and watched as she disappeared into the back. She knew that she fucked up. Victor was supposed to be a one night stand thing and that was it. She was supposed to take her one night affair to her grave and leave it there. She never thought that she would let it happen again. She couldn't quite put her finger on it, but it was something in his deep-stroke that made her want more. She knew that Victor was nothing but a waste of her time because they could never be together but her body needed to have him.

She almost craved him. It was like she had to have him. Making love to him was like a high that she couldn't come down from. The way he made her feel seemed to slow down time. After splashing some cold water on her face she gathered her withered heart and headed back out to face him.

"You a'ight now." Victor smiled, knowing he had tore her shit up.

"Ha ha, funny." She tried to hide embarrassment. "But look, Victor, we need to talk."

"What's the deal now, Ma?" he asked sitting back in one of the chairs.

"Don't be difficult, Victor, I'm being serious."

"I am, too. You don't feel the chemistry between us, Mina?"

"I do, but I shouldn't be. Last night and today was cool, but it was a mistake. I shouldn't have let it happen."

"So you telling me you didn't enjoy that?"

"Yeah, but I gotta let you go."

"What's the problem, Ma? You got a man that's willing to do anything to be wit you and you gon' pass that shit up?"

"I want to be with you, Victor, but I can't!"

"Quit fighting it, Ma. It's inevitable. We gon' to be together."

"I told you that I'm feeling you! Why can't that be enough?"

Standing up, he walked over to Mina and gently caressed her face.

"Because you got me feeling things I ain't never felt before," he said as he wrapped his arms around her.

"I can't remember feeling like this, either. The shit is scaring me for real," she whispered.

"It's scaring me, too, Ma, but I got you, I ain't going nowhere." Victor turned her face to him.

Hugging him back, she inhaled his scent. She was contemplating leaving Andrew when her cell phone began to ring.

"Don't answer it."

"I gotta see who it is," she replied, while digging around in her purse. Frustrated, Victor sat back down in the chair.

"Hello? Hey, baby, yeah. I'm just running a little late…" She spoke while eying Victor. "I'll be home in about fifteen minutes. I love you, too, bye."

"So what now?"

"I'm going home to my fiancé and I'm going to pretend like this never happened and I suggest you do the same."

"If that's what helps you sleep better at night then go on keep lying to yourself."

"Look, I gotta lock up so…"

"I'm gon' check on you later. Meet me at the Amoco station on Kingshighway tonight around nine. I got something special planned for you," he said as he walked past her.

"Victor," she called, but he ignored her and kept walking.

Chapter Six

Volume Up

As she stood in front of her full-length mirror, listening to Faith Evans' song "Catching Feelings", Mina examined herself. With a dispassionate eye, she studied herself. Suddenly she wondered what men found attractive about her. Yeah, she had a pretty face, but that was about it. There were millions of women who looked like her and even better. Why Andrew and Victor chose her she could never figure out. Pulling her hair up with her hands, she tried to remember how she used to look. She desperately missed the old Mina. This new girl was an imposter and was not her at all.

The long hair, false eyelashes, pounds of makeup, and expensive clothes were all so superficial. Most women indeed would love to be in her shoes, but Mina felt suffocated. Andrew turned her into something she was not and she only had herself to blame. After rushing home that night and preparing dinner for him he opted to stand her up. Sitting on the couch she counted every minute that passed until he called.

At around eight o'clock, after blowing out the candles, she decided to go upstairs and get ready for bed, but before she climbed the stairs, the phone rang. It was Andrew. He called with the excuse that he was tied up campaigning for his father. Not wanting to hear any more of his lies, she told him that she was going to bed and hung up.

* * *

Truth be told, Andrew was on the other side of town having a threesome with Christi and Congressman Davis.

"Baby, come to back to bed," Christi whined as she pulled the satin sheets up over her breasts.

"I can't risk anybody seeing me leave your house this late. You know that," he said, becoming annoyed.

"But, Drew, I need you," she purred this time.

"I need you, too, darling, but we have to be careful. I will not jeopardize my career or my father's for you or anyone else. I thought that you understood that!"

"How long do you expect me to keep up with this charade?" Christi barked back.

"Um, this was nice guys but I have to get home before the wife has a fit," Congressman Davis said, placing his suit jacket on.

"Bye, Brandon," Andrew said, hugging him.

"Bye, babe, I had fun," Congressman Davis replied, kissing him on the lips.

"Bye, Brandon. Did you hear me, Andrew? How long do you expect me to wait?"

"We've already discussed this, Christi," he replied as he buttoned up his shirt.

"I just need to hear it one more time." She rubbed his back.

"I will only be married to Mina for a year and then you

and I will be together."

"I don't know how you do it. How can you stand being around that girl? I break out in hives after five minutes of being around her. You would have thought after being around a woman like me that by now she would be able to fit in. But no matter what she still looks like she belongs in the slums."

"Darling, I know I have tried, my mother has tried, but we just can't seem to break Mina of that ghetto mentality."

"So, honey, you haven't thought about sleeping with Mina since you've been with her?"

"What's with all the questions, huh? How many times do I have to tell you I don't look at her like that? Mina means nothing to me! Do you want me to sleep with her because if you keep on with the nagging, I'm not sure what I'll end up doing."

"I'm sorry. I just get a little jealous. You know I want you all to myself. Hell, I even hate sharing you with Brandon. I can't stand being here all alone at night when I know that you're across town... with *her*."

"I understand, but it's you I love. You have nothing to worry about when it comes to Mina."

"Oh, baby, I can't wait to wake up next to you everyday. You make so happy," Christi said as she kissed Andrew intensely.

"I have to go, Christi," he said as he tried to pry her off of him.

"But, Andrew, I need you," she growled as she pushed him down on the bed. Easing her way down she unzipped his pants with her teeth as her pink perky breasts dangled in the air. Inhaling deeply Andrew closed his eyes as Christi wrapped her mouth around his dick and sucked.

"Okay, but after this, I'm gone," he moaned.

"I'm sure," Christi looked up and smiled.

* * *

Checking her watch, Mina saw if she dressed quickly she would still have enough time to meet Victor. Racing back into her room she hurried and took a shower, applied her make-up, then stood in front of her walk-in closet. Mina's closet was magnificent. It held five hundred outfits and well over three hundred pairs of shoes. Everything was color coordinated and was put together according to style and season. She even had a rotating rack installed. If she wanted a specific outfit, instead of digging for it, all she would have to do is press a single button located on her wall.

Since she didn't know where they were going or what he had planned, she chose a simple, deep v-neck, pink spaghetti-strapped baby doll dress. Since it was a little chilly out, she adorned her arms with a pink shrug.Matching the dress with a pair of silver Gucci heels, she decorated her ears with a pair of diamond hoop earrings by Harry Winston. Delicious had already styled her hair into a bun and the M.A.C makeup she applied was flawless. Grabbing her silver clutch purse and keys, she headed out the door.

Twenty minutes later Mina was at the Amoco station on Kingshighway. She looked on as Victor stepped out of his Navigator. Everytime she saw him she was amazed at how good he looked. Victor had to be the finest man that she ever laid eyes on. His hair and goatee were freshly cut and perfectly lined. His kissable lips looked good enough to eat. Just the sight of him turned her on. His grey Sox baseball cap, R.I.P Escobar Gonzalez tee shirt, jeans, white S. Carters and an iced out chain brought out the thug in him that she loved.

"You look nice," she said, gathering her composure.

"Thank you." Victor smiled as she got out of the car. "You're going to ride with me. My man is going to watch your car while we're gone." A little unsure but not wanting to seem like a punk, Mina agreed. Walking over to his car, she wondered if he was going to tell her that she looked nice.

"I'm glad I wore this dress 'cause it's hot out here." She fanned herself, trying to get him to acknowledge her outfit.

"Yeah, I'm glad too. I wouldn't want you to be uncomfortable." Rolling her eyes as he opened the door for her, she got in.

"So where you wanna go?"

"Excuse me? You asked me out, not the other way around," Mina was confused.

"I know I did. I just figured you might want to go somewhere special."

"I thought you had something special planned."

"Nah, I changed my mind. So where you wanna go?"

"Wherever you want to is fine with me," she sucked her teeth.

"A'ight then. Let's go to the movies."

"To the movies?! Do I look like I'm dressed for the movies?"

"You said wherever I want to go you were cool with. I want to go to the show. There's a new Martin Lawrence movie out I want to see."

"Whatever. Let's just go so we can hurry up and get this thing over with." Halfway to the theater, Victor made another suggestion.

"You know what, I don't feel like going to the show tonight after all. Let's go to my crib and chill," he exhaled, smoking a blunt.

"Your house?" Mina said, fanning the air, mad that the weed smoke might get into her clothes.

"Yeah, let's just kick back, watch TV and order a pizza."

"Are you fucking kidding me?" she asked, ready to go off.

"Do I have to remind you about what you said?"

"No!"

Mina couldn't believe the outcome of their date. So far it was the worst date she had ever been on. Victor was conceited, selfish and inconsiderate. How she ever found him attractive, she would never know. She cursed herself for allowing herself to fall for him. Pulling up to a house in Spanish Lake, Mina sat with her arms crossed. She was pissed.

"What's wrong? You mad?" Victor asked, trying his damnest not to laugh.

"Shut up talking to me," she snapped.

"My bad. You coming or what?"

"You're not going to open the door for me?"

"You got two hands, don't you?"

"Ughh!!" Mina hopped out of the car and stomped up the steps behind him. After this night she vowed once more, this time meaning it, to never to talk to him again. Opening up the front door, he grabbed Mina's hand.

"Don't touch me," she yelled as he pulled her into the house. Stepping into the house Mina found a completely empty living room filled with thousands of pink and red rose petals scattered across the floor and a candlelit table set for two. Over twenty tea candles were lit around the room as Anthony Hamilton's "Since I Seen't You" played in the background. The only thing Mina could do was smile. She was so overwhelmed.

"You said whatever I wanted to do was fine with you, so I'm here to let you know that the only thing I want tonight is to be alone with you so we can spend some quality time together," he said sincerely.

"I can't believe you did all of this for me," she blushed.

"I told you that I wanted to take care of you. What, you thought I was bullshittin?" Leading her over to the table, Victor took her purse and helped her into her chair. Sitting across from her, he called out for the chef that he hired for the night.

"Good evening. I am Patrick, your chef. Tonight I have prepared a three course meal for you. First we will start off with grilled marinated shrimp, served on a bed of Polenta with a spicy pepper sauce. For the main course we have shrimp and bay scallops sautéed with garlic, tomato, white wine, arugula and basil served over spaghetti. And to top that off, for dessert, I have prepared for you my world famous chocolate caramel cheesecake."

"Wow, sounds good to me."

"Thank you Patrick," Victor said.

"You're welcome sir. Your appetizers will be out shortly."

"I don't know about the garlic, your breath gonna be stanking," Victor teased.

"Nigga, you eating the same thing," she laughed. "But anyway my breath won't be stinking because I always carry a toothbrush with me."

"For what? I wasn't gonna kiss you," he laughed.

"Ahh, that's messed up. I still can't get over all of this." She glanced around the room at the candles, roses and table.

"Your man ain't never done anything like this for you?"

"I don't want to talk about him," she answered, caught off guard by the mention of Andrew.

"I got yo' ass didn't I?"

"Yes you did."

"You should've seen your face. You were pissed off." He laughed and Mina liked the sound of his laugh. It was a deep baritone laugh that sounded sincere. Not phony like Andrew's laugh.

"I was 'cause you were getting on my nerves."

"See, I was just trying to surprise you. You feel stupid don't you?"

"You ain't got to rub it in."

"Yes, I do," Victor laughed as Patrick brought out their appetizers.

The two fed each other as if they were long time lovers. All the while, getting better acquainted. What more could they ask for...good conversation, good company and a connection so strong, nothing had ever felt so right before. After dessert Mina excused herself to restroom. Standing in front of the sink, after brushing her teeth, she examined her face in the mirror. Pleased with the way she looked she rejoined Victor in the living room.

"So are you enjoying yourself?"

"Yes, I am."

"Tell me something about yourself that most people don't know about you."

"Um, let me think... I love kids. I want to have a big family. Family and friends mean the world to me."

"How many kids do you want to have?"

"Maybe three or four, it all depends."

"Depends on what?"

"If I find the right man or not, plus I heard labor pains are a muthafucker."

Laughing at her last statement, Victor asked, "And what is the right man for you?"

"He has to be smart, sexy, funny, a little thuggish, loving, caring, attentive, respectful and honest. Oh and it doesn't hurt if he's good in bed," she laughed.

"So let me guess, that nigga you wit don't have none of those qualities 'cause if he did you wouldn't be here with me." Looking away she tried not to show how she really felt but was unable to. All of the pent up frustration she had felt over the past year began to spill out of her. Turning her head and wiping the tears from her eyes she tried not to let Victor see her cry.

"It's a'ight Ma, I got you," he said hugging her.

"I'm cool." Mina pushed him away. Showing her weaknesses was something Mina rarely did especially in front of a man. She didn't know how to handle Victor's sincerity.

"Come here," he took her hand guiding her into the middle of the floor.

"What are you doing?"

"Shh, just chill." Wrapping his arms around her waist, they danced to Donny Hathaway's, "I Love You More Than You'll Ever Know".

"I'm sorry for pushing you away."

"It's cool," he stroked her hair.

"I hate that I feel so calm when I'm around you."

"Why? That's a good thing."

"Nothing in my life has ever been calm. I don't know how to react when things are going good."

"Look, I ain't out to hurt or lie to you. If you haven't noticed, I'm feeling you like crazy."

"Me too." She flashed him a smile of contentment and laid her head on his chest as they swayed together in sync.

"Ay, blow out those candles for me," Victor asked, letting her go as the song went off. At first she was about to throw another hissy fit but after taking another glance around the room she thought different. Victor went through all the trouble to set up a private dinner for her in his house, the least she could do was blow out some candles.

"You know the words to this song mean a lot to me," he said as the song played again.

"They do?" she asked surprised.

"Yeah, every time I listen to it, I think of you," he said as he lit the fireplace.

"I don't know what to say."

"You ain't got to say nothing Ma, it's cool. I'm just letting you know that I'm feeling you."

"I'm feeling you, too, Victor." Mina turned around and smiled at him.

"To be honest with you, I haven't met a chick in a long time that made me want to spend all of my time with her."

"Oh, so you want to spend all your time with me?"

"Yeah. I told you I want to be your man," he said, watching her stop to pick up a light blue box in front of one the candles.

"What's this?"

"Open it." Biting down on her lip, she opened up the Tiffany box to find a diamond and platinum tennis bracelet.

"Victor!" Mina exclaimed with her mouth wide open.

"I know we don't really know each other that well, but I ain't never felt this way about a woman before. I ain't saying that we gon' be together or that this thing between us will work, but I promise to do all I can to be the man you deserve."

Feeling like she was going to pass out, Mina sat down on the floor to catch her breath. She didn't know what to do. Things were beginning to get out of control with Victor. He was just supposed to be a fuck, not the man she had secretly dreamed of her whole life. Thoughts of Andrew entered her mind, but the heart never lies and hers was screaming for her to give into Victor.

"Whaaat? Somebody shut up Mina?" Victor teased, sitting down in front of her.

"This is moving too fast for me."

"I know, it's moving fast for me, too, but I can't help the way I feel, Ma. I see you sitting here trying to be strong, but you don't have to do that. I got you and the quicker you admit it the better off you'll be." He stroked her cheek.

"I guess," she trembled at his touch.

"Nah, you know." Victor kissed her lips roughly as Alicia Keys' "Diary" echoed throughout the room.

Victor placed his body on top of hers as he ran his tongue in circles across her neck. Mina moaned. Caressing her breasts with his hand, he used the other to pull the straps of her dress down, Mina was all too ready get dicked down. After removing her dress, Victor planted small kisses all over her body.

Once he stopped at her thong, he looked up at her and gently removed it from her curvaceous hips. Surprised but pleased to see that her clit was swollen and extremely wet, he smiled. Taking his hand, Victor massaged her clit with his thumb. Not able to control herself anymore, Mina began rotated her hips to Victor's rhythm.

Removing his thumb, he began to flick her clit with his tongue. Shivering shots of electricity coursed through her body. In absolute heaven, Mina screamed from sheer ecstasy. Victor sucked her throbbing clit like there was no tomorrow, swirling his tongue up, down, from side to side and around. Nearing her first orgasm, Mina grabbed his head, begging for mercy. Not letting up he inserted two fingers inside while still sucking her clit. Cumming in his mouth, Victor enjoyed the taste of her sweet juices.

Whimpering and moaning she sucked his bottom lip. She wanted to taste the rest of him so she licked his neck and nipples as well. Eager to see what awaited her she pulled out his dick. Although familiar with his dick, she was always amazed to see that she could take all of him. Victor was straight packin'! Once she released the tool that was made to please her, he was completely naked.

Positioning herself between his legs, Mina laid on top of him. In her hand was the one thing that she craved the most. Lowering her head she placed her lips around the tip of his mammoth dick. She ran her tongue around the tip, then while holding the shaft, she bobbed up and down. Her hand was her guide as she sucked his dick until his body began to convulse.

Knowing what this meant, she eased up, looked at him with lust in her eyes and kissed him. Victor kissed her back so passionately, he began to scare himself. Taking control again, he placed himself in between Mina's thighs. With one swift move he was inside of her. He pushed deep inside her vaginal walls as he gripped her waist and slid all the way to her soul.

"Ahh!" Mina yelled as her eyes rolled into the back of her head.

Stroking her, Victor said, "You gon' quit fighting me now?"

"No," she said, knowing her response would make Victor work harder at what he was trying to accomplish. Victor laughed and placed her feet on his shoulders. Lifting her ass off the floor, he thumbed Mina's clit and began pounding harder and deeper into her pussy—a pussy that was a perfect fit for his dick.

"You gon' quit fighting me now?"

"Yes, baby, yes," Mina moaned in ecstasy as Victor's movements became faster. She grabbed his ass, wanting to cum with him. Their bodies moved together as they both came. After the mind-blowing orgasms, they were both drenched in sweat.

"Good," Victor said as he kissed her lips.

Chapter Seven

Previous

Two hours later, Mina was back at the Amoco station to pick up her car. Reluctantly hugging Victor goodbye, she got into her car and headed home. Safely back in the confines of her home she lay thinking about the men in her life. She figured as much that Andrew was cheating on her, but what could she do?

Thinking of Victor was the only thing that would keep her sane and warm at night. Her heart wanted him, needed him, but Andrew held this cloud over her that she felt she never could escape. She vowed to herself that after tonight she would never see Victor again, no matter how much it hurt. For nights, Mina cried herself to sleep because Victor was on her mind.

She wanted to hear his voice, feel his touch, just to be with him. He had tried calling her, but she would never answer the phone. After a week of chasing her he gave up and gave up his pursuit. She thought that everything was over between them.

Unbeknownst to Mina, Victor was across the street at the store watching her every move. Even though he tried, he couldn't go a day without seeing her. Somehow, she had stolen his heart and refused to let go. At night he would long for her, for them. During the day he would try to remember how her skin felt against his. He memorized everything that made her blush. Behind the clothes and makeup, he saw who the real Mina was on the inside – a young woman still trying to find herself. The way she smiled and the way her eyes sparkled under the moonlight showed her true beauty.

Victor could tell that behind her smile, she was hurting. Whoever her man was, he wasn't treating her right and he knew it. He just wished that Mina would give him the opportunity to show her what she was worth. She didn't even understand her affect on him. To him, whenever she was around, the world seemed to be better. All he wanted was to love her, but she wouldn't let him… if only she would let him.

Mina tried getting over Victor, but each day that passed only intensified her pain. Every hour seemed like a year and the lonely nights made her want him even more. Occasionally, Andrew would drop by and make her life a living hell. His lies and deceit were a known fact and he didn't even bother to cover them up anymore. One day, while washing his clothes, she found lipstick on his collar.A couple of days later he came by reeking of another woman's perfume. The following week, they accidentally switched phones so, when Mina went to answer what she thought was her phone, she was greeted with a warm "Come fuck me."

When the caller realized that it was Mina, she hung up. She wanted to be fed up, needed to be fed up, but Andrew held her future in his hands. Mina knew that she deserved better. She needed to feel what real love felt like as she never felt it before.

Love is what she felt whenever she was around Victor, but sadly enough, their love was forbidden. Weeks later she still cried herself to sleep. She wanted to wrap her arms around him or at least touch him. It was funny how he came into in her life and everything that she thought she knew suddenly wasn't true anymore.

For both Mina and Victor, this is how they felt. He wanted to love her but niggas like Andrew made her throw her guards up. Mina was sick and tired of being lied to and used. There was no way she could, or would, let that happen again.

Victor, on the other hand, knew this and was willing to do anything in his power to prove her wrong. He was not about to be blamed for the way Andrew treated her. He was going to show Mina that there was a better way. Anything that she wanted, or needed, Victor was willing to provide. He knew that to get Mina he had to take drastic measures. His mind was made up, he wanted her and would have her.

"Mina, you have a phone call on line two," Jodie said.

"All right, thanks. Hello?"

"Hey, Fat Momma," her mother spoke.

"Hi, Ma." Mina rolled her eyes, wishing she hadn't answered the phone. "Guess who I got to DJ the wedding," Rita said excitedly.

"Who, Ma?" Mina asked dryly.

"DJ Tossin Ted! Girl, your reception is gon' be off the chain!"

"Okay, Ma, good."

"What's your problem? You could be a little more enthu-siastic. Don't let all this glitz and glamour go to yo' head. You still my daughter and you still come from po' folks."

"Momma ain't nobody letting nothing go to they head! It's ya'll who are getting all caught up in this whole wedding fias-co!"

"Who are you yelling at, Mina Elise Matthews? Don't make me come up there and put my foot up yo' ass!"

"I'm sorry, Ma, I'm just stressed out and you're not helping by antagonizing me every five minutes."

"Well, I'm sorry for trying to help my child plan her wedding. You won't hear nothing else from me." Rita hung up.

Rolling her eyes to the ceiling, Mina hung up the phone. She knew that she had to make up with her mother so she made a mental note to go see her before the week was over. Glancing down at her bracelet her thoughts went to Victor. Pushing him out of her mind she continued with her work. Not even five minutes later, Jodie buzzed her again.

"Can you take a message, I'm busy?" Mina replied, annoyed.

"It's Andrew."

"All right. What is it, Andrew, I'm busy?"

"That's no way to talk to your future husband, sweetie."

"I don't have time for this today. What is it?"

"Have you gotten your dress for the Mayor's ball yet?"

"How many times do I have to tell you, I'm picking it up next Wednesday?" she answered, frustrated.

"You really need to check that tone of voice that you're using with me."

"I'm sorry. I've just been stressed out lately." She spoke in a softer tone.

"Well, I have great news. My father and I are going after one of the most dangerous drug cartels this side of the river."

"What?"

"You know that father needs something that is going to make him stand out against Carol Leverly so he's planning on, with the help of the Chief of Police, to bust this major Latino drug lord."

"That's great news, Andrew," she said unenthused.

"I may be a little late for dinner tonight so make sure that my food stays hot and that you're wearing something sexy, okay."

"Andrew, I am tired and I don't feel like cooking tonight."

"You feel like cooking when you want to feed your face! Have we forgotten who put up the money to open your lil' rinky dink, ghetto hair salon? The only thing I ask of you is to have dinner on the table and you can't even do that! Don't make me go there Mina, please don't."

"Why do you even want to marry me, Andrew? According to you I'm just some fat ghetto girl with no class that you spruced up and made better. Why would you even want to make me, of all people, your wife?"

"Because it makes me look good. Plus, marrying you will assure that my father gets the poor peoples' vote. Yeah, you're a little on the chunky side, but with a personal trainer, that can be solved."

"I hate you, I hate that I have to look at you, let alone marry your sorry ass!" Mina spoke through clenched teeth as she seethed with anger.

"Oh, is Mina mad? Trust me, sweetheart, you'll grow to love me just as much as I love you. Sooner or later, you'll get into the swing of things. But I have to go so have dinner on the table and wear that little black see through teddy for me tonight, a'ight. That is how you people say it, a'ight?" He laughed, hanging up.

Mina trembled with anger as she slammed the phone down. *How much longer can I put up with him, Lord?* she wondered. Pacing back and forth across the room she tried to regain her composure but found it next to impossible. Needing some fresh air, she grabbed her purse and sunglasses, and headed toward the front door.

"Mina, Mo is on line three," Jodie replied.

103

"Tell her I'll call her back later. I'm going to be gone for the rest of the day." She called over her shoulder as she rushed out the door.

"But, Mina," Jodie shouted after her.

Once Mina walked out of the door, she was faced with more bad news. Victor and some unidentified woman were leaving a store, Sole, together hand in hand. The sight of them stopped Mina dead in her tracks. Looking her way, Victor smiled and kept on moving.

Mina rushed to her car and got in, wanting to cry. Continuing to watch them through her rear-view mirror she tried to steady her breath. Victor held the beautiful Latino sistah's hand as she got into the car. Leaning over into the car he kissed her lips and stroked her hair. Mina became distraught as she remembered his words and everything he said to her. For a minute there she actually began to consider his feelings for her as being true.

Now standing up straight, Victor and the unknown woman continued to talk. He knew that Mina was watching them. Victor hated to do this to Mina, but it was for her own good. She needed to see what she was missing. She needed to realize that he was the one she needed. After another goodbye kiss, Victor's female friend left and he began to walk toward the Bread Company.

"Who the fuck was that?" Mina yelled across the street to him.

"You talking to me, Shorty?" he asked running across the street.

"Yeah, I'm talking to you. So… you've moved on to the next bitch now?"

"I don't know what you talking about, Shorty."

"You know damn well what I'm talking about, Victor! Last month you were all up in my grill telling me how much you loved me and now, you all out in the middle of the street kissing some video hoe reject. What you call yo' self—spittin' game to me or something?"

"Don't try to play the victim wit me, Shorty. You told me to move on so I did. Now you want to get mad 'cause I found somebody else. You need to make up your mind Ma, 'cause you confusing me."

"It doesn't matter what I said. You still ain't got no business flaunting that bitch in my face!"

"So you jealous?"

"Jealous? Jealous of what? That bitch can't make you feel like I do."

"Oh, for real?" he said as he leaned up against her pinning her to the car while holding her hands.

"What are you doing?" she whispered as she inhaled his breath which smelled like honey.

"Kiss me."

Grabbing his face, Mina kissed Victor with all of her might. Deep down inside, she knew in her heart that with him is where she needed to be. Victor kissed her lips, cheeks, eyes and nose while caressing her cheek.

"I'm sorry," Mina pleaded.

"I know."

"Do you really like her?"

"Fuck nah, I just used her to make you jealous," he laughed.

"You dirty muthafucker," she said, pounding her fist into Victor's chest. "Don't do me like that again, I was gonna kick your ass." Mina pushed him, laughing, too.

"It worked though, I got you back," he said pulling her into him.

"Yeah, it did work." Hugging him tightly, she smiled.

"So you mine? You ready to leave ol' boy now?" he asked

seriously.

Mina tried to find one reason to say no but she couldn't as she gazed into his eyes. Seeing him with another woman, and how she reacted to it, only showed her that being with him was what she wanted. Leaving Andrew would be difficult. He was going to do everything in his power to make her life miserable but having Victor by her side would make the ride all that better.

"Yeah, just give me a week to get my stuff in order and I will be all yours," she kissed him again.

"Don't be on no bullshit, Mina."

"I'm not. With you is where I want to be."

"Come see me tonight."

"I can't." Mina sighed and dropped her head thinking of Andrew.

Holding her chin up he said, "I got you Ma, I ain't going nowhere. Whatever you need to do to get away from that nigga, you do it. I'll be here waiting for you."

Later that night as she prepared dinner for Andrew, Mina danced her way around the kitchen listening to Keyshia Cole's "I Changed My Mind." She'd already made an appointment to talk to a lawyer the next day. There had to be a way to buy Andrew's share of the salon. Besides, the shop, her house, car, credit cards and bank accounts were in his name, so without him, she had nothing. She couldn't believe how she let him control every aspect of her life. Just as she was about to rethink her decision, Victor's face appeared in her mind. Smiling to herself she knew that with him everything would be okay.

"Mina, honey you home?" Andrew yelled.

Rolling her eyes, she stood frozen stiff. She couldn't wait for the day that Andrew would be out of her life for good.

"I'm in here," she yelled.

Walking into the dining room Andrew found that the table was set for two. Mina put out her best china and the room was lit by two candles and soft music was playing in the background. To him the room was set for love.

"Sweetheart, you've outdone yourself. I almost thought for a second that you might disobey me," he said as he kissed her on the cheek.

Rubbing her cheek she tried to erase his kiss.

"What's with the robe? You're ruining the visual I had of you."

"Excuse you, but I was cold. It ain't like I got that many clothes on up underneath here."

"Well, take if off. You're ruining the moment."

Beyond annoyed, Mina untied her robe and let it fall to the floor.

"What the hell is that you got on?"

"What you don't like it?"

"I told you to wear your black teddy not some old, holey, Guess T-shirt."

"You said to wear something sexy. This makes me feel sexy."

"You're really pushing it, Mina."

"Whatever. You ready to eat 'cause the food is getting cold."

"Yeah, maybe your cooking will be better than your outfit."

"I'm sure you'll love it." Mina smirked as she left the room.

"So what's for dinner?" he asked cheerfully as if nothing happened.

Returning to the dining room, she told him to close his eyes.

"This must be good." Andrew smiled, rubbing his hands

together.

"Okay, open your eyes."

Standing back she crossed her arms and waited for his reaction. Andrew sat looking at the Ramen noodles with hot dogs floating around in a bowl like at any moment it would come alive.

"Is this some kind of joke?"

"No, this is what us po' folks like to eat."

"What is this?" he asked angrily.

"It's Ramen noodles and hot dogs. Everybody in the hood eat this."

"Are you trying to make me angry?"

"How much longer did you think I was going to put up with your bullshit?" Mina shouted.

"Who are you talking to?"

"You, muthafucker! What, you thought I was just gonna sit by and let you treat me like shit! Whose number is 566-5128?"

"Just who do you think you're talking to, Mina? This is my house! I pay all the bills up in here! You don't question me, I question you!"

"Fuck you, nigga, you don't run me!"

"You still don't get it, do you? I do run you, I run everything up in here!" he yelled, pushing her up against the wall.

"I ain't got time for this shit, Andrew! I don't love you anymore!" she pushed him back. Without even an ounce of hesitation, he drew his hand back, and punched her in the face. Holding her eye, she wondered whether or not she should hit him back.

"I'm sorry, I didn't mean to do that." He apologized trying to come near her.

"Get away from me!"

"You just get me so riled up sometimes. I don't blame you,

Mina, I haven't been a good fiancé to you but I'm willing to try."

"Well, I don't want to try anymore! That lame-ass apology you just gave is not going to make me feel any different!"

"I just wanna make it up to you, Mina. Let me make it up to you. Let's make love." He tried to hold her.

"What? So it can last three minutes."

"No, correction it's only three minutes with you!" Andrew yelled as he grabbed his suit jacket and left.

Chapter Eight

Volume Down

June 15, 2005, a month and a half before the wedding, and Mina was on her way to work. She didn't want to go, but later on that day, she had a meeting with her contractors for the new salon. With over sized Fendi glasses covering her eyes, she pulled up to the curb and parked in her spot. Getting out of her car she tried her best to avoid Victor, only to run into him anyway.

"What's up, lil' Momma? I missed you last night," he said, approaching her.

"Hey, Victor," she spoke solemnly, trying to conceal her face with her hand.

"What's up? What's wrong?" Victor could tell through her demeanor that something was wrong.

"Nothing, I'm just a lil' tired," she said, trying to avoid his eyes.

"Give me a hug." Standing still, she let him wrap his arms around her. "You not gon' hug me back?" Reaching her arms around him, she half-heartedly hugged him back.

"What kind of hug was that? I know you can do better than that Ma. Show yo' man some love." Hugging him again, this time with feeling, she tried her best not to cry.

"What's the deal? You mad at me or something?"

"No," she whispered with her head down.

"Why you got your head down and what's with the glasses? It's not even sunny out." He tried to take them off.

"Look, just leave me the fuck alone!"

"Yo', calm down! What the fuck is wrong with you?"

"I just don't feel like being touched right now!"

"Something ain't right Ma. What's up?

"Will you just leave me alone!" she yelled trying to walk away.

"Mina, come here!" Stopping dead in her tracks she knew that Victor wasn't going to give up until he found out the truth. "I don't know what the fuck is wrong is you! But this pushing me away shit ain't gon' even work! Now tell me what's wrong wit you!"

"Victor, just let me go okay? I will talk to you later," she said as tears fell from her eyes. Walking up behind her he placed his arms around her and kissed the back of her head.

"I'm sorry, Ma, I didn't mean to yell at you. I just want to know what the problem is. Is it that nigga? Did he do something to you?" Mina was silent. "Did he hurt you?"

Staying silent, she nodded her head. Turning her around, Victor lifted her head up, and slid the glasses from her eyes. Mina winced as he pulled the glasses from her face, then she looked the other way.

"What the fuck happened to your eye?"

"He hit me last night when I told him I didn't want to be with him anymore." She sobbed.

"Where he at? I put that on my old dude, he's dead!"

"No, you can't go anywhere near him Victor. I can handle him."

"Ma, the nigga hit you in the eye. I don't call that handling him. You're coming home with me tonight."

"I can't."

"It's nothing. I told you from day one that I got you."

"I still have some things that I need to take care of. Besides, I don't want you to get involved in this. By the end of the week I will be free. You have nothing to worry about."

"I don't know Ma. What kind of man would I be if I didn't handle this for you? You questioning my manhood right now, Mina."

"I'm not questioning your manhood because I know exactly what you would do and that's why I don't want you involved. Just let me handle this my way, okay."

"A'ight, I will, but after you leave that nigga, he's mine."

* * *

Mina's one-week agreement with Victor was almost up. The lawyer she consulted with didn't help the situation at all. At their meeting, he divulged to her that there was really nothing at all she could do but stay with Andrew, or leave, and lose everything. All of her assets were actually his so if she left him she would leave with nothing.

The only way she could attain any of the assets was if she were to marry Andrew and then divorce him. That was only if they were without a prenuptial agreement. The only thing that Mina could do at that point was cry. Leaving Andrew would cost her everything. *Is being with Victor really worth it?* she questioned herself on the ride to the shop. Parking her car directly in front she looked across the street at the FootLocker in hopes of seeing Victor but he wasn't there.

"What's up, ya'll?" she said as she entered the shop.

"Hey, Mina Diva," Janiya spoke while lining up one of her

clients.

"The cleaners called, Mina. They said you can come pick up your clothes today," Jodie informed.

"Anything else?'

"Oh, yeah, your friend from across the street came in here looking for you earlier."

"What did he say?" Mina asked, excitedly.

"Nothing really. He just asked if you were here and I told him no."

"Did he say that he was gonna come back later?"

"No, sorry."

"Looks like Rio Grande over there got you all shook up." Delicious grinned, while reading *The Ex Factor* by TuShonda Whitaker.

"Shut up, Delicious," Mina said, blushing while smiling for the first time that day.

"For real, gurl. It's written all over your face," Janiya said.

"It's that obvious?" she asked as she slumped down in an empty chair.

"Honey, you been moping around here all week. Hell, I get depressed just looking at you and what's up wit the glasses? You've been wearing them all week?" Delicious questioned.

"I don't know, I just like wearing them," Mina lied, hoping he wouldn't pry any further. Changing the subject she said, "Ya'll just don't understand the kind of situation I'm in."

"What's the 411, Hon?" Delicious asked, putting down the book.

"Okay, you know that I'm supposed to marry Andrew soon."

"Right."

"The thing, is I don't want to be with Andrew any more. I want to be with Victor."

"The plot thickens." Delicious excitedly rubbed his hands together.

"But, if I leave Andrew, he is gonna take the shop, my house, my car and every other thing that I have."

"How could he possibly take all your stuff away from you?" Janiya questioned.

"Easy. His name is on everything, not mine."

"Girl, is you crazy? You don't let no man run yo' life like that. I could slap you in yo' mouth Mina." Delicious began pacing the floor.

"I know, I'm sorry ya'll." Mina broke down and cried.

"Don't pay him no mind, Mina." Tiffany gave Delicious the evil eye.

"No, he's right. I'm stupid. All of this is my fault. I was in such a rush to get out of the hood that I believed everything Andrew said to me. I never once sat back and peeped the situation like I should have. He basically owns me, and if I leave him, I will basically be leaving him with nothing but the shirt on my back."

"He won't get away with it, Mina. I won't let him," Mo declared as she walked into the shop.

"There ain't nothing we can do. I'm gon' have to live the rest of my life with a man that I don't love."

"Sweetie, you said that you were leaving Andrew for Victor. Victor got money, don't he?" Mo asked.

"Yeah, but I love Victor too much to ask him for anything. I haven't even told him who Andrew is yet."

"You mean to tell me that Chiquita Taco Bell don't know that the Mayor's son is your fiancé?" Delicious questioned.

"No, I haven't told him yet. I didn't think it was that important."

"You better hope not," Mo said.

"I asked Victor to give me a week so I could get myself

together but today is the last day and I still haven't broken up with Andrew. As a matter of fact, today is the Mayor's Ball and I have to attend the party with him tonight."

"You have to tell him tonight, Mina," Tiffany spoke.

"You're right. I have to end all of this madness tonight. Whatever happens, happens. I can't continue to live my life in fear of Andrew and his family."

"Child, don't worry about us we are going to be fine. Now, you just pull yourself together and go on in that bathroom and splash some cold water on your face. I can't have you going to a ball with bags under your eyes." Delicious hugged her, trying to make her feel better.

"Thank you, Delicious," Mina hugged him back.

"Go on now."

Watching her until she disappeared into the back, Delicious turned around to the girls and said, "Ain't no way in hell we gon' let that token fag take our shop away."

"What the hell is a token fag?" Mo asked.

"It's what Andrew is, honey. A man that denies he is gay."

"Get out of here." Janiya waved him off.

"I'm telling you that boy ain't nothing but an angel with a dirty face."

"A what?" Mo asked.

"You know, a tambourine player."

"When you say tambourine player what do you mean?" Jodie asked.

"Do I have to spell it out for you bitches? Andrew is gay," Delicious shouted, not knowing that Mina was standing right behind him.

"What?" she shrieked, dumbfounded.

"Dear Lord, forgive me for I have sinned," Delicious said as he turned to face Mina.

"Andrew is what?" Mina asked again.

"Is it just me or do ya'll feel a little faint?" he said in his best Southern accent.

"You need to learn how to shut your mouth sometimes," Tiffany said as she rushed over to Mina's side.

"No, I think Delicious is right," Mo agreed.

"You think that my Andrew, the man that I have been with for over a year, is gay?"

"Yes." Delicious answered.

"Don't you think if Andrew were gay, I would know?"

"Sometimes they can slip under your radar, honey."

"You're wrong, Delicious. There's no way that Andrew could be gay," Janiya argued.

"Look a here, honey, I know a man lover when I see one. Why do you think this whole time I have been referring to Andrew as my future baby daddy."

"We all thought you were just playing," Jodie whispered, almost as distraught over the news as Mina.

"Mina, sweetie, I am so sorry that you had to find out this way but your man is bi-sexual."

"I don't know, Delicious," she replied, still unsure but thoughts of Andrew and Congressman Davis in the bathroom together continued to pop in her head.

"I'm telling you, girl, you know that I would never steer you wrong."

"This is just way too much for me to deal with right now. I have a ball that I have to attend so can we just drop this whole thing? Delicious, you have thirty minutes to do something fabulous to my hair."

* * *

Three hours later Mina stood by Andrew's side as they mingled with friends. That year's ball was decorated beautifully. Gold hanging lamps hung from the wall, giving the room a Moroccan feel. Still, the day's events hadn't left Mina's mind.

She would catch herself every now and then surveying Andrew's body language and gestures. Nothing about him spoke gay to Mina. Andrew was just an ordinary, square brother.

"Andrew, darling, how are you?" Christi purred as she kissed him on the cheek.

"How are you, Christi? You look absolutely ravishing tonight," he responded.

"Doesn't she? Christi you out do yourself every time," Mrs. Wellington agreed, taking a sip from her fifth glass of champagne.

"Thank you. I try."

"Mina, you look nice," Christi spoke dryly as she glanced over Mina's black halter Versace dress that hugged every curve of her body.

"Thank you," Mina replied back in an even drier tone.

"I think the dress is a little too tight but you know that's how Mina likes it," Mrs. Wellington chimed in.

"The dress is supposed to fit tight. That's how the designer cut it to fit," Mina shot back insulted.

"Now, now ladies calm down," Andrew refereed.

"Mother Wellington, I do have to come by for tea one day soon," Christi said.

"Yes, dear, I would love that."

"Why don't you, Mina and Mother make it a date?" suggested Andrew.

"Dear, now you know that high tea is not Mina's thing. I'm sure she has other things she would like to do besides hang around Christi and me."

"She's right, Andrew. Mina has her, how do you say, 'shop' to attend to," Christi snickered.

"Well, I think that it would be great if you started to include Mina in more. Mina dear what do you think?" Andrew asked.

"There ain't no way in hell that I would have tea with money bags and Christi Love here if you paid me," she said as she rolled her eyes and walked away.

"Well, I never!" Mrs. Wellington put her hand over her heart and gasped.

"And you never will," Mina shot over her shoulder at them.

"I told you, she has no class whatsoever." Christi shook her head.

"I can't wait until the day that scallywag is out of our lives," Mrs. Wellington exclaimed appalled.

"Excuse me, ladies and gentlemen, dinner is now served," the Master of Ceremonies announced.

After being seated for dinner, Mina sat quietly picking at her food while everyone else chit-chatted. Whenever she did pay attention to the conversation, she would catch Christi and Mrs. Wellington looking at her while whispering to one another. She couldn't take it anymore after tonight. No matter what, she was leaving Andrew. No longer could she tolerate him, Christi, or his family. Accidentally dropping her fork she bent to pick it up when a waiter bent down to grab it for her. Before she could even say "thank you" she noticed Andrew eyeing the waiter's butt out of the corner of his eyes.

"I'll be right back, let me get you another fork, ma'am," the waiter spoke.

"Okay," Andrew answered for her.

With her eyes scrunched, she sat shocked. When Andrew caught her staring, he asked, "What?"

"Uh, nothing," she said.

Returning with a clean fork, the waiter went to hand it to Mina but Andrew graciously eased it from his hand. Gazing up at the waiter, he smiled and said "thank you" almost as sweetly as Delicious would. At any moment Mina thought that she would throw up. Delicious was right. Andrew was gay. Disgusted, yet at the same time overjoyed, she knew that ousting Andrew was the only way to get him out of her life for good.

With dinner finished everyone gravitated to the dance floor. Dancing closely to Andrew for the first time in almost a year, Mina smiled. She didn't even mind being close to him because she knew that after tonight she would never have to be again. Dreaming of running into Victor's arms, she hugged Andrew even tighter. Resting her head on his shoulder, she pretended like he was Victor. Closing her eyes, she swayed to the beat and dreamt of him. Mina was so far off in la la land that she didn't even notice the photographer taking pictures of them.

Chapter Nine

Rip

The next day couldn't come fast enough for Mina. She couldn't wait to get to the shop to tell Delicious and the crew the news. Grabbing her purse out of the backseat of her car she rushed into the shop.

"Mina!" everyone shouted as she walked through the salon doors.

"What's up, everybody?" She smiled, hugging Delicious, Janiya, Tiffany, Neosha and Jodie. As she hugged everybody, she noticed Mo, on the phone, having a heated conversation.

"Nigga, fuck you!" Mo yelled into the phone.

"What's wrong with her?" Mina whispered to Delicious.

"What ain't wrong with her? It's Quan's ass again," Delicious pursed his lips and rolled his eyes.

"I should've known but look, I got something to tell you."

"*Heeey*, turn that up," Janiya requested as the Ying Yang Twins song, "Wait" began to play on the radio.

"Ah, uh, that song gets no play in my shop." Mina shook

121

her head.

"Why not, girl? This is my jam." Janiya stood up and danced, bouncing her big booty.

"Girl, you got too much ass back there to be bouncing yo' booty like that," Delicious teased.

"Don't hate. Come on, Mina. Let me turn it up."

"No, them niggaz is disrespecting woman to the fullest. *Ay, bitch, wait till you see my dick.* I think not."

"I heard they handicapped," Neosha added.

"Now ain't that some shit." Tiffany doubled over in laughter.

"Ain't no need for ya'll to be talkin' about the Ying Yang Twins. Half of ya'll daddies in here retarded," Delicious teased.

"Delicious, you need to quit," Mina cracked up, holding her side.

"Whatever, nigga! I know you were with her last night! You know what? Quan go and be with the bitch!" Mo yelled, hanging up in his ear.

"Girl, if you don't calm down, I'm gon' put yo' ass out," Mina said, seriously. "My bad, girl. He just get under my skin."

"Tell me what happened." Mina sat beside her.

"I just found out he fucking with some chick named Sherry."

"How you know that?"

"Because the bitch been playing on my phone and shit. Leaving messages talkin' about how they just got done fucking. I know the bitch ain't lying because she's telling me what he had on that day down to his drawers."

"What you wanna do? Do we gotta beat a bitch's ass?"

"Nah, fuck her. I'ma fuck his ass up. That's what I'm gon' do."

"Girl, why don't you just leave his ass?"

"'Cause that nigga paid, plan and simple."

"You deserve so much better though, Mo."

"You got that right," said one of ladies in the shop.

"Look, when it all boils down to it, it's up to you to decide whether or not you wanna leave. Because we ain't the one sleeping in your bed at night, you are," Mina replied trying her best to give some advice when her own life was fucked up.

"I know, but hey, it ain't like I ain't doing my thing too."

"I guess but let me tell ya'll what happened last night!" Mina yelled amped.

"What? Nelly finally came to his senses and left that non-singing, two left feet having, skank Ashanti alone?" Delicious asked, seriously.

"No, Delicious. I got something even better than that." Mina jumped up and down with anticipation.

"Well, spill the beans, honey," he said.

"Andrew is gay."

"Girl, that's old news. I told you that yesterday," Delicious rolled his eyes and waved her off.

"I think he might only be attracted to white men though."

"Ohh... he's one of those, I see," Delicious said, scratching his chin, thinking.

"One of what?" Janiya asked.

"Andrew, my dear, is what we gay folks call a *Dairy Queen*."

"A what?" Neosha laughed.

"Hold up sweetie let me school these chicks," Delicious placed down his comb speaking to one of his clients. "Let me break it down for you heterosexuals. A *Dairy Queen* is an African American, Hispanic, or Asian man who is only interested in white men as their sexual partners. They normally are attracted to white men with blonde hair," Delicious spoke in his best school teacher's voice.

"Enough of that nonsense so Mina, how did you figure it out?" Jodie asked.

"We had just been seated for dinner and I dropped my fork, right? Well, I lean over to pick it up, but a waiter reaches and gets it before I do."

"Let me guess. He was white with blonde hair." Delicious's eyes danced with mischief.

"Yeah, I ain't ever seen Andrew act so fruity in my life!" Mina laughed.

"Oh my, God! What did he say?" Tiffany asked.

"He was like thank you," Mina said, doing her best gay impersonation.

"Eww. Yo' man an ass hound." Janiya danced around like she had the he-be-je-bes.

"Shut up, Janiya, 'cause Andrew is not my man anymore."

"Well, it sure looks like he's your man in this newspaper," Delicious handed her the morning paper.

Mina gazed down at the newspaper and sat down, astonished. She didn't even know that the photograph was taken. Feeling herself becoming faint she exhaled and let out a much needed breath. Praying to God, she hoped that reading the paper was something Victor didn't do.

"What's wrong, Mina?" Jodie questioned.

"Nothing."

"She worried about Fat Joe and the Terror Squad seeing that picture 'cause if he do he gon' lean back on dat ass," Delicious joked.

"What am I gonna do? If Victor sees this he is gonna flip."

"Just tell him, Mina," Tiffany urged, holding Mina's hand.

"Yeah, if he cares about you as much as he says he does, then he'll understand," Neosha agreed.

"I hear you, but I don't know."

"Mina you better make sure you get an AIDS test done."

Tiffany warned fearing for the worst.

"Oh, girl, you don't even have to worry about that. I made sure Andrew always stayed strapped. Besides, I haven't fucked him since I started fucking Victor. "

"Good." Tiffany blew out a sigh of relief.

"LOOK, girl, if that fine, viral, sexy, handsome, thugged-out Latino stud doesn't understand then FUCK HIM! I mean a man that fine doesn't come along that often, but you'll get over it eventually." Delicious tried to help but really could not.

"Once again, Delicious, thank you for your words of encouragement." Mina looked at him, rolling her eyes.

"Hey that's what I'm here for. I see how my wisdom and encouragement feeds ya'll's misguided, underachieved minds. Ya'll know I'm the gay Oprah. I fix lives."

"Delicious, *SHUT UP*! You don't help shit around here. All you do is run yo' goddamn mouth," Neosha shot.

"Have you been sent here to hurt me? Is the devil knocking on my door? What did I do to get such treatment from you," he said pretending, to cry.

"Huh. Delicious, I'm sorry. I didn't mean it." Neosha hugged him.

"I know you didn't, *girl*. I forgive you. You do love me after all don't you?"He asked smiling ear to ear.

"We all love you, you big dork. Now can we get back to Mina." Tiffany interjected.

"Oh, no, she didn't!" Delicious snapped his fingers.

"Oh, yes, I did." Tiffany shot back, getting into Delicious' face.

"WILL BOTH OF YA'LL JUST SHUT UP," Mina scolded.

"On… that morning...when… this… life… is over…I'll fly away," Jodie sang.

"Now what was that for?" Delicious asked.

"It was too much evil in this room. All ya'll need some

healing."

"I'm sorry, Mina," Tiffany said, ignoring Jodie.

"Yeah, Mina, me, too," said Delicious.

"It's cool. I just gotta get out of here," Mina grabbed her purse and headed toward the door.

"Remember. We're here for you Mina, and Jesus is too," Jodie yelled after her.

"Okay, Jodi," Mina yelled back.

Jumping in her car she drove forty minutes to Victor's house. Her heart didn't know what to expect once she reached the door and knocked. After pulling her hair up into a ponytail she gave herself the once over and walked up the long flight of steps. Blocking the fear that lay deep down in her, she knocked. With her ear next to the door she listened as footsteps neared the door.

"Hello?" Julisa, the maid from the last time she was there asked.

"Hi, do you remember me? My name is Mina and I'm here to see Victor."

"Is Mister Gonzalez expecting you ma'am?"

"No, he isn't. This is a last minute visit but I'm sure it's okay." Mina bogarded her way through the door.

"You can't just come in here unannounced ma'am," Julisa shouted, trying to catch up with Mina.

"Which room is he in?" Mina said, opening up each door as she walked down the hallway.

"Armando, we have an intruder," Julisa yelled into the walkie talkie.

"Trust me, you won't get in trouble," Mina said as she rounded the steps two at a time. Opening one of the doors, Mina found a room built for a little princess. Shocked, she stopped for a moment, until she saw Julisa the maid approaching.

"If you stop now we won't call the police," Armando the

driver yelled. Running now, Mina opened another door and found Victor but he wasn't alone. In front of him was a large, round, mahogany table. On it were stacks of money with bricks of cocaine and heroin sitting beside it. Confused she locked eyes with Victor.

"Mina, what are you doing here?" he asked.

"I'm sorry sir, I tried to stop her but she got past me," Julisa pleaded, out of breath.

"It's okay. Leave us alone for a minute," Victor instructed.

"Yes, sir," Julisa replied, closing the door behind her.

"You should've let me know you were coming."

"What's going on?" she asked still staring at the contents of the table. Taking her by the hands, Victor searched deep within her eyes and wondered if she could handle what he was about to tell her. Seeing only confusion, and a woman clearly afraid, he told himself that it was now or never. He had to tell her the truth if they were ever to be together.

"Victor, answer me what is this shit!"

"Mina, calm down. I've wanted to tell you something for the longest but I just didn't know how to."

"Tell me what!?" she asked frightened.

"I know you've heard in the news about how the Mayor is trying to end any and all drug trafficking here."

Nodding, she agreed.

"Well, I'm the one supplying all of those drugs. But I'm about to forget all this shit and go legit. In a couple more months I will be done," he said, trying to make the situation better than it was.

Snatching her arms from his she yelled, "You lied to me?"

"I didn't lie to you I just never mentioned it before." Victor tried to hold her hands again but she only squirmed away. Pacing the floor she tried to comprehend what she had just been told.

"Listen, Mina, I like you. Sometimes I even think I love you but this is what I do and that's not gonna change. At least not now it isn't."

"So when were you going to tell me about this, Victor?"

"I don't know. Whenever the time was right."

"There was never going to be a right time! This is my life that you're playing with. I have a legit business that I'm trying to run! I can't be tied to a fucking drug dealer!"

"Why not?"

"What part of that didn't you understand!?"

"Shorty, I would never put you in harm's way."

"You're not God. You can't protect me! And I was actually going to leave my fiancé for you," Mina said, shaking her head. Holding her in his arms, Victor tried to ease the hurt she felt.

"I got you, Shorty, I told you I'm not going no where. If you need some time to think then that's cool. But I'm not giving up on you that easily," Lifting her chin up he stared her directly in her eyes and kissed her lips. Mina couldn't help melting in his arms as she wrapped her arms around his neck and kissed him back.

"Sometimes I just wish that I could leave you alone," she whispered.

"But you can't," he said kissing her again.

"Yo', Victor, check this out! That bitch Mina on the front page hugged up with the Mayor's son!" Dro yelled as he entered the room.

Releasing his lips from hers, Victor's face turned to stone as soon as the words left Dro's mouth.

"What did you say?" Victor seethed with anger as he forcefully pushed Mina away.

"Let me explain," Mina said, for the first time feeling afraid of Victor.

"Explain what—that you a snake? I told you that bitch wasn't no good." Dro handed Victor the newspaper. Skimming over the article he read that Mina and Andrew were engaged and that they had were together for almost two years.

"It isn't what you think," Mina protested, hyperventilating.

Pulling his silencer from out of his pants Dro pointed it towards Mina's head.

"Oh, my God," Mina screamed.

"Yo' let me gon' ahead and murk this bitch," Dro said with his finger itching to pull the trigger.

"You've been lying to me?" Victor was finally able to ask.

"I didn't know how to tell you," Mina cried.

With his lips trembling, Victor continued, "I get it, they've been using you to get information on me."

Shaking her head no, Mina didn't know what he was talking about.

"She probably got on a wire now," exclaimed Dro with wide eyes.

Throwing the paper down to the floor Victor viciously tore opened Mina's blouse. Mina jumped, trembling with fear at the sound of her shirt beginning torn open.

"I swear I don't know what you're talking about, Victor! Just let me explain! I was gonna leave Andrew today, I swear!"

"She lying, dog!" Dro instigated as he eyed Mina's breasts. Finished searching Mina, Victor stood back up.

"She ain't got no wire on." Victor breathed heavily.

Pulling her shirt back together, Mina covered her chest up. Sniffling she tried to reach out to Victor but he smacked her hand away.

"Bitch, don't touch me!"

"Bitch?" Mina asked hurt.

Easing her way around the gun that was pointed at her face, she followed Victor across the room.

"Just me give me the word dog," Dro said eager to pull the trigger.

"You believe me, don't you?" Mina asked.

"Even if you are telling the truth how could I ever trust you? You're fucking engaged to the Mayor's son!" he yelled, startling Mina. "Do that nigga know about me!?"

"No!" she yelled back.

"Why are you still talking to this bitch, man?" Dro questioned.

"Man, shut up! And put that gun away!" Victor tried to clear his mind.

"Listen to me, baby. Just... let me explain," Mina tried once more. Now seated on the couch Victor held his face in his hands and tried contemplating the situation.

"Get the fuck out." Victor finally replied, still confused.

"What?" Mina asked.

"You heard me. Get the fuck out," he yelled once more.

"You just gon' let her go?" Dro asked in disbelief.

"So that's it? You're not gonna even let me explain?"

"If I have to tell you one more time to get the fuck out of my crib, I swear to God I'ma kill you myself," Victor shouted, shooting daggers with his eyes.

Wiping her face, Mina summoned what was left of her dignity and pride and left.

Chapter Ten

Eject

The ride home from Victor's was a blurred one for Mina because her eyes were clouded with tears. Putting it all together, she figured out that Victor was the Latino drug lord that Andrew was talking about. She couldn't believe that Victor treated her that way. She thought they meant more to each other than that.

Mo and Delicious continuously called her on her cell since she left the shop earlier that day, but she was too drained to answer. Peeling off her clothes, she stepped into the shower. Mina let her tears flow freely as she stood underneath the hot running water. Once she finally stepped out she realized that she had been in the shower for almost an hour. Thanking God that it was a Saturday she knew that she had two days to pull herself together before she would have to face everybody at the shop.

Sunday and Monday came and went and Mina still hadn't moved from the bed. She laid in bed the entire weekend, listening to Mariah Carey's "We Belong Together" thinking of Victor. Only getting up because she had to pee she headed to the bathroom. Smelling herself she noticed the stench coming from under her arms for the first time. After peeing she was just about to hop into the shower when she heard a knock on the door. Hoping it was Victor, she raced down the flight of stairs and opened it without asking who it was.

"Lawd, save me. It's the exorcist," Delicious shouted, frightened by her appearance.

"I ain't got time for yo' shit today, Delicious," Mina warned as she turned and left him and Mo standing.

"Girl, what is up wit you? We have been calling you since Saturday," Mo questioned.

"Yeah, we figured you were up in that big ol' mansion wit Victor getting your freak on, so we let you be. But clearly that wasn't the case." Delicious eyed her appearance once more.

"That was until Jodie said you wouldn't be coming to work today," Mo said.

"Let me guess? He didn't take the news well," Delicious asked.

"No, he didn't and it's all because of Dro, that funky ass cousin of his," Mina said, angered all over again.

"What happened?" After telling the story of what happened, Mina was in tears. "Oh, no, that nigga did not play my girl like that," Delicious declared.

"Yes he did. He played me for a fucking a fool. I actually let myself believe that that nigga cared about me," she cried.

"Oh, pooh pooh everything's gonna be all right," Mo said, hugging her.

"Girl, don't be sittin' up there letting that Enrique Iglesias-looking muthafucker make you cry," Delicious demanded.

"I know, I'm sorry. It just hurts."

"Do you still want to be with Victor?" Mo asked.

"Yes, but it's over," Mina answered.

"It's not over. As of right now your, little pity party is over. If you still want Victor, then Victor is what you're going to get," Mo declared.

"Right, by the time we're done with Lil Ricky, he will be eating out of the palm of your hand," Delicious added.

"Are you sure?" Mina asked.

"Was Ashanti sure when she cut those Elvis side burns off? Yes because album sales went up. Was Beyonce sure when she booty hopped her way all the way to Grammys? Yes because she won five Grammys for showing some skin and backing that ass up. Was Puffy's baby momma Kim sure when she filed child support on that ass for their son and her son by another man? You goddamn right because the bitch went from getting five thousand a month to goddamn near thirty grand a month! Was Usher sure when he lied about having a chick on the side, pregnant, just to boost album sales? HONEY, YES, CAUSE NOW THE NIGGA IS THE NEW KING OF POP," Delicious boasted.

"Boy, you are crazy." Mo broke out laughing.

"I'm telling you, girl, you better listen. Now go on in that bathroom and clean yourself up. We got work to do," Delicious said, helping Mina up.

"Look, I thank ya'll for trying to make me feel better but it's over between me and Victor. He thinks that I lied to him and I am too drained to try and explain what went down. In two weeks I will be marrying Andrew Wellington II, and that's that."

* * *

After some major persuasion, Delicious and Mo finally talked Mina into coming to work that day. Grabbing her Dior bag from out of the backseat of her drop top convertible, she headed into her popular salon, Mina's Joint.

"Mina!" everybody in the salon yelled as she walked through the door.

"What's up, ya'll?"

"Child, hurry up and get in my chair 'cause you look a hot mess by the head," Delicious declared, still disgusted by her appearance.

"Shut up, Delicious. Don't start with me."

"Somebody need to start with you."

"Just because I don't have on a full face of makeup like you don't mean that I look bad."

"Girl, you better take a page from my notebook. What if a news reporter caught you looking like that?" he asked.

"And if they did, so what? I am a regular person just like anybody else. We all have our bad days."

"Mina," Delicious said, knocking on her forehead. "You are still engaged to the Mayor's son. Ain't nothing ordinary about that."

"I ain't trying you to hear you Delicious. It's too early in the morning to be having this conversation wit you. I'm going to my office."

"You gon' need my advice one day and when you do... I'm gon' give it to you."

"Hey does anybody want anything from the Bread Company? I'm getting ready to run down there," Mo asked.

"No, thank you," everyone replied.

As Mo was leaving, the girl Sherry who Quan was cheating with, walked in. Not knowing who she was, Mo continued to walk past her, only for Sherry to bump into her on purpose.

"Excuse you," Mo spat, holding the door open.

"No, excuse *you*, bitch."

"Bitch, you bumped me! What the fuck is your problem?"

"You're fucking my man, that's the problem!"

"Who the fuck is your man?"

"Quan!"

"What did you say?" Mo said, coming back into the shop.

"Do it look like I stutter? I said Quan!"

"Uh oh, looks like its gon' be some head bussin' up in here today ya'll," Delicious instigated.

"Yeah, bitch, I'm Sherry! The one your man be fucking every night!"

"So you're the stank bitch that's been playing on my phone?"

"I ain't no stank bitch, but, yeah, that's me!"

"Okay and? Is that supposed to mean something to me? Bitch, I don't give a fuck about you fucking Quan!"

"If you don't give a fuck then why won't you leave him alone?"

"'Cause that nigga caked up! He buys me whatever I want! You see that drop top BMW sitting out there, that's mine, courtesy of Quan! My bills stayed paid and I ain't got to work or do shit! That's why I'm not leaving him! So go right ahead, bitch, keep on fucking him! I don't give a fuck! I don't want to fuck his fat ass anyway! You're making it easier for me!"

"You just mad 'cause he don't want you no more!"

"Whatever, continue to talk your nonsense! I ain't got time for this!" Mo said turning to walk away.

Mina came out from the back station. "What's going on? I can hear ya'll all the way from the back," Mina questioned.

"Quan told me everything! He told me that you can't even have kids! He told me that ya'll been trying for the longest and you still can't get pregnant! Well, guess what, bitch? I'm two months pregnant with his baby."

"Oh, naw, bitch, you wrong for that!" Delicious shot up.

"Bitch, get yo' broke, trifling ass out my shop!" Mina said, pushing Sherry out the door.

"Don't touch me!" Sherry yelled.

135

"You better be glad I don't whoop your ass," Mina slammed the door in her face. "You okay, girl?"

"I'm cool. Fuck that bitch. Let me run up to this store. I'll be back in a half an hour," Mo said trying her best not to show her true feelings.

"Okay," Mina replied unsure of what to say or do. Turning around Mina saw that everybody was still standing around, gossiping. She threw her hands up and shooed them back to their stations. "The show is over!"

* * *

It took Delicious approximately two and a half hours to fix Mina's hair and to get her back looking the way she normally did. She had decided on an upsweep hairdo that would show-case her high cheekbones and sultry eyes. Since it was the middle of afternoon and business had slowed down, Mina, Mo and the entire staff decided to head out for lunch. A buffet meal was on everyone's mind so they made the ten minute ride to the nearest Ponderosa. After ordering and being seat-ed, they all grabbed a plate and tore into the buffet. As they all stood in line, Mina turned to Mo and brought up the sub-ject of Quan and Sherry.

"Are you sure you're all right?"

"Girl, I'm fine."

"What are you going to do if she is pregnant?"

"I'ma keep doing me. I can't be worried about Quan's tri-fling ass. I got better things to worry about."

"Are you sure, Mo-"

"Look, Mina, I know you're trying to help but I don't want to talk about it."

"Subject dropped."

"Mo, yo' fat ass bet not eat all of the chicken," Delicious warned, returning from the restroom.

"Just for that yo' black ass gon' have to wait for the next

batch of chicken to come out, Na," she said, sticking out her tongue.

"I swear the next time you're in my chair I'm gon' burn you." Delicious pounded his fist into his hand while staring at Mo.

"They got some baked chicken over there." Neosha pointed out.

"Sorry, sweetie, I just took the last piece," Janiya grinned.

"Now ya'll need to quit! Ya'll know I'm on Atkins," Delicious said, upset.

"Didn't nobody tell you to take yo ass into the bathroom and touch up yo makeup," Tiffany said, laughing.

"A *diva* must always be presentable."

"Well this *diva* is getting ready to fuck this chicken up." Mo took a huge chunk out of a thigh and eyeing Delicious.

"Die, bitch, die." Delicious pointed his fork in her direction.

"You know you ain't right. I'm getting ready to go sit down," Mina said, after fixing two plates.

"Me, too," the other girls replied. Back at their table they all said grace and prepared to eat.

"Oh, I love their mashed potatoes and gravy." Mina savored each bite.

"I love their salads," Jodie chimed in.

"Girl, I love a big dick on a rainy night," Delicious said, sitting down.

"Keep me near the cross, Jesus." Jodie shot Delicious a look.

"You are so nasty," Mo said, ready to vomit. "Don't you see us eating?"

"What? What I say wrong? Don't front like I'm lying."

"He is right. Ain't nothing better than making love to your man when it's raining outside," Tiffany replied, with her eyes closed reminiscing.

"I can't even front 'cause Quan was digging all up in these guts last night," Mo declared with a smirk on her face.

"You was backing it up on him, girl?" Delicious put his hand in the air to get a high five.

"And you know it," Mo snapped, giving him a high five.

"You don't know nothing about backing it up, Mo," Neosha teased.

"Girl, please. You got her fucked up. She been fucking since she was twelve," Delicious joked.

"Fuck you, Delicious," Mo said, giving him the finger.

"Speaking of backing it up, Mina, did you see your boo from across the street today?" Janiya questioned.

"Nah," she answered. Disappointed, she bit her lip to keep from crying.

"Did somebody forget to give this dumb bitch the memo that said don't talk about Victor," Delicious said as he smacked Tiffany upside the head.

"What? I didn't know and if you hit me one more time I'ma cut yo punk ass."

"Come on, Miss Tiffany. We can do this! I will fuck yo' big ass up!" Delicious declared with hands up in the air signaling for her to bring it on.

"Delicious, you better calm your ass down. Tiffany ain't no joke with them hands," Janiya teased.

"Girl, please, I will go Kill Bill on that ass. Please believe I take Judo classes three times a week. " Delicious broke out laughing.

"I don't know what I would do without ya'll." Mina laughed, too.

"Well, you'll never know." Mo hugged her neck.

"Oh, ain't that cute? Look at the ghetto version of Tia and Tamara," Delicious joked.

"Fuck you," Mo said, hitting him in the face with a sweet roll.

"So what's the plan? How are we going to get Mina and Victor back together?" Tiffany asked.

"Ya'll can forget about it. Victor doesn't want anything to do with me," Mina answered.

"But you have to try at least one more time."

"I tried. He didn't want to listen to me so fuck him."

"So that's it. You not gon' even try?" Delicious asked.

"No, and I don't wanna talk about it anymore."

"Leave the girl alone. If she doesn't want to fuck with Antonio Badhairday no more then that's her business," Mo joked.

"Shut up, Monsieur Georgia Mae Parthens," Mina teased.

"Ooh, no, you didn't," Mo threw down her fork.

"Oh, yes, she did," Delicious instigated.

"Georgia Mae? Your middle name is Georgia Mae?" Tiffany laughed, spitting food out of her mouth.

"Yes, it is. I was named after my grandmother," Mo tried to explain. Everybody still laughed, though. "Ya'll know better than to make fun of the dead. And, Daniel, I know you ain't joning."

"Delicious, your real name is Daniel?" Neosha laughed.

"Bitch, I will cut you. Don't be laughing at my name."

"Delicious, yo' momma get an F for naming you Daniel," Janiya teased, while they all laughed.

Chapter Eleven

Next

"I told you not to fuck with that cunt, dog! I don't see why you over there looking all crazy! The bitch was a snake! You should have let me off the bitch when I had a chance!"

"I don't know, man. I kinda think shorty was telling the truth," Victor said, smoking a blunt while looking out of the living room window.

"Nigga, have you lost your mind? The bitch is engaged to the Mayor's son. She had to have known that they were going after you!"

"She seemed too shocked, though."

"That's because the slut had a heater to her brain! Think, dog, think! Just tell me that you ain't tell her none of our business."

"I told her that I sold some work and that I was going to be out of the game in a year."

"You told that bitch that and you ain't let me kill her! I swear this is just like that Samia shit!" Before Dro could take the words back or apologize Victor was already at his throat.

"You ever let her name slip out your mouth again and it's like that for you, blood or no blood," Victor said calmly, bringing his face two inches away from Dro's face.

"My bad, dog, I wasn't thinking."

Turning his back to him, Victor took another drag from the blunt and returned to his place back in front of the window.

"All I'm saying is we need to take care of the situation before things get out of hand."

"Leave it to me. I'll handle Mina."

* * *

A couple of weeks had passed and Mina still hadn't heard from or seen Victor. She missed him tremendously. She tried calling him but he would only pick up the phone to hang it up on her. Mina figured that things were over between them so that morning she and Mo went to get their last fitting done on their dresses for the wedding. Finished with their fitting, Mina drove down the highway while talking to Mo.

"Guess who I was wit last night?"

"Who?" Mina asked.

"That nigga Chantez."

"Chantez from back in the day? When ya'll start back fucking around?"

"Girl a couple of weeks ago. He saw me coming out of Princess Beauty Supply on Natural Bridge and flagged me down."

"Is he still cute?"

"Fuck cute! That nigga is fine!"

"Let me guess. You fucked him?"

"You damn right I did and my pussy been thanking me ever since. Let me tell you, the nigga work it so well I'm starting to think Quan might notice a difference. Girl, Chantez be having this pussy on swole."

"Okay, T.M.I. muthafucker, T.M.I. So what's going on wit you and Quan?"

"He finally broke down and told me the truth. The bitch Sherry is pregnant for real."

"For real, Mo? What are you going to do?" Mina asked shocked.

"Nothing. He has to deal with the bitch, not me. As long as my bills stay paid, I'm good. But I did have to tell Chantez the other night he can't be beating up my pussy."

"Why not?"

"'Cause you know Quan ol' average size ass ain't putting in no work like that. That nigga gon' fuck around and notice a difference," Mo cracked up laughing.

"Unnn, Mo, you are so nasty," Mina said shaking her head.

"Bitch, please, don't act like two weeks ago Victor wasn't tearing your shit up. Shit you're engaged to be married, I'm not. That nigga ain't got no claim on me."

Ring, Ring!

"Hand me my phone," Mina said to Mo. "Whose number is it?"

"I don't know it says unknown number."

"Hello?"

"Mina, baby, it's your momma."

"What's up, Ma? Where you at?"

"You not gon' want to hear this but me and yo Aunt Bernice up here at the St. Ann Police Station."

"What for?"

"Um…"

"Um, what, Momma?" Mina yelled.

"We kinda got in a fight this morning at Wal-Mart and we can't post bail so we need you to come pick us up."

"How much is your bail, Momma?"

"Bail?" Mo whispered, tapping Mina on the arm.

"Five hundred dollars."

"I'll be there in ten minutes," Mina said, hanging up.

"Rita and Bernice got locked up?"

"Yeah, for fighting at Wal-Mart of all places."

"Hell, nah." Mo laughed.

"It ain't funny, Mo. You know this shit gon' be on every newspaper in St. Louis."

"Oh, damn, I forgot about that." Pulling up to the police station, Mina saw three news reporters already on the prowl.

"Shit!" Mina pounded her fist on the steering wheel of the car.

"Just don't say nothing."

"I'm not."

"Miss Matthews, can you tell us what happened today to your mother and aunt?"

"Miss Matthews has nothing to say," Mo said as she stopped to pose to have her picture taken by the paparazzi.

"Mo, bring yo' ass!" Mina hissed.

"My bad, girl. You know I can't pass up a photo opportunity."

"Hi, I'm Mina Matthews. I'm here to post bail for my mother, Rita Matthews and my aunt, Bernice Stapleton."

"So, you're related to those two?" the officer whose badge identified him as Officer Wilkinson, said pointing to the holding cell where her mother and aunt were.

The two were sitting on the bench looking a tore up mess. Bernice looked like an aging hooker. She had the nerve to have on a blue jean halter dress that hugged the belly tire she had stretched across her stomach. Her black fishnet stockings looked like they were a size too small. They were so tight that it looked like the fat from her thighs was popping out the holes.

The blonde, wet and wavy weave that Delicious put it in the day before made her look like Rick James before he was released from jail. And to top it off, she had on a pair of sky-blue open toed sandals that tied up the leg which knocked the whole outfit off track. Her mother, on the other hand, opted for a more sophisticated B-girl look.

Rita paced the holding cell floor with her burgundy pixie braided wig swinging in her hand. Her stocking cap was pushed back on her head and one gold door knocker earring swung from her ear.She also had on the gold herringbone necklace that her father bought her for Christmas with a pink, too tight Velour Roc-a-Wear jogging suit that showcased her panty line as she walked. And what really messed Mina up was the fact that her forty-seven year old mother had on a pair of pink and white Air Force Ones.

"Yes. I'm sorry to say that this is my mother and aunt. What did they get locked up for?"

"Apparently, Wal-Mart was having a Fourth of July sale this morning. Your mother and aunt were caught on camera, tripping and pushing customers so that they could get to the merchandise first."

"What?! That doesn't make any sense!"

"I'm not through. The big one with fishnets assaulted a young lady by the name of Tameka Jackson. Apparently, your aunt picked up the last APEX DVD player that was on sale for $19.99. You know, I wanted to get one of those but the wife said no—"

"Could you get back to the story, please?"

"I'm sorry where was I? Oh, yeah, your aunt picked up the DVD player after Miss Jackson put it down. Well, Miss Jackson claimed that the DVD player was her—"

"The bitch gon' walk up on me like I was a punk or some-thing! She thought 'cause she was younger than me that I was gon back down! Huh you know how I get down! When she came walking up in my face talking that noise about the DVD player being hers I told the lil' girl to get somewhere and sit down," Aunt Bernice explained.

"But the lil' bitch wouldn't listen! Talking about we betta gone somewhere wit our old selves! Now you know she had to get it, Mina! 'Cause ain't a damn thing old about me!" Rita replied.

"You know I wasn't gone let her talk crazy to my sista so I slapped the lil' heffa! The next thing I know we banging! Yo' momma and me against three girls!"

"Aunt Bernice, hush! Sitting over there looking like Nick Nolte's mug shot!"

"Oh, no, you didn't!"

"Mina, we tore into them lil' girls!I don't let nobody talk crazy to my sista so I jumped in and told the girl she betta step before I got to stomping in my Air Force Ones!" Rita said proudly.

"Momma!"

"What?!"

"Just stop it! I don't want to hear anymore! How could you embarrass me like this right before my wedding?! It's already bad enough ya'll country as hell, but now you gotta go embarrass me like this! I already got people laughing at me and here you go making it worse! I can't deal with this right down! Here is their bail money, I'm out!" Mina, yelled heated. She stomped out of the police station.

"Mina, honey, wait," Rita called after her.

"No, Momma, I'm through talkin' to you!"

"Could you at least stop and get your Aunt a package of Benson & Hedge's menthol on the way home? My blood pressure done went up and I ain't got my pills!

Chapter Twelve

Pause

"Are you sure he's going to come?" Delicious asked as he and Mo sat at a restaurant called Tomato. Seated right by the window they both sipped on their complimentary glass of water.

"Yes, Delicious. I talked to Victor earlier and he said he was going to be here."

"Well, he sure is late. The nigga could have at least called. A bitch do have things to do. I did plan on going to the gym today and besides, I'm hungry." He crossed his arms and legs, all the while rolling his eyes.

"Well, go ahead and order then. Damn you getting on my nerves!"

"Who are you talking to?"

"You!"

"Bitch, I ain't Sherry! I will whoop yo' ass!"

"Fuck you. I'm gon' smack the shit outta you, you keep on playing with me," she laughed. "But anyway, what the fuck do you have on? You couldn't save your girlie wear for the shop," Mo said eyeing his oversized Fendi glasses and purse, rhinestone tank top, fitted jeans and stiletto pumps.

"Squeeze me? I know you ain't even trying to size me up, Miss Thing. For your information this is Chanel. Say it with, me Cha-nel. Not Chantell like that fake shit you got on."

"Whatever. He's here." Standing up, they both greeted Victor.

"What's up, Mo?" Victor said, giving her a hug.

"How you doing lateness?" Delicious said sarcastically.

"Shut up, Delicious. Excuse my friend, Victor. He's on medication."

"Anyway, when you gon' stop being an ass and get back with my girl?"

"Delicious!"

"What?! That's what we're here to find out, ain't it?"

"I am so sorry, Victor."

"It's cool, Ma." Victor's face softened into a laugh.

"So?" Delicious asked.

"I've been thinking a lot about what happened and I overreacted. I should have listened to Mina."

"Yes, you should have," Delicious agreed.

"You got a lot to say, don't you?" Victor asked.

"I'm sorry, Poppi, please don't kill me. I'm too cute to die."

"We're cool as long as you never call me Poppi again."

"Would you all like to order?" the waitress asked.

"Not yet. Can you give us a second?" Mo asked.

"Sure. Take as much time as you need."

"I really do love Mina and I want her back."

"Well, you're going to have to tell her soon because she's getting married in less then than a week."

"Damn, that soon?"

"Yeah, you might wanna try catching her tonight after the

Cancer Research fundraiser. I'll give you her address before we leave."

"Cool. Thanks, Mo."

"No problem. Anything for a friend."

"Good. Let's order because a diva is hungry," Delicious snapped.

* * *

Later that afternoon, standing in front of the store window, Mina stood wondering about her upcoming nuptials. She hoped and prayed that Victor would've called and forgiven her but he never did. She couldn't fathom living the rest of her life with Andrew, but as each day passed, it became clearer and clearer that Andrew would be the one that she would be marrying. Closing her eyes she said a silent prayer to God.

God, please guide me to make the right decision right now. I need your guidance, lead the way o' Lord. Show me your path. I need your help. In your name, I pray, Amen.

Reopening her eyes, she saw Mo and Delicious pulling up in front of the shop.

"Mina, you have a call on line two," Jodie said.

"Hello?"

"Mina, it's your Mother."

"Hi, Momma."

"I called to apologize again about what happened the other day."

"It's okay. I'm sorry for the way I acted. I shouldn't have said the things I did. I've just been under a lot of stress lately."

"I understand. Well, I'm gon' let you go now."

"Momma."

"Yes."

"I'm singing tonight at the Cancer Research fundraiser. They're having a talent show this year to raise money so I'm going to perform. If you, Daddy and Smokey want to come you're welcome."

"Are you sure? We don't want to embarrass you or anything."

"I love you just the way you are, Momma, you know that. Don't go changing yourself on my account."

"I love you, too. Is it okay if your aunt and uncle come, too?"

"Yeah, sure why not."

"Okay, we'll see you tonight. I gotta go pick me out an outfit."

"Okay," Mina said, hanging up, dreading the worst. "Where have you two been?" she asked Mo and Delicious.

"Out minding our business," Delicious answered.

"Keep it up, Delicious. I'm gon' punch you dead in your mouth."

"I love you, too, boo."

"I brought you back some fettuccini alfredo." Mo handed Mina the to-go plate.

"Thaaank you."

"You're welcome."

"Are ya'll coming to the fundraiser tonight?"

"Yeah, why not. I ain't got anything else to do. Delicious, you want to ride with me?"

"Sure, sweets."

"Okay. Well, I'm getting ready to get up outta here. Thanks again for the food Mo, and I will see ya'll later."

* * *

Although Mina left the shop early in order to get ready for the fundraiser, she was still an hour late. When she got home, instead of eating and showering, she ate and went to sleep. She had been feeling extremely tired and nauseated for some reason. Once she got into a good zone in her nap, she was awakened by the sound of her phone ringing.

"Hello?" Mina answered in a raspy tone.

"Where the hell are you?"

"I must have fallen asleep."

"Can you ever do anything right?!"

"Andrew, I'll be there in a minute."

"Hurry, the talent show is about to start and you're the fifth one to go."

"All right, I'll be there." Hanging up she got up, took a shower, and dressed. In less than an hour's time, she was at the auditorium. Searching through the sea of people she found Mo, Andrew, Delicious, her dad, Smokey and Uncle Chester seated at a table near the front of the stage.

"Sweetheart!" Andrew exclaimed.

"Andrew."

"It's about time you made it. We were all worried sick about you," he kissed her on the cheek.

"I just bet you were." It was obvious to Mina that he was putting on a show for her family.

"Hey, Fat Momma, give your daddy some suga."

"Hey, Daddy."

"How is my favorite niece?" Uncle Chester asked.

"I'm your only niece, Uncle Chester."

"Well, actu—"

"Um, Mina, honey, your Momma and you aunt decided to perform in the talent show, too," her father interrupted.

"Oh, my God, are you serious?"

"Yes, honey, just wait and see." Delicious smirked.

"I'm not gon' even say anything. What's up, lil' boy," Mina teased playing with her brother.

"Nothing. So, Mo, when me and you gon' be together?" Michael wrapped his arms around her.

"Mina, you better get your brother before I fuck him."

"Mo!"

"I'm just playing."

"No, she not." Delicious belted out a hoop of laughter.

"Have a seat, dear," Andrew replied, pulling out her chair.

"What's wrong with you? You look kinda pale?" Mo whispered into Mina's ear, not missing a thing.

"I don't know I think I might have food poisoning or something."

"Umm hmm. I just bet you do."

"Andrew, where are your parents?" Mina asked, looking around for them.

"They're over there sitting with the Fitzgeralds," Turning around, she found the Wellingtons seated a couple of tables back from them. Catching their eye, she waved.

"I, myself, think it's kinda rude. They ain't come over here and speak or nothing," her daddy said.

"Come on, Daddy. Don't even worry about it. Remember we're here to have fun tonight."

"Next up to perform, we have Rita and Bernice performing…excuse me, is this correct?" the white female MC asked poking her head back in the curtain. "Okaaay we have Rita and Bernice performing Push It by Salt & Pepper."

"It's Salt 'N Pepa not Salt & Pepper," Rita yelled.

"I'm sorry Salt 'N Pepa."

The next thing Mina knew the lights went off, the curtain opened and different colored strobe lights filled the stage.

"Oh baby, baby, ba-ba-ba-ba-baby, Get up on this!"

Closing her eyes tight, Mina tried to forget what she had just seen. Her Mother and Aunt were up on stage, in front of over a hundred people, in black spandex catsuits. Her Mother had on a red furry Kangol hat, red leather bomber jacket, red high top Princess Reeboks and gold Bamboo earrings. While her Aunt chose a yellow Kangol hat, yellow bomber jacket, yellow Princess Reeboks and gold dolphin earrings. Reopening one of her eyes, Mina looked at them once more and became sick to her stomach. To make matters worse, when Mina opened both of her eyes and looked closer she saw that her eighty year old grandmother was behind a turntable with head phones wearing a purple leather jacket.

"Rita 'N Bernice here, and were in effect
Want you to push it, babe
Coolin' by day then at night working up a sweat
C'mon, girls, let's go show the guys what we know
How to become number one in the hot body show
Now push it."

Hot body show? Wit all them rolls? Oh, hell no," Mina thought. She couldn't believe her Mother and Aunt. They were actually on stage humping and pumping like they were in their twenties. Standing in the middle of the stage they both broke out doing the Kid 'N Play. They even did the Whop and the backbend that Salt 'N Pepa did in the video but when Bernice went down to do a split she couldn't get back up. So Rita had to stop pumping up the crowd in order to help her up again.

"Yo, yo, yo, baby, pop, yeah, you come and give me a kiss
Better make it fast or else I'm gonna get pissed
Can you hear this music pumping hard?
Now push it,"

her Aunt said, now in the crowd, talking to Uncle Chester. Surprisingly enough the crowd seemed to love their act. Everyone was up on their feet smiling and applauding their effort. Even Mrs. Wellington's drunk ass was up cheering. Looking over at Andrew, she saw that he wasn't pleased at all.

His face was stone and he hadn't cracked one smile. Mo and Delicious were up on their feet hooting and hollering though, they enjoyed every minute of it. Once the song was over Rita, Bernice and Nana Marie stood center stage and took a bow. As soon as they left the stage, Andrew grabbed Mina and hauled her off to the lobby.

"What is your problem? Let me go! You're hurting my arm!"

"Did you not just see that fiasco?" he yelled, holding her arm even tighter.

"Everybody loved it. Why are you trippin'?"

"How am I going to explain this to my colleagues when they ask me about this? It's bad enough I had to defend Ren & Stimpy when they got locked up, but now this! You better get control of your hillbilly family before I do!" he warned, shoving her into the wall.

Wanting to cry for the harsh words Andrew said about her family, Mina held every last tear in. At that moment, she knew that she couldn't do it anymore. She couldn't continue living a lie and put up with Andrew's abuse. Mina ran into the nearest ladies' restroom.

Standing in front of the restroom mirror she gave herself one good look. Mina couldn't believe that she had let herself get this way. She let money and material things run her life for too long.

Laughing, she couldn't believe that in another week she was actually going to marry a gay man. She didn't care that people were staring at her like she was crazy. Maybe she was but for the first time in over a year she felt free. She was finally free of Andrew and his abuse because that night she finally decided to leave him for good. Holding her head up high she left the restroom and headed for the stage.

"Next up on our list we have the beautiful fiancé of Andrew Wellington, II. Mina Matthews is performing a song by Tweet called 'Iceberg'." Walking onto the stage Mina was welcomed with thunderous applause.

"Hello, everyone, I hope you're enjoying yourselves tonight because I am. Before I perform, I want to give a shout out to my family."

"Do yo' thang, girl!" Delicious shouted from the crowd.

"That's my baby!" Rita added, still sweating from her performance.Holding the mic in her hand, Mina looked directly at Andrew and said, "This is for you, sweetie." The lights went off again but instead of strobe lights, Mina had one single light shining down on her from above. In a white Carolina Herrera halter dress that hit mid thigh, silver heels and her hair in an upsweep, Mina placed a white gardenia behind her ear. Red lipstick adorned her lips and her skin was flawless. Mina looked like a new age Billie Holiday.

"Search the world over, until I found you
Thanked Jehovah... for you
Didn't know your occupation or what you do, it didn't matter
Linen Hers & His
When I shopped with you
Everyday a happy day beeeeing in love
You had me sewed up
So sewed up
Search the world over
Until I found yooou
Thanked Jehovah for you
Didn't know that his creation... was a crazy fool
And now the situation is low
No me and you
And I shoulda prayed that you changed then."

Mina could hear gasps in the audience as she sang but she kept on going anyway. Her voice was thick and filled with emotion. Everything that she was feeling came pouring out. As she sang, tears began to well up in her eyes.

"Yoooou...oh you, you turned so cold
Oh, you... turn so cold
Tell me why, Why
Why'd you have to do this here
I did everything you like
You know I did, ohhhh
Love from my family
Close with all my friends
They said you were no good for me naw
But I didn't listen
Made a claim that you would love me always and I made
them stay away so they wouldn't persuade me
Nothing was safe no... not for me
No not, Not for me."

The tears that had formed were now streaming down her face at full speed. Everyone at her family's table was crying, too, except for Andrew. He was utterly embarrassed because everyone knew that the words from the song were directed at him. Keeping her eyes on Andrew, Mina continued to sing her heart out.

"I slipped up and fell in love with an iceberg
How could you turn so cold?
I gave you all I had, yes I did
Such a fool
Why
You... turned... cold
Turned cold
You... turned... cold
Turned cold."

Wiping her face, Mina gave Andrew one last look and walked off the stage and out of the auditorium without looking back.

Chapter Thirteen

Burn

Mina ran back and forth from her closet to her bed placing clothes into suitcases as she listened to 702's song, "Feelings". She knew Andrew would be home at any moment so she had to hurry. Grabbing ten pairs of shoes at one time she stuffed them all into their own separate suitcase. Marc Jacobs bags, Valentino dresses, Manolo Blahnik heels and Agent Provocateur underwear were thrown everywhere.

She couldn't wait to be up outta there. No more living like a caged bird that could sing. Mina was finally going to be free. Walking past a mirror she caught a glimpse of her engagement ring in the mirror. Stopped dead in her tracks, Mina looked down at it, and with little or no hesitation she slid the five carat rock off of her finger. Sitting it down on the dresser she knew that she would miss the ring, not the meaning behind it.

"Mina!" Turning around quickly she found Andrew standing in the doorway of their bedroom. She didn't hear him come in over the loud music. "How could you do this to me?!"

"Do what to you, Andrew? Tell you the truth?" she asked rolling her eyes.

"I have done nothing but love you since we've been together! I didn't deserve that! I thought that things between us were good."

"You call cheating on me and whooping my ass a good relationship? Things between us were never good! I was with you for two years and all you did was cheat and lie! The only reason you kept me around is because I was your little trophy piece! Well, guess what? I'm sick of it! Where were you, Andrew, when I was at home alone at night? Huh, tell me!" she yelled, finding a new found confidence.

"First off, don't question me about what I do when I'm not with you! You have a roof over your head, clothes on your back, and you stay putting food in your mouth! So what if I was cheating? A man has needs and lately you haven't been fulfilling them! All you do is sit up all day and eat!"

"What? You think that's supposed to hurt me!" she yelled secretly knowing it did. "You think that's supposed to mean something to me? You can take all this shit back because I don't need none of it! Here take yo' shit!" she yelled grabbing clothes from out of her closet onto the floor.

"I don't give a fuck about that shit!" he yelled throwing a glass vase across the room. Jumping back, Mina moved out of the way so that none of the glass pieces would cut her. "I should beat your ass!"

"It's not like you've never hit me before!"

"Are you fucking somebody else?"

"What you think?" Mina crossed her arms, staring at him.

"I should've known, you fucking whore! You were nothing but a piece of trash to me anyway! Tell me, Mina," Andrew said in her face, with a sinister look in his eye. "What does his cum taste like?"

"It taste like yours but sweeter, you fuckin' fag!" Mina yelled spitting in his face.

"What did you say?" he yelled, pushing her down into the closet then getting on top of her.

"Get off of me!"

"What did you call me?!" Andrew began slapping her in the face repeatedly. Mina tried hitting him back. She reached out and tried to scratch his face but she was too slow. Andrew already had her hands pinned to the floor. Not able to defend herself with her hands she kneed him in the groin causing him to fall back in pain. "You fucking bitch! When I get up I'm going to kill you!" He groaned in agony.

"Fuck you, nigga, now what!" Mina said with her hands up in the air signaling for him to bring it on. Noticing that he was back on his feet she took off running heading for the stairs, only for him to grab her by the back of her hair. Pulling her back down onto the floor he took his right foot and kicked her in the side.

"Where you think you going?!" he yelled kicking her again and again.

"Stop!" she screamed hoping that someone would hear her but the loud music drowned out her voice.

"Shut up!" he yelled, back-handing her.

Harking up as much spit as she could, Mina spat in his face. After wiping his face, Andrew took his hand and back slapped her face once more. Screaming all types of obscenities at her, Andrew repeatedly slammed Mina's head into the floor. He then took his fist and punched her directly in the eye causing it to swell immediately. Using her hands, Mina dug her fingernails into his skin. As he continued to abuse her body, Mina clawed his face while kicking and screaming the entire time.

"Stop it," Mina cried, feeling like her head was on fire.

Not listening to a word she had to say, he continued to drag her across the floor, kicking and screaming. Picking Mina up, Andrew body slammed her already battered body onto the hardwood floor. As her body hit the ground, Mina's head bounced off the floor causing her vision to blur for a moment. Andrew placed both his hands around her neck and began to choke her unmercifully.

Light-headed, Mina tried her best to fight back but the little air she had seemed to be escaping quickly. The room began to go dark and all the blood in her body had rushed to her head. Not able to breathe anymore, Mina's eyes closed and her body went limp. Letting her go, Andrew inhaled deeply, wiped the sweat off his forehead and gazed down upon her still body.

Andrew clenched his fists and paced across the room, wondering what he should do next. He didn't know if Mina was dead or alive. Realizing this time he had gone too far, Andrew grabbed his keys, ran down the steps and left. Unbeknownst to him, just as he was pulling away, Victor was pulling up. Stepping out of his car, he watched as Andrew sped off. Victor saw that the front door was still open as he walked up the steps. Knowing that something was wrong, he pulled out his Berretta.

"Mina!" he bellowed out frantically as he searched the first floor. Not finding her, he ran up the steps still calling her name. "Mina!" he called out again.

To his surprise, he found her lying on the floor battered, bruised and unconscious. Kneeling down beside her, Victor pulled her close.

"Wake up, baby! It's me, Victor! Can you hear me?!" He shook her body trying to wake her up.

Victor checked her pulse and felt that she still had one. Immediately he called 911. Five minutes later an ambulance was outside of Mina's door. Victor was beside himself with grief as the paramedics began to resuscitate her. He knew that Andrew did this to her. *If only I would have come sooner*, he thought.

"She's breathing," an EMT shouted.

"Thank God," Victor yelled, overjoyed.

"Do you know who did this to her, sir?" one of the officers asked him

"Nah, I came over, the door was open and I found her like this," Victor lied. He was going to make sure that he personally took care of Andrew.

"We'll need you to come down to the station to fill out a report."

"Can I go to the hospital with her first?"

"Yeah, sure. Do you know how we can notify her family?"

"I don't know her parents' number but I do have her best friend, Mo's."

After following the ambulance to the hospital, Victor sat in the waiting room praying that Mina was okay. Her family was contacted and were on their way. Victor knew that they would have all sorts of questions, but he wasn't quite sure how he was going to answer them. The only thing he knew was that if he lost Mina he would never forgive himself.

"Where is my baby?" Rita shrieked as she and Mr. Matthews, Smokey, Nana Marie, Aunt Bernice, Uncle Chester, Mo, Delicious and the stylist walked behind her.

"Ma'am, who are you here to see?" a nurse asked.

"My daughter, Mina Matthews, was admitted about a half an hour ago."

"Okay, ma'am. The doctors are in with her right now. If you'll just take a seat they'll be with you in a moment."

"Bitch, does it look like I have a moment? I want to know how my daughter is! Now!"

"Rita, calm down, the lady is only doing her job," Mr.

Matthews said trying to calm her down.

"Victor! How is she? How is Mina doing?" Mo exclaimed, rushing over to him.

"I don't know. I'm still waiting to hear, too."

"Who the hell are you?" Aunt Bernice questioned.

"I'm Victor." He extended his hand.

"Okay.That's still not telling me anything."

"This is Victor. We all went to school together," Mo tried to explain.

"Were you the one who found Mina?" Nana Marie asked.

"Yes ma'am I went by to see her and the door was open. I went in and called out for her but she didn't answer so I ran up the stairs and found her on the floor."

"Was she badly beaten?"

"Yes, ma'am, and… she was unconscious."

"Sweet Jesus!" Rita shouted.

"I think her fiancé did this," Victor continued.

"What are we gon' do if we lose her, Ed?! What we gon' do?!"

"Everything is gonna be all right, Rita." Ed hugged her.

"Mo, you didn't know anything about this?" Aunt Bernice asked.

"No. I mean, we all knew that Andrew could be an asshole sometimes but we didn't know that he would be capable of doing something like this. She never told us that he was hitting on her."

"Excuse me. I'm Dr. Townsend."

"How is my daughter?" Rita asked.

"She's in stable condition and breathing on her own, which is a good thing."

"Thank you, Jesus," Nana Marie whispered.

"So she's going to be all right," Rita asked.

"Yes, I will say though, she was badly beaten and whoever

did this to her meant to kill her. Just thank God that your friend got to her in time."

"Can we go in and see her?"

"Yes, but only for a minute. We have her on pain medication that is causing her to sleep."

Rita and Ed didn't know what to expect when they entered Mina's hospital room but what they saw shook them to the core. Mina lay in a comatose like sleep. Both of her eyes was swollen shut. Her bottom lip was busted open and black and blue marks filled her face, neck, and arms. A clump of her hair had been pulled out when Andrew dragged her. They didn't know if their beautiful Mina would ever look the same.

"Mina, baby, it's me, your momma."

"And your ol' man is here too sweetie."

"Oh, Mina, we love you so much," Rita cried.

"Just hurry up and come back to us, dear." Before leaving out, they both placed kisses on her forehead.

"Momma, you and Smokey can go in and see her now," Rita replied. Holding his Grandmother's hand, Smokey led her into the room. Standing beside her bed, neither of them said a thing. Seeing Mina in so much pain was too much for either of them to bear. Kissing her cheek, Nana Marie said a silent prayer and left the room. Afterwards, Aunt Bernice and Uncle Chester, Mo, Delicious and the rest of the stylists went in to see her.

"Girl, look what you gone and done now," Mo said as tears streamed down her face. "I love you too much for you to go and scare me like this. But, don't worry, 'cause no matter what, I got your back."

"This is too much, girl! This is just too much." Delicious wept, holding a handkerchief up to his nose.

After each of them told Mina they loved her, Victor finally got a chance to see her. It was his first time since he had found her lying on the floor. Victor hated hospitals. The smell of disinfectant and decaying bodies made him sick. But for Mina, he would withstand it all. Pulling up a chair, he sat beside Mina and gazed at her face. No matter how many bruises splattered her face, he still could only see the beautiful woman he fell in love with.

"Damn, Ma, you had a nigga scared there for a second. I thought I lost you. I love you too much for you to leave and I realized that the minute you walked outta my door that day. Just hurry up and come back to me okay," Victor silently cried. Taking her hand in his he gently kissed her palm. Wiping his face he stood up and headed for the door.

"Victor, don't leave," he heard Mina's voice say. Stopping dead in his tracks he smiled and turned around. Mina's hand was up in the air reaching out for him. Rushing back over to her side he took her hand back in his and kissed it once more. "Don't leave. Stay here with me," she whispered barely able to speak.

"I got you, Ma, I promise I ain't never gon' leave you again."

* * *

The next three days, as promised, Victor stayed by Mina's side. The only time he would leave was when he needed to go home and change. During the day he would watch her as she slept and by night, he would lay beside her in the hospital bed. Sleep or eating wasn't even factor. He would not be okay until he knew that Mina was.

Being with her in the hospital really gave him the opportunity to see how much she was loved. Flowers and get-well cards filled the room. Everyone from customers at the shop to church goers came to visit her. Her parents and family also stayed by her side faithfully. At first, her mother and father were hesitant about Victor being around so much but eventually they warmed to him. Rita didn't really know that much about Victor but from what she saw she liked.

After her three-day stay in the hospital Mina was finally able to go home. The only problem was she had no home to go to but that was the least of her worries. The police had been in and out of her hospital room the entire time she was there. They had wanted to know who tried to kill her but she wouldn't give up any information.

"I told you I don't know who it was. The guy had on a ski mask," she lied.

Mina wasn't about to tell the police that Andrew damn near beat her to death. They would never believe her, and besides, Mayor Wellington had every judge and policeman in his back pocket. To Mina, telling the truth would only conjure up more drama that she just didn't need nor want. Her family, on the other hand, didn't understand her logic at all. They wanted Andrew's head on a platter.

"I just want to move on with my life," she told them.

But the Matthews clan was not trying to hear it. It took all of the little strength Mina did have to get them to understand. Finally, they all gave up pursuing justice and let things be. Standing in the hospital room, Mo helped Mina ease her arm into a sky blue Roc-a-Wear jogging suit jacket.

"Oww, oww," Mina moaned.

"You all right?"

"Yeah, I'm cool. It still hurts a lot."

"Well, at least you look better. Your eye is starting to go down."

"Don't even mention my face. I look horrible. I don't how Victor has been able to look at me the past couple of days." Mina gazed into the mirror at her black eye and swollen lip.

"That boy loves you to death. He doesn't care how you look."

"Praise Jesus, the dead has arisen," Delicious declared as he entered the room.

"Hi, Delicious," Mina said.

"Chile, what are we gonna do about this head of yours?"

"Boy, I ain't thinking about my hair."

"You might not be but I am."

"Whatever."

"Well, honey, I don't how you're gonna feel about this, but I have some bad news."

"What now?"

"Andrew has changed all the locks to the shop and he has a sign up that says '*Closed until further notice* '."

"What?! He can't do that!"

"Calm down, sweetie. You don't want to get too worked up," Mo warned.

"I can't believe this shit!"

"Believe what?" Victor asked as he entered the room.

"Andrew closed down the shop."

"Can he do that?"

"Yes, because technically he owns it. Are the other stylists talking about going to another shop?"

"No, not yet. I mean everybody wants to stay with you, but folks got bills to pay," Delicious answered.

"What I'm going to do?" Mina said, plopping down onto the hospital bed.

"I'll pay your entire staff until we can get this thing settled."

"Victor, I can't let you do that. You've already done enough as it is."

"You can and you will. I told you I got you, Ma."

"Well, that's settled. Can I get paid today?" Delicious asked with his hand held out, palm turned upward.

"Delicious," Mo scolded.

"What, girl? I was just playing," he lied, knowing damn well he was wasn't.

Suddenly Dr. Townsend interrupted their repartee. "Excuse me. May I speak to Mina alone, please," he asked.

"We'll be outside, Mina," Mo said.

"Is something wrong?"

"That depends on you."

"I don't understand."

"Well, when I got your bloodwork back yesterday, I found out that you are expecting."

"Expecting what?"

"Expecting a baby."

"You got to be kidding me," she said not believing the news.

"Doctors tend to not kid about things like this. You need to set up an appointment with an OB/GYN soon for your pre-natal exam."

"Okay," she said, still in daze.

"Congratulations."

An hour later, Mina lay in Victor's king size bed, pretending to be asleep. The news of being pregnant had her confused and totally shaken up. With two thousand thread count sheets wrapped around her body and plump plush pillows under her head, she lay contemplating her next move. The decision of whether or not she was going to keep the baby had already been chosen, but how Victor would feel about the news, would be another story.

Hearing him coming, she closed her eyes and played possum. Entering the bedroom Victor smiled. He envisioned this day since he returned to the states. Mina was the love of his life and he would do whatever was possible to keep her in his life. Too much had already been taken from him and he wasn't about to lose Mina as well. Climbing into bed with her, he laid beside her just like he did while she was in the hospital.

"Wake up, sleepyhead," he said, as he kissed her forehead.

"What time is it?" she asked, gazing into his deep brown eyes.

"Five o'clock."

"Wow, I really slept in." Mina said, rubbing her eyes. "Oww! Shit, that hurt!" Mina winced forgetting that her eyes were still sore.

"You okay?" Victor asked concerned.

"Yeah, I'm fine."

"Are you sure 'cause I could get you an ice pack," Victor tried to get up.

"I'm fine," Mina pulled him back down onto the bed.

"I got something I need to talk to you about then."

"Okay about what?" Mina sat up.

"Since we're taking our relationship to the next level there's something I need to tell you."

"I have something I need to tell you, too."

"Let me go first."

"What is it?"

"I have a seven-year-old daughter."

"What?" she said, taken aback by the news.

"I didn't tell you about her before because that would have meant me telling you what I do for a living. You already know that I export drugs but it goes deeper than that."

"How deep?"

"My family is a part of one of many drug cartels in Cali, Colombia. We're called the Gonzalez cartel. The reason I left when we were younger, was because my Grandfather Escobar Gonzalez died, and it was time for my father, Jesus, to run the business. A lot of people thought that someone else should have been chosen to run the business since my father married outside of his race. But even though my father caught a lot of slack, he proved himself and brought in more money in five years than my Grandfather did his entire run. Ten years later my father became sick and died. That's when I took over."

"Okay, now, where does your daughter fit into all of this?"

"Right after I took over, I met Samia. We fell in love instantly and shortly after, we married. A year later my daughter, Lelah, was born. Everything was going cool. I had my wife and daughter, money was stacked to the ceiling and then everything went wrong. Lelah was two and Samia had taken her out shopping without a bodyguard. Some local thugs ended up kidnapping her and Lelah. A ransom was put out for a million dollars. Since I don't trust the police, I decided to handle it myself. I paid the ransom but when it came time for the exchange, Lelah was the only one to return. I found out later that Samia was killed after trying to escape."

"Victor, I am so sorry," Mina replied, hugging him.

"I know I should have told you this in the beginning but I didn't know where things were gonna go. I wanted to tell you that I am going to do everything in my power to keep you safe."

"Where is Lelah now?"

"She spends the summer with my family in Miami. I have to go and get her in two weeks."

"Does your family know about me?"

"Yeah, I've told them all about you and they can't wait to meet you."

"When you said that you had some news I surely wasn't expecting that." Mina climbed out of bed and paced the room.

"I'm sorry, Ma, I should have told you." Victor became worried that she might leave.

Mina looked him dead in his eyes and knew that she could never be mad at him. His presence commanded her attention and just the sight of him turned her on to the fullest. Looking over his olive skin, tall frame, chiseled chest and sexy mouth she envisioned how their son would have the same features. "Come here."

Walking over to him she placed her body into his welcoming arms. "I love you. I've loved you since you were eleven and I was thirteen. I should have believed you when you came to see me that day. I regret that I let you leave every time I think about what that punk muthafucker did to you. I promise that I will never leave you again. You believe me?"

"Yes," she said as tears streamed down her face.

"What are the tears about?" he asked as he wiped her face for her.

"I'm pregnant."

"For real?"

"Yes." She nodded.

"When did you find out?"

"When Dr. Townsend came in to see me right before I was discharged."

Shocked by the news Victor said, "Yo', I ain't trying to be cruel or no shit like that but is it mine?"

"Yeah, it's yours!" Mina shrieked, shocked by the question.

"Ay, calm down. It's just that you still were seeing ol' boy. I don't know if ya'll was still fuckin' or not."

"Well we weren't. I stopped fuckin' him once we hooked up. Plus, he and I always used condoms, unlike you and I," Mina snapped, still upset. "Look if you don't believe me we can get a paternity test done when the baby gets here."

"Yo', it ain't even that serious. I just asked you a question. Of course I believe you when you say it's mine. Calm down." Victor took her into his arms and hugged her tight.

"You're not mad?"

"Nah, why would I be? You're about to birth my seed."

"You have to promise me one thing though."

"Anything, what?" he kissed her lips.

"Promise me that you will not go after Andrew."

"Nah, I can't do that! Uh uh!" he yelled, releasing his arms from around her waist.

"I can handle Andrew. Just let me take care of him."

"You're pregnant. I'm not about to let you go anywhere near that nigga!"

"You told me to trust you and I did. Now I'm asking you to do the same. Trust me, I can do this."

"Did you not just hear me when I told you what happened to Samia?! I'm not about to let the same thing happen to you! I forbid you to go anywhere near him! You hear me, Mina? Promise me you won't go near Andrew!"

"I promise," she said with her fingers crossed behind her back.

Chapter Fourteen

Shuffle

"Calm down, everything is going to be all right."

"How do you know, Dad?" Andrew asked as he paced back and forth across his father's office floor.

"It's been over a week now and the police haven't even contacted us. If Mina said anything to them, they would have knocking on our door by now.

"Your father's right dear, you have nothing to worry about," Mrs. Wellington waved him off as she took a drink of special tea.

"If that bitch says one word, my life is over!"

"Sweetheart, calm down. You're going to tear a hole in your father's Arapaho rug."

"How could you let things get this far, Andrew? You were supposed to keep your temper in check, remember. You were to marry Mina and get it annulled a few months later. I would've been a shoo-in for Governor and you would have been solidified as a saint in the community. I believed in you son, how could you let me down like this?"

"I tried, Father! What more do you want from me?!" Andrew cried.

"I'm sorry, son. I shouldn't have come down so hard on you," Mr. Wellington said, hugging his son.

"My poor baby. I knew that no-class scallywag would be the downfall of you," Mrs. Wellington cried as well.

"Don't cry, Mother."

"I'm sorry, I just hate seeing you like this."

"I'll be fine, Mother."

"This is just too much. I need another drink. Cook!" she cried out as she left the room. Taking his son by the shoulders, Mr. Wellington looked him square in the eyes. "You know what must be done, son."

Nodding his head, Andrew agreed. Getting rid of Mina once and for all was the only way to handle the situation.

* * *

"How are you doing, Mina?" Dr. Frager said, entering the examination room.

"I'm fine," Mina replied lying back on the exam table.

"And are you the father?"

"Yes, this is my fiancé, Victor."

"How you doing?" Victor extended his hand.

"Nice to meet you. Okay, lets see how far along you are. If you will, Mina, will you raise your top up some."

Pulling her shirt up, Mina watched as Dr. Frager squeezed a cold blue substance onto her stomach. She placed a monitor onto her stomach and Mina and Victor watched as their baby's picture came onto the screen. Mina couldn't believe her eyes. She was actually seeing her baby for the first time. The baby was so small. It was almost the size of a golf ball.

"Victor, look," Mina said, pointing to the screen.

"I know, Ma, how many months is she doc?"

Ring...Ring...

"Hold that thought." Victor stepped off into the corner to answer his cell phone. "Hello?"

While Victor talked on the phone, Dr. Frager wiped the gel off of Mina's stomach and excused herself from the room. With the picture still up Mina continued to stare in amazement at her baby.

Her excitement was interrupted by Victor's loud bellows. "Yo', what the fuck I tell you dog! Handle that shit! Don't call me! That's what I pay you for! Just do it!" Victor hung up the phone in a huff. "Dumb muthafuckers."

"What's the matter?"

"Don't worry about it. Ain't nothing concerning you." Victor said with an attitude.

"Well, fuck you, too, muthafucker," Mina retorted.

"My bad, Ma." Victor laughed and took her face into his hands and kissed her lips.

"That's better." Mina brightened up and smiled.

"Sorry for the wait, guys," Dr. Frager reentered the room.

"No problem. So how far along is she?" Victor asked.

"From the looks of things, Mina, you're about three months pregnant. The baby should be here in February. I want you to start taking these vitamins, and iron pills, starting today," Dr. Frager said handing her some samples, and giving her prescriptions. "Congratulations and I will see you back in a month."

* * *

Standing in front of the mirror Mina observed her shape. She was already a size fourteen and she knew since she was pregnant that she would gain even more weight. Victor said that he didn't care about her size but she knew deep down inside that all of that would change once she got bigger. Frowning at her reflection she tried to picture how she would look if she were thinner.

"What are you doing?" Victor asked, catching her posing in the mirror.

"Nothing," she lied, embarrassed.

"Come here," he said sitting down on the side of the tub. Taking her place on his lap sideways she looked into his eyes.

"I know what you were doing and you need to stop it now. How many times do I have to tell you that you are beautiful? You are beyond beautiful and you know why? Because not only are you beautiful on the outside you're beautiful in here," he said pointing to her heart. "I love you, Ma. I always have and I always will. Nothing will ever change that."

Smiling, she hugged his neck tight.

"I love you."

"I love you too. Now get up."

"What are you doing?" Mina asked, perplexed.

Victor leaned over and turned the faucet on. Going through a rack of toiletries that he bought for her, he found a bottle of Bath & Body Works Cucumber Melon bubble bath and poured that in to the water. Taking a lighter out of his pocket he lit the four candles that were strategically placed around the tub. Mina sat on top of the let down toilet seat while Victor removed her wooden wedge-heeled sandals.

Helping her back up, Victor peeled the Evita tube dress she was wearing down revealing her bare breasts and white thong. He kissed her stomach softly while sliding her moist thong off. Turning the light off, the bathroom was set for seduction. Mina didn't know whether she was coming or going she was in so much bliss.

"What are you doing to me?" she asked, trembling from the touch of his lips on her skin.

"Shh… let me take care of you," he whispered as he placed her body into the steamy hot bath.

"Umm this feels nice, thank you. How did you know I needed this?"

"You deserve to have this done every day," he said as he looked into her eyes and stroked her arm.

"Oh really."

"Yeah."

"What CD do you want to listen to?"

"Umm Floetry Live would be cool." Turning the CD player on, he played "It's Getting Late."

"This must be your thing," Mina said.

"What's my thing?" He kissed her lips.

"Seducing women."

"Actually, you're the first woman that I've ever done this for," he replied truthfully.

"You didn't do this for Samia when she was alive?"

"Nope, I didn't have enough time. I was always too busy working or running the streets but I have vowed that I will always put you, our baby and Lelah first."

"What kind of thug are you?" she laughed.

"I'm not a thug. I'm a man, baby girl," he replied, grabbing a white sponge and the Sandalwood Rose Aromatherapy Body Wash.

Sitting on the side of the tub, he ran the sponge across her neck while kissing her collarbone. Victor then ran the soapy sponge down her chest and over her hardened nipples. Mina moaned as she enjoyed his every touch. Caressing her breasts, he kissed each of them until Mina couldn't take anymore. As his hand reached her navel, she parted her legs so the sponge could find her center. In circular motions, he moved the sponge around. He watched as her back formed an arch.

"Ahh." Mina's moans slipped out and she almost didn't recognize her own voice.

Teasing her insides with his fingers, Victor playfully

seduced Mina's nipples with his tongue. Mina took his face
into her hands, then sloppily kissed his lips. Mina sucked on
Victor's tongue while feeling herself nearing an orgasm.
Shivering uncontrollably, she came all over his fingers.

"Can we please fuck?" she asked out of breath.

Ignoring her, Victor continued to wash her. Standing her
up, Victor turned on the shower so that she could rinse off.
When he was through, he helped her out of the tub and towel
dried her body slowly. Back in the bedroom, Victor laid her
down on her side. He went back into the bathroom and got a
bottle of Jasmine Vanilla massage oil. Returning to the bedroom, he took off his Timbs and got into bed with her.

"Close your eyes," Victor instructed.

"Why? What are you up to?" Mina grinned.

"Just be quiet and enjoy this, Ma."

"You're the boss," she closed her eyes.

Turning the bottle over, Victor poured a handful of oil into
the palm of his hand. Mina sighed as he glided his hands
across her back. Victor then kissed her cheek while massaging
her neck and shoulders. Using his thumbs he massaged her
shoulder blades. Mina was in absolute heaven. Every since she
had come home from the hospital Victor had been waiting on
her hand and foot.

Victor was a man full of surprises and just when she
thought she had him figured out, he would surprise her with
something new and different. Mina saw the need in his eyes.
He wanted to be with her physically but unable because she
was still sore. But now, she was fully healed and ready to get
her freak on. Now on her back she let him run a trace of oil
over her breasts. Staring into each other's eyes she watched as
his slippery hands ran across her aching nipples. Using her
own hands, Mina joined in and massaged her breasts as well.
Still staring into each other's eyes they connected on an erot-

ic level.

"Make love to me," she demanded, grabbing his neck and pulling his face toward hers.

The sexual tension between the two manifested as they kissed each other hungrily causing an electricity of heat to go off inside of both of them. Sitting up she unbuckled his belt, slid his shorts and boxers down. Victor then helped by pulling his wife beater over his head and kicking his shorts off.

Mina looked at his dick, and saw that it was throbbing and had a curve to it. She couldn't wait to feel him inside of her. Running her fingers down his six pack, she bit into her bottom lip.

"I love you, Mina," Victor moaned as he slid his way into the slit of her warm wet pussy.

In response, Mina wrapped her arms around his neck and moaned from the pleasure that his dick was giving her. Thrusting in and out he enjoyed the tightness of her center.

Wanting to go in as deep as he could, Victor gripped both of Mina's thighs tightly and grinded slowly. Scratching his back, she called out his name. The more he increased speed the more turned on she became. Sitting up she pushed him back and began to ride him.

Gliding up and down his dick, Mina began to feel weak as her body convulsed. Every stroke of his thick hard dick made her head spin. Her eyes rolled to the back of her head as she neared her first orgasm. Victor pumped hard while holding Mina's waist as her body began to tremble. As he thumbed her clit, Victor caused her orgasm to intensify. Always the one to please her man, Mina wiped off his dick with her hand and took it hungrily into her mouth. The first lick tasted like honey. Wanting another taste, she wrapped her mouth around the head licking the tip.

"Fuck!" Victor yelled. Deep throating him she sucked and

licked him repeatedly until he was ready to explode. Not wanting to disrespect her he pulled out and came on the sheets. Both of their bodies were filled with sweat and the room smelled of sex. "That was the shit."

"I know, baby, that was some good dick," she purred, massaging his dick.

Ring...Ring...

"I'll get it. Hello?"

"Why haven't I heard from you?"

"Momma, I've been resting. I am still sore you know," Mina lied, knowing good and well she had been getting dicked up on a regular basis.

"Well, you know Smokey is leaving in a few in a weeks to go to school so you and that new man of yours are gonna have to come to the going away dinner."

"Okay. Oh, Momma, I forgot to tell you that I'm going out of town the end of this week."

"Going out of town? Where? I thought you were still sore?"

"I am, but Victor wants me to go to Miami with him to pick up his daughter."

"His daughter? That nigga got kids?"

"Yes, Momma." Mina rolled her eyes to the ceiling.

"And you're okay with that?"

"Yes, Momma, I love him," Mina said, stroking Victor's dick.

"Okay, I'm gonna trust your judgment, but if that Julio Iglesias-lookin muthafucker lay one hand on you, it's on! You hear me!"

"I hear you, Ma," Mina laughed.

"All right, nah. You be safe and call me before you leave."

"Okay," she hung up.

"Baby, why yo' dick so big?" she purred, sucking on his bottom lip.

"Keep it up and we gon' be going for round two."

"I would but I promised Delicious and Mo that I would meet up with them later."

"Cool, I gotta take care of some business anyway," he said, easing out of bed. Gazing at his naked body Mina became turned on and wanted to fuck again but quickly pushed the thought out of her head. Rubbing her stomach she thought, *That's how I got pregnant in the first place.*

"Armando is going to drive you," Victor shouted from inside the shower.

"Just because I'm pregnant doesn't mean that I can't drive myself."

"I don't trust that nigga Andrew. Who knows what he might have up his sleeve?" Realizing that he was right, Mina decided not to put up a fight.

An hour later she and Armando were pulling up in front of Delicious' crib.

"Thanks, Armando. I'll call you when I'm done."

"Mr. Gonzalez instructed me to stay with you at all times, ma'am."

"No, it's okay I will be fine."

"Sorry, I have to follow the boss' orders."

"Okay." Mina rolled her eyes, feeling like an invalid.

Knock, Knock!!!

"Who is it?" Janiya asked.

"It's me, girl, open the damn door!"

"Hey, girl! Oh, my God! You cut your hair?"

"You like?"

"Yeah, girl! You just like that girl Meesa now."

"Where is everybody at and what the hell is all of that noise?" Mina questioned as she walked through Delicious' brightly decorated home. Even though he had loud colors in his home it was decorated well. Delicious had a citrus color theme going on throughout his house. Since his favorite era was the sixties he also had a lot of retro furniture as well.

"Delicious is doing his Ciara impersonation again."

"Oh, my God, I gotta see this."

"I bet you want the goodies, bet you gotta have it," Delicious sang as he stood in the middle of the floor with a honey-colored wig on, a white cut off T-shirt, low rise jeans and sneakers. The nigga really thought he was Ciara. Mina had to give it to him. He had the routine down pat.

"Go Dee Dee, Go Dee Dee," the girls cheered.

"Ya'll know ya'll need to stop egging his crazy ass on," Mina shouted over the loud music.

"Mina!" everyone screamed, running toward her.

"You look so cute," Tiffany exclaimed.

"Delicious, you hooked her hair up," Neosha replied.

"Yeah, I want my hair like that," Jodie added.

"Miss Thang look a'ight."

"Nigga, quit hatin'. You know she look good. Girl, you look just like Halle Berry."

"More like Chuck Berry," Delicious teased.

"Fuck you, nigga," Mina said, hitting him.

"You know I'm just playing. Let me look at you. You look Fab-o-lous!" Delicious snapped his fingers.

"Thank you, baby."

"What's up with the glow?" Mo asked, eating a bag of chips.

"I got good news ya'll. I'm pregnant!"

"What?!" everyone yelled.

"How far along are you?" Mo asked.

"Almost three months, but you can't tell my momma and them, though. I'm going to tell them at Smokey's going away dinner."

"I'm gonna be a God Momma!" Mo shouted out, excitedly.

"Congratulations, Mina," Tiffany said.

"Have you heard anything from Andrew?" Neosha questioned.

"Nope, it's like he's vanished or something. I guess that nigga laying low."

"I wouldn't say that," Delicious spoke up.

"What's the 411, Hon?"

"A friend of mine said they saw him coming out of Magnolia's a couple of nights ago drunk as a skunk."

"For real?"

"Honey yes—"

"Mina, will you tell Victor that we all said thank you for paying us?" Jodie replied, interrupting Delicious.

"I sure will but I called this meeting."

"Next time speak when I finish." Delicious rolled his eyes at Jodie.

"Boy you betta shut up."

"I see ain't nothing changed. But for real ya'll, I called this meeting because I want to take care of Andrew once and for all. " Mina laughed.

"What are you gonna do—report him to the police?" Janiya asked.

"Nope, better than that, I'm going to blackmail him."

"How?"

"We all know that Andrew is gay, but the world doesn't know it…yet. If we can get Andrew on tape in a compromising situation and then threaten to expose him with it, I'm more than sure that he will turn the shop over to me in no time."

"Sounds good to me. When and how do we do it?" Mo asked.

"I was thinking that Delicious could use one of his friends

to bait Andrew and then put him in a comprising situation. That way we can have a hidden camera set up in the room, catching it all on tape."

"I have just the person to do it." He picked up the phone and immediately dialed Stiletto's number. Stiletto was a drag queen friend of his from back in the day. Thirty minutes later, Stiletto arrived. He was Caucasian, tall, blonde and blue-eyed, just the way Andrew liked them. Stepping out of his drop top Chrysler Sebring, he looked as if he could have been a young Brad Pitt. The man was absolutely divine. Approaching the steps, he was stopped. Armando had gotten out the car and frisked him.

"Who does that big, burley stud think he is?" Stiletto asked as he entered the house, a little flustered by the whole situation. Looking at one another, the girls wondered how such a feminine voice came out of such a muscular man.

"I'm sorry, Stiletto, if he offended you in any kind of way. That was my driver/bodyguard Armando," Mina said, trying to stifle a laugh.

"No problem, chile. To tell you the truth, I kinda enjoyed it. So what's the deal? Ya'll want me to set up the Mayor's son?"

"Yes."

"So, Mr. Andrew is among the A-List Elite?"

"What is the A-List Elite?" Mo asked.

"Damn, Mo! Don't you know anything? The A-List Elite are gay men who have money, power and privilege. Haven't you heifers been around me long enough to know all of this. Shit, ya'll making me look bad in front of my girl." Delicious scrunched up his face.

"Boy, don't nobody be listening to you."

"I heard over the years that he was gay. If I would have known it was true I would have reeled that big fish in a long time ago."

"If you want him, you can have him, but he does have an abusive side."

"A man beater, oh, hell no! Girl, he hit you?"

"Yep."

"Oh, we got to get that switch hitter now." Laughing at him, Mina knew that Delicious couldn't have picked a better person to trap Andrew. Stiletto was just as wild and flamboyant as he was. The girls could easily tell how the two become friends. After telling Stiletto her plan and offering to pay him five thousand dollars, he agreed. Everything was set up to go down as soon as Mina returned from Miami.

* * *

"Baby, that flight was crazy."

"I know my ears are still ringing," Victor replied, holding Mina's hand as they walked to the Lincoln Town Car that was awaiting them.

"Buenas tardes, Dro," spoke the family driver, Thomas.

"Yeah, what's up to you, too," Dro said with a slight attitude.

He was annoyed the entire plan ride. He didn't expect Mina to accompany them. To him it was already bad enough that the two were back together but to see them all lovey dovey made him sick to his stomach. He couldn't stand Mina and he made sure that she knew it at all times.

"Buenas tardes, Vencedor. Es bueno a encontrarse contigo." (Good afternoon Victor. It's good to see you.)

"Buenas tardes, Thomas. Aqui esta mi novia, Mina." (Good afternoon, Thomas. This is my girlfriend, Mina.)

"Good afternoon, Mina. It's a pleasure to meet you."

"El gusto es mio," she smiled. (The pleasure is mine.)

"Since when do you know how to speak Spanish?" Victor asked.

"I've always known how. You just never asked." She chuckled.

"See, that's why I love you so much. You keep a nigga on his toes."

"Can we go now?" Dro said, feeling like he had to throw up.

"Yeah, man. Bring you ole hatin' ass on. What you need is some pussy. Maybe you'll lighten the fuck up then."

"Fuck you, nigga," Dro replied underneath his breath.

Ten minutes later they were pulling up in front of Dro's parents' five million dollar bayfront villa. Mina never saw anything so beautiful. The house was surrounded by palm trees and shrubbery that gave the home a tropical vibe. Jaguars, Porsches and Bentleys adorned the spiral driveway and the sounds of insects and birds danced around her ears.

"Is that my handsome son?" A beautiful African American woman, who looked to be in her forties, reached her arms out to Victor.

"How you doing, Momma?" Victor said, hugging her back.

"You're getting skinny, boy. You need to eat."

"I have been eating, Ma. Mina's been taking care of me."

"*Mina*, I've heard so much about you. Welcome to the family, sweetheart." His mother hugged her.

"Thank you, Mrs. Gonzalez."

"Please call me Faith."

"Where is Lelah?" Victor asked.

"You know your daughter. She's in there making sure that she's as pretty as ever for her daddy."

"¿Es mi hijo? Ven acá. Dame un abrazo." (Is that my boy? Give me a hug.)

"What's up, Pop?" Dro hugged his father.

"You're looking good, son."

"Is that my baby?" Dro's mother yelled as she came running out of the house to greet her son.

"Hi Ma."

"Is that all I get? Hi, Ma. I haven't seen you since Christmas boy. You better give me a hug."

"I'm sorry, Ma," he gave his mother a hug.

"Victor, introduce us to your friend," Dro's father said.

"I'm sorry, Mina, this is my Uncle Emilio and my Aunt Alita."

"Como esta usted? Mucho gusto." (How are you doing? It's nice to meet you.)

"Ohh, you know how to speak Spanish?" Emilio asked.

"Yes sir, I speak Spanish fluently."

"Well, son, you've done good for yourself," Emilio said pleased.

"Thank you." Victor smiled.

"Isn't she beautiful?" Faith replied.

"Yes, quite lovely. The baby is going to be absolutely gorgeous," Alita gushed, rubbing Mina's stomach.

"You told them already?"

"Yeah, I know I was supposed to wait until we got here but I just couldn't."

"My son has always been impulsive that way," Faith laughed.

"Daddy, Daddy!"Gazing up at the door, Mina saw the cutest seven-year-old girl. Lelah was caramel, with slanted brown eyes and a heart-shaped face. Her silky black hair was pulled up into a ponytail. Three carat princess cut diamond earrings sparkled in her ear and a platinum charm bracelet decorated her wrist. A yellow Juicy Couture tube dress and white Prada sandals were on her feet. Lelah was a little fashionista.

"Ven acá, mi hija hermosa," Victor yelled, scooping his daughter into his arms. (Come here, my beautiful baby)

"I've missed you, Daddy."

"I missed you too, princesa."

"Do you like my dress?"

"Yes, it's the most beautiful dress I've ever seen. Lelah, I want you to meet somebody. Lelah, this is Mina. Mina, this is Lelah."

"Nice to meet you, Miss Lelah. You look so pretty today."

"Thank you," she spoke shyly hiding her face in her father's chest.

"Enough chit-chat. Let me show you the house. Your cousins are in the house," Emilio said.

Once they reached the indoors, Mina was greeted by Dro's bother Rico and Victor's other cousin Hector. Holding both of his girls' hands, Victor escorted the ladies throughout the 6,200 square foot home. The entire house was decorated in spring and summer colors. The walls were crown-molded and the arched doorways were adorned with French doors.

Emilio and Alita had everything from fine marble stone to hardwood and terracotta floors. There were six bedrooms, five bathrooms, a pool and a deck. Each room had an amazing view of the lake. By the time they finished touring the house Mina was wiped out. The baby was telling her it was time for her daily nap.

While Mina napped, Victor pulled his uncle aside to discuss business. Wanting a quiet place to talk, they headed out to the deck. Passing his nephew a Cuban cigar, they sparked up and looked at the lake for a while before either of them spoke.

"This is beautiful, Unc. I gotta get me a spot down here, too."

"I know, me and your aunt love it down here and ever since your mother moved down here your aunt has really been having a ball."

"I'm glad Momma's happy. You know, after Pop died, I couldn't get her to do anything."

"I know. I remember but that's all in the past. Everybody's doing well now and we have to focus on the good, not the bad."

"You're right Unc, that's why I want out."

Sitting for a moment, Emilio sat and pondered Victor's words. He knew that Victor's flying out to Miami had more to do with business than pleasure. When his brother Jesus died, leaving the business to Victor, they all wondered if he made the right decision. Quickly they learned that he did. Victor did an extraordinary job running the Gonzalez cartel. Money was pouring in from all different states and countries. Emilio was too old to run the business so the question of who Victor wanted to appoint leader needed to be answered.

"You want out?"

"Yeah I mean, I've had a good run. I've made the family a lot of money. None of us will ever have to work a day in our lives." Victor turned facing his uncle.

"That's true," Emilio said, still staring at the lake.

"And now that Mina is pregnant, I don't want her, or my baby, to go through what Samia and Lelah went through."

"I hear you."

"I'm twenty-eight years old and I have yet to really enjoy my life. Yeah, I take care of Lelah financially and I make sure that she goes to the best school but I haven't been there for her like I should have. I don't want to make the same mistake twice."

Leaning forward, Emilio placed the cigar in the ashtray. Sitting back again he continued to stare at the lake.

"You know once you're out, you're out. There's no coming back."

"I understand."

"How much money do you have saved up?"

"One hundred fifteen mil and I will still have funds coming in from my businesses and from the stock market."

"You did good, son."

"Thank you."

"You know that I have always looked at you like my son. I only want the best for you so if you really want out then you're out as of today."

"Thank you. I really do want out; this shit is for the birds. I'm trying to live like you and Auntie," Victor smiled.

"So who do you have in mind to run the business?"

"I was thinking about Dro."

"I disagree with that. Dro is not ready yet. He's too impulsive, a hot head and doesn't manage money well. No, I think Rico would do much better."

"You knew I was going to tell you that I wanted out, didn't you? That's why you invited Rico down here for the week."

Smiling to himself, Emilio said nothing.

"Still two steps ahead of everybody else huh Unc," Victor laughed.

As the two shared a laugh, Dro stood outside the door listening to their every word. He couldn't believe that his father had chosen Rico over him. It was his time; he was supposed to the run the business. He secretly hated his father and Victor's relationship over the years but now the hate multiplied. Furious beyond words, he vowed that he would have his revenge on the both of them if it was the last thing he did.

Chapter Fifteen

Mute

The last night at the Gonzalez villa was an extraordinary one for Victor and Mina. The entire family sat around a large rectangular table outside sharing a feast fit for a king. The sun had gone down and the torches that were placed around the yard were lit. A full moon was out and the surround sound speakers played soft jazz music. Wine was steadily being poured and everyone was happy. Mina never enjoyed life so much. In a week's time she and Lelah had grown close and her relationship with Victor's mother would forever be cherished.

Faith was the nicest woman and she always made Mina feel at home and welcome. At that moment, gazing around at all the different faces, Mina felt complete. *This is how it should've been when I was with Andrew*, she thought to herself. The Gonzalez's never judged and always had a good time no matter what. She knew that her family and Victor's would get along perfectly.

"Mina, will you pull my hair back in a ponytail for me?" Lelah asked.

"Of course, come sit on my lap."

Watching as his daughter climbed onto Mina's lap, Victor smiled. When they broke the news to Lelah that Mina was pregnant she took it quite well. She said that she couldn't wait to be a big sister. Victor couldn't have asked for more. His two favorite girls in the world were getting along better than he could have ever imagined. He was out of the business and his mother was doing well. At that moment, he knew that from that day forward, his life would be good.

"There you go, all done. You look fab-o-lous, Lelah," Mina said, imitating Delicious.

"Thank you, Mina," Lelah hopped down, returning to her game of jump rope.

"What's wrong cousin? You've been quiet all week," asked Hector.

"Nothing, I'm cool."

Taking his word Hector continued to eat.

"So when is the baby due, Mina?" Rico questioned.

"February."

"I can't wait. I'm going to spoil him or her to death," Faith added.

"Oh, I love this song," Alita said as Norah Jones' song "Come Away With Me" played.

"I do, too," Mina agreed.

"Come here then." Victor extended his hand to dance.

Mina smiled from ear to ear as she joined him in the middle of the lawn. Victor pulled her close and wrapped his arms around her waist while she placed her head onto his chest. As she swayed back and forth, Mina listened for the sound of his heartbeat. Rubbing the back of her head, Victor kissed her forehead.

Seeing how much they were enjoying themselves, Alita and Emilio joined in. Side by side they all drifted off to another place. Little did they know that this would be their last time together. With a smile on her face Faith gazed at her son and future daughter-in-law. Lighting a cigar, Dro's upper lip curled while the veins in his neck popped out. He wanted them both dead, including his father.

"I got a surprise for you," Victor whispered softly into Mina's ear.

"What?" she grinned, knowing it was going to be something good.

"Look up." Staring up at the night sky, she watched as a Goodyear Blimp flew by. Shocked beyond words, she read the words *"Will You Marry Me, Mina?"* as they ran across the screen over and over. Everyone had their eyes on her as they awaited her reply. Mina focused her attention back on Victor and found him on one knee with a Tiffany box in his hand. Gasping for breath she saw the most beautiful ring ever. It was a ten carat, flawless, square cut engagement ring. The ring made Andrew's ring look pathetic.

"So, will you marry me?"

"Yes," she yelled so that everyone in the universe could hear. Taking her hand he slid the engagement ring onto her ring finger.

"Congratulations, son," Emilio said hugging Victor.

"Thank you." Having seen enough, Dro quietly went into the house refusing to acknowledge what he just witnessed.

"Congratulations sweetheart," Tears filled Faith's eyes as she hugged Mina.

"You're going to make a beautiful bride," Alita added.

"Thank you." Mina began to cry tears of joy.

"Is Mina going to be my new Momma now?" Lelah questioned.

Bending down on one knee, he grabbed his daughter's hand and said, "No one can ever take the place of your mother, princess."

"Right honey, I would never try to take your mother's place. But I will say that I'm going to love you like you were my own," Mina said.

"I loved your mother very much, but Daddy has to move on with his life. I will always love your mother because she gave me you. But now I have Mina in my life and the new baby on the way and I want for all of us to be one big happy family. Do you understand that?"

"Yes," Lelah nodded.

"Okay, give Daddy a kiss."

Kissing her father on the cheek, Lelah then gave Mina a hug around the waist. "I'm glad that you make Daddy happy," Lelah said to Mina.

"I'm glad that your Daddy makes me happy," Mina answered.

* * *

The following Sunday afternoon, the house was quiet and everyone was gone shopping except for Emilio. All of the servants and the cooks had the day off leaving Emilio alone. There couldn't have been a better time for Dro and his father to have the conversation that he had been dying to have the entire week. Sneaking back into the house after everyone was gone he found Emilio in his favorite chair watching television. Taking his chance, Dro took a seat directly in front of his father only to freeze up. Seeing that his son wanted to talk, but was unsure of what to say, Emilio started up the conversation.

"What is it, son? You got something on your mind?"

"Yeah, I've wanted to talk to you."

"I know you have. I've been waiting."

"I overheard the little conversation you and Victor had the

other day.""Is that right?" Emilio said in a thick Spanish accent.

"Is that all you have to say? You chose Rico over me! I should be the one to lead the family, not him!" Dro yelled, furious.

"You're not ready yet, Alejandro," Emilio replied as calm as can be."Fuck that! That's bullshit and you know it! I should have been the one to run the business when Uncle Jesus died! Only full blooded Puerto Ricans should run the family business! Victor shouldn't have even been a thought to run the business! It should have been me then and it should be me now!"

"Alejandro, I've always detected that you were jealous of your cousin but never this much. You speak with such larceny against your own blood. That's why you will never run the business," Emilio spoke, keeping his eye on the flat screen.

"Look at me!" Dro turned his father's face in his direction. "You never loved me! You always loved Victor more than you love me! I have hated you and that half-breed muthafucker my entire life but now it's time for me to get mine!" Dro said, pulling out a syringe filled with Sodium Thiopental, a fast acting sedative.

"What are you doing, son?" Emilio asked as Dro injected him with the drug."I'm doing what I should have done years ago muthafucker!" Taking out another syringe filled with Pancuronium Bromide, Dro injected that into his father's veins which caused his muscles to become paralyzed. Unable to defend himself Emilio stared at his only son hoping that he would come to his senses.

"Die slow, muthafucker," Dro said as he injected his father with the last syringe filled with a lethal dose of Potassium Chloride, which would stop his heart.

"I've always loved you, son," Emilio said as his eyes closed and his soul went to heaven. Watching as his father's body go limp, Dro let one tear slip only to wipe it away. Running outside he made sure that the coast was clear and threw the syringes in the lake. Busting a window and stealing $50,000 from the safe he called the police and told them there had been a robbery. Before the police came, Dro ran out to the lake once again, this time throwing in the gloves and the duffle bag filled with money.

An hour later, the entire Gonzalez family was in shambles. Alita was hysterical with grief. Emilio was the love of her life and the father of her children. She could not fathom her life without him. Holding his mother tight Dro told her that everything would be all right. Crying into her son's arms, Alita told him that now he and Rico were all she had.

Victor went crazy upon hearing the news. *Who would possibly want to kill him?* was the question that kept popping up in his mind as he cried. Emilio didn't have any enemies as far as he knew. *Maybe it was the Diablo family,* he thought. Whoever it was he was sure to get revenge. Mina tried to console him but he was inconsolable. The only thing he could do was cry. Emilio was like a father to him after his own father passed. Who would he turn to now when he needed fatherly advice?

Their flight back to St. Louis was set to leave the next day but that had to be canceled because they had a funeral to plan. When the autopsy report came in showing that Emilio was poisoned with the same drugs used to do lethal injections, Victor lost his mind. He knew that whomever killed his uncle was demented and cruel. Being the leader of the family, Victor had to keep his cool, but at night while lying in Mina's arms he let any and all frustrations out.

Family and friends from all over the United States and Colombia attended the vigil and funeral. At the vigil they all prayed for Emilio and all other deceased individuals. Since the funeral would be covered by the media, Victor showed up in a black Hugo Boss suit, white button up shirt, black silk tie, and Kenneth Cole shoes. Mina chose to wear a fitted Christian Lacroix pinstriped suit with a pair of Michael Kors heels. Up until the funeral, Mina had no idea how well-known the Gonzalez family was. Alita had been outside herself with grief. The family didn't know if she would be able to go on.

When it came time to the view body, she fainted, and the church attendants had to use smelling salts to revive her. Victor felt so bad for his aunt because he watched his own mother go through the same thing years back. Throughout the entire funeral service Victor sat stone-faced. He knew that everyone was watching him, wondering what his next move was.

Crime families from all over the country came to show their respects and give their condolences to the Gonzalez family. Victor shook hands with every last one of them, thinking in the back of his mind, *one of you killed my uncle.* No one knew that Rico was appointed the new leader of the Gonzalez cartel, not even Rico, and Victor wanted to keep it that way until he found out who killed Emilio.

Mina tried to stay strong throughout the long week but on the inside she was scared to death. She constantly wondered if someone would try to kill Victor as well. She wanted to voice her concerns but Victor was already going through so much so she opted to keep quiet. For the first time since she arrived in Miami she was ready to return home. Mina had never missed her family more.

* * *

The next day they all stood outside hugging and saying their goodbyes as Thomas loaded their luggage in the back of the car. With Lelah in his arms, Victor told his mother that he loved her while hugging her goodbye.

"I'm gonna miss you, too, baby. You two be safe," she cried, speaking to Victor and Mina.

"We will," Mina assured.

"Where is Alejandro?" Alita asked, blowing her nose.

"He's still inside. I'll get him," Rico said.

"Now call me when you get home okay," Faith said again for the fifth time.

"We will, Ma, I promise. Besides, I'll be back in a couple of weeks," Victor replied.

"Victor, we have to get going or you're going to miss your flight," Thomas said.

"Remember to listen to the guards and don't go anywhere without them," Victor told his mother, aunt and Rico.

"I'll keep an eye on them, Vic," Rico complied.

"A'ight, Momma, I'ma call you when I get home." Dro hugged and kissed his mother.

"Okay, baby, I love you."

"Give Granny some suga," Faith said to Lelah. Leaning over, Lelah kissed her on the cheek.

"A'ight, ya'll. We out," Victor said, getting into the car.

"We love you," both Alita and Faith yelled, holding onto one another.

"We love you, too," Victor and Mina both said at the same time.

Chapter Sixteen

Record

Mina finally returned home and everything was set into motion to trap Andrew. Janiya and Tiffany were outside of Magnolia's, parked, waiting for Andrew to make his entrance. He would usually show up for the country-western themed night on time but for some reason he was late. The girls started to wonder whether or not he would show up. Just when they thought it was all a lost cause, Andrew pulled up. Picking up her Nextel, Tiffany spoke into the phone and said, "The eagle has landed. I repeat, the eagle has landed."

If you didn't know how Andrew looked you would have thought he was a regular club-goer. Gone were his thousand dollar suits and five hundred dollar Scooby Doos. No, he was undercover – a fitted baseball cap, T-shirt, khaki shorts and trainer tennis shoes were his new attire. Entering the club, he surveyed the purple-walled building for any possible pick up but didn't see any.

Taking a seat at one of the empty tables he ordered a Red

Bull. Back outside, Janiya two-wayed Stiletto letting him know that Andrew was in the house. Spotting his target instantly, he popped an Altoid into his mouth and proceeded toward Andrew. Noticing the Brad Pitt look-alike coming toward him, Andrew immediately became aroused.

"How you doing there, big boy?"

"I'm fine and you," Andrew answered a little nervous.

"Don't be afraid, I won't bite, at least not until I get to know you a little better," Stiletto teased, picking up on his nervousness. "So what brings you into a place like this?"

"I wanted a drink so I decided to come in," he lied.

"A drink, honey? Red Bull is not a drink. Let me get you something with some *umph* to it." Getting back up, Stiletto sauntered over to the bar slowly, making sure Andrew caught his every move. "Hi I would like a Vodka on the rocks for that fine gentleman sitting over there by himself and a water with ice for me. And keep them coming but don't tell him that I'm having water. I don't want him to think I'm a light weight." Stiletto laughed, sliding him a fifty dollar bill for his trouble. "Here you go, lover."

"What is this?" Andrew asked.

"Vodka on the rocks, I'm having the same thing too."

"Oh."

"Let's make a toast."

"To what?"

"To new beginnings," Stiletto smirked.

"To new beginnings," Andrew said, clinking glasses with him. Knocking his first drink back, Andrew felt somewhat refreshed. For the first time in weeks he felt calm. Four drinks later he was past tipsy and slurring his words.

"Let's dance." Stiletto reached out his hand.

Taking his hand Andrew joined him on the dance floor. The DJ was bumping the club version of Amerie's "1 Thing" and every gay man and woman was on the floor doing their thing. GoGo dancing, Stiletto backed it up on Andrew, showing no mercy. Liking his moves, Andrew held onto his waist, making sure he felt his manhood harden. Taking that as his cue, Stiletto made a suggestion.

"Why don't we go back to my place?" Stiletto whispered into his ear.

"Okay," Andrew smiled, feeling his manhood rising.

Hand in hand, they left out together. Andrew hopped back into his car while Stiletto got into his. Unbeknownst to Andrew, Tiffany and Janiya were taping the entire scene. Watching as they pulled off, Tiffany buzzed Mina again this time saying, "The king has left the building. I repeat, the king has left the building."

* * *

Fifteen minutes away, Neosha and Jodie sat in front of Stiletto's apartment building awaiting his and Andrew's arrival. Upstairs in his apartment Mina, Mo and Delicious were busy setting up the video camera.

"Girl, how did you get past Victor, Armando and the guards?" Mo questioned.

"Victor and Dro are at the club tonight. After he left, I told Julisa and Armando that I would be in my room asleep for the rest of the night but Julisa kept on coming in asking me if I needed anything, that's what made me late. Finally after an hour, I made a fake body under the covers with some pillows and crept downstairs to the garage."

"You better hope Victor doesn't find out that you're gone."

"I called him before I left and told him I was going to bed. Besides, I transferred the house phone to my cell just in case he decides to call."

"I knew you were a sneaky bitch," Delicious joked.

"I learned from the best."

"So where are we going to set up this thing?" Mo asked.

"I was thinking right over there in that laundry basket. That way the clothes can cover the camera."

"Good idea, Dee."

"I hope these clothes are clean." Mina tooted up her nose.

"They're clean. I already checked," Delicious answered.

"That's set, so what do we do next?"

"Wait, I guess."

"Has anyone thought about where we're going to hide?" Mo questioned.

"Right there in that closet, we can all hide up in there. That way we can get a good view," Delicious answered.

"I don't want to see that shit," Mina hissed.

"I don't know about you, but I do. I always wanted to see how two men look

when they're having sex." Mo grinned.

"Where did you come from?"

"How has Victor been since you all returned home?" Delicious asked.

"He's okay. He's really sad though. Emilio was like his second father."

"How is Dro?"

"Actually, he's taking it quite well."

"Really?" Mo said.

"Yep, better than I would be."

"They're here, they're here," Mina heard Neosha's voice coming through her Nextel.

"Okay ya'll, time to hide," Delicious said, rushing them into the closet. "Remember, we have to be quiet so have a seat on the floor and don't say a word." Hearing Stiletto's voice they all sat frozen stiff inside of the closet.

"Would you like something to drink?"

"No, I drank enough," Andrew replied, rubbing his temples.

"Ahh, is somebody not feeling well? Come on. Let Momma fix it," Stiletto said, taking Andrew's hand, and leading him into his bedroom.

Pushing him down onto on the bed he began to untie his shoes. Placing his hand inside of his pants, Andrew began to massage his dick. Removing his hand, Stiletto saw just how aroused Andrew was. His dick imprint could be seen from a mile away.

"I see somebody's hard," Stiletto licked his lips.

Overly aroused Andrew took Stiletto's face and began to kiss his lips passionately. Lying on top of him Stiletto kissed him back with as much intensity.Back inside the closet Mina's jaw dropped to the floor. She couldn't believe what her eyes were seeing. She knew that Andrew was gay but to see him in the act was a story all in itself. Mo, on the other hand, was enjoying every minute. Delicious stared at the two of them making out as if it were nothing.

Passionately kissing one another, Andrew ran his fingers through Stiletto's hair just like he would a woman. Playing the role of the dominant one, Stiletto ordered Andrew to undress him. Not used to taking orders, Andrew reluctantly slid down Stiletto's pink panties. Naked from the waist down, Andrew began to massage Stiletto's dick with his hand.

"*Let me cater to you…*" Mina's cell phone began to ring. It was Victor.

"What was that?" Andrew asked.

"That was my cell phone. Baby, please, don't stop," Stiletto moaned.

Knowing they had almost been caught, Mina said a silent prayer to God. Mina looked through the slits of the door as she watched Andrew pull Stiletto down to the edge of the bed. Hungrily he took his dick into his mouth, and began to suck sloppily. With her eyes wide open, Mina had to cover her mouth so she wouldn't throw up.

Andrew was sucking Stiletto's dick like there was no tomorrow. With his dick in one hand he jugged his balls in the other hand while running his tongue up and down his shaft. Andrew then turned him over and used his hands to spread Stilettos' ass cheeks apart. Licking his ass from top to bottom, he tickled his asshole with his tongue.

"You got a condom?" Andrew asked, pulling down his pants.

"Yeah, look in my pants pocket," Stiletto said breathing heavily.

Taking the condom out Andrew tore it open with his teeth and slid it on. Not able to watch anymore, Mina closed her eyes. She had no idea that things were going to go this far. Stiletto was only supposed to make out with Andrew, not have sex with him. Easing his way in, Andrew began to pump in and out of Stiletto's ass. With her eyes closed shut, Mina heard a bunch of "oohs," and "ahhs," coming from the other side of the door. Mo's freaky ass had her face damn near planted on the door. Five minutes later, Andrew was stuttering, talking about he was cumming.

"No, baby, not yet! It was just starting to feel good!" Stiletto whined. Sliding out Andrew pulled the condom off and jerked off onto Stiletto's butt.

"Damn, that felt good," Andrew said, his head tilted back, massaging his dick.

"Good? You betta get yo' five-minute ass up outta here with that bullshit! Stiletto don't want no one-minute man! Stiletto likes to cum!" Stiletto said, putting his pants back on.

"I'm sorry, I just get a little excited sometimes. We can try again if you want."

"Do I look like Aaliyah? Get it right the first time and you won't have to try again," Stiletto said, snapping his fingers in Z style formation. "It's time for you to go, Twista!"

"Twista? Who is Twista?"

"Twista flows as fast as you cum! Now gets… to… steppin'…little man," Stiletto instructed, holding open the front door.

"Maybe we can get together again someday," Andrew said, leaving.

"When you see me on the streets, remember you don't know me!" Stiletto yelled quoting lyrics from T.I.'s song.

Slamming the door shut, he watched as Andrew got into his car and left. Seeing the coast was clear Janiya, Neosha, Jodie and Tiffany all hopped out of their cars.

"Ya'll can come out now," Stiletto bellowed opening the door for the girls.

"Thank God," Mina said.

"Where is the tape? We want to see what happened," Tiffany said excitedly.

"Ya'll go head on. I can't see that again." Mina shook her head, trying to escape the visual.

"I'm going to go take a shower," Stiletto said as he went into the bathroom.

Rewinding the tape, Delicious played it back so everyone could see. The girls couldn't believe their eyes. Neosha and Jodie covered their eyes while Tiffany and Janiya gasped from sheer shock. Once the tape was done playing they all sat quiet for a second.

"I think I'm gonna be sick," Mina said, turning purple. She raced to the trashcan and heaved up the Popeye's chicken from earlier that day.

Mo followed behind her. "Are you okay?" Mo asked, rubbing her back.

"Yeah, I'll be all right." Mina wiped her mouth with the

back of her hand.

"Here, honey, drink a little bit of this." Stiletto handed her a 7Up.

"Thank you."

"Well at least we got what we need to save the shop," Tiffany said out of the blue.

"I'm sorry ya'll. I know I wasn't supposed to have sex with the boy, but shit it started feelin' good. I hope you're not mad, Mina," Stiletto asked.

"Nah, I'm not mad it's just… that…I can't believe I gave two years of my life to his sick ass."

"But check it, Mina, if you hadn't gone through all of that drama with Andrew, you wouldn't be where you're at now. You have a wonderful man who loves and adores you and a baby on the way. What more could you ask for," Janiya encouraged.

"You're right; I have all I could have ever wanted. Fuck that bitch, Andrew! It's payback time!"

* * *

"Baby you almost dressed?" Victor yelled. knocking on the bathroom door.

"In a minute. Bay!"

"Yeah, girl, so you mailed the tape off this morning?" Mina whispered into her cell phone while putting on her make-up.

"Yep, I made four copies. One for me, one for you, one for Delicious and the other one, I sent to Andrew," Mo replied.

"Where's the original?"

"I got it. I'm going to give it to you when I see you this afternoon."

"Okay."

"Mina!" Victor yelled.

"Let me get off this phone before this boy loses his mind."

"A'ight, see you later."

"Bye."

Smoothing down her skirt, Mina opened the door, only to find her handsome fiancé standing there.

"How do I look?" she smiled, turning around.

"Beautiful," Victor said as he took in the crème crochet crop jacket, crème camisole, denim pencil skirt, Balenciaga bag and gold Charles David heels. Mina's short hair was perfectly spiked and curled, and the four-carat diamond earrings and engagement ring had her blinging the fuck out. "Yo', let me get some of that before we leave," Victor kissed her lips and caressed her butt.

"No we have to go, remember," she pushed him away. "You look good too, boo."

"Thanks," Victor said as he put on his red, black and white Nike Huarache tennis shoes that matched his red and white Ecko shirt and black baggy shorts.

"Daddy, can we go now?" Lelah whined.

"Yeah, since somebody's actin' funny," he said, referring to Mina.

"Whatever playa, I'll hook you up later."

Forty-five minutes later, the couple along with Lelah, arrived at the Matthews' household.

"Okay, guys. Here are the rules," Mina said, getting Victor and Lelah's attention. "Ignore everything my mother, aunt, and cousin Nay say. And…"

"Baby, calm down. Everything is gon' be fine," Victor assured.

"No, you don't know my family like that."

"I will get to know them if you let me get out this car."

"All right don't say I didn't warn you."

"Who is that out there in that Lincoln Town Car like they the president," Nay shouted holding the screen door open.

"It's me, Nay," Mina replied as Armando opened the door

for her.

"Damn, girl, you don't waste no time do you?"

"Nay, this is Victor and his daughter Lelah."

"Do you…a…speak…a… ingles?"

"Nay, what are you doing?"

"I'm speaking Spanish. What does it look like I'm doing?" she snapped, dressed in a red *Old Navy* tank top with her stomach protruding out, denim booty shorts and flip flops. With a wrap that was long on one side and short on the other, black lipstick, add-a-bead chain and red see through pager, Nay thought she was the shit.

"Whatever, where is my momma?"

"They in the kitchen."

Walking into the living room, Mina was hit smack dab in the face with decorations. Rita had everything from a banner to streamers. Balloons, party hats, foil horns, plastic tambourines and even a pin the tail on the donkey graced the wall. Mina didn't know if she was at a going away party or a child's birthday party.

"Is that Nana's baby?" Nana Marie asked, sitting in her favorite chair.

"Hey, Nana," Mina gushed, hugging her grandmother.

"Don't you ever go away that long again. You hear me?"

"Yes, ma'am. Nana Marie, you remember Victor, don't you?"

"I sure do. How are you doing, son?"

"I'm fine and you?" Victor kissed her cheek.

"I'm doing okay. Who is this pretty lil' thing?"

"This is my daughter, Lelah. Lelah say hello."

"Hello."

"Hello. She is too cute." Nana Marie smiled.

"What up, big head?" Smokey said, hitting Mina in the back of her head.

"Smokey you better gone! Don't hit me no more!" Mina punched him in the arm.

"Shut up. What's up, man? I'm Smokey, Mina's brother. We ain't get a chance to really talk at the hospital." Smokey gave Victor a handshake.

"What's up?"

"Bout time you decided to show yo' face." Rita smirked, standing in the door with a cigarette hanging from her lip. With the top of her hair pulled up into a burgundy and black ponytail, and the back hanging, she donned a too tight Blazer's asymmetrical jersey dress, red & white tube socks, and fake Manolo Timberland boots.

"Hey, Ma," Mina cringed, feeling sick all over again.

"You look different. You got something you need to tell me?"

"No," Mina shrieked.

"Hello, Mrs. Matthews." Victor kissed Rita's cheek.

"Boy, don't be kissing on me like that. Something might pop off."

"Oh, my God," Mina shook her head, embarrassed.

"Hey there, pretty girl. I'm Mina's momma, Rita. What's your name?"

"Lelah."

"Well, Lelah, you gon' on in the back and play with the kids."

"Can I, Daddy?"

"Sure, sweetheart."

Watching as Lelah joined Jimmy Jr., and Jasmine, Victor and Mina smiled.

"Where's Daddy, Momma?"

"In the backyard wit yo' uncle barbecuing."

"Mo just called and said she and Delicious are on their way," Aunt Bernice shouted, coming down the steps. Shaking her head, Mina couldn't help but to laugh at her appearance. Aunt Bernice sported a turquoise backless halter top that showcased her back rolls, patchwork jeans and clear platform sandals. Her usual heavy makeup and blonde wet and wavy weave was in, but this time, she added platinum blonde highlights.

"Hey, Aunt Bernice."

"Hey, honey."

"Hi, Bernice," Victor spoke.

"Why, hello, there, handsome. Give Aunt Bernice some suga." Taking her into his arms, Victor kissed both sides of her cheeks. "Now that's what I'm talkin' about! Mina baby you better hold onto this one!"

"The meat is ready, we can eat now," Uncle Chester yelled, coming into the house.

"Hey, Uncle Chester." Mina gave him a hug.

"How you doing, Fat Momma?"

"Fine. Uncle Chester, this Victor."

"How you doin', son?"

"I'm doing good and you?"

"I can't call it. I'm just trying to do me, you feel me."

"I feel you." Victor laughed at the old man.

"That's a nice piece of artillery you got on yo' finger, Mina." Uncle Chester stood back on his legs, eyeing her engagement ring.

"Let me see that," Nay said, snatching her finger. "Girl, where you get that from, the Home Shopping Network?"

"No, Victor gave this to me. We're engaged."

"Congratulations, sweetheart," her father said, coming into the kitchen.

"Thank you, Daddy." Mina hugged him.

"All I have to say is you better treat her right," Ed voiced to Victor.

"I will, sir. You have nothing to worry about."

"A'ight now."

"I thought you didn't have nothin' to tell me," Rita said, looking at Mina sideways.

"I wanted it to be a surprise."

"You knocked up, too, ain't you?"

"How you know?"

"I had a dream about fish last week. I knew I wasn't pregnant, yo auntie can't have no mo kids, and Nay already pregnant so that only left you and Smokey fast-ass girlfriend Sharnetta."

"Hi, Mrs. Matthews," Sharnetta spoke.

"Hey, there, baby. How you doin'?" Rita asked as fake as she could be, extending her arms for a hug.

"Fine," Sharnetta said, none the wiser.

"We fixin' to eat soon so you make yourself comfortable, okay."

"Okay."

"Come on, ya'll. Let's say grace," Aunt Bernice ordered. "'Cause I'm hungry than a muthafucker."

"Auntie! There are kids in the room," Mina scolded.

"My bad, damn. Quit being so sensitive."

"Whatever," Mina mumbled under her breath. After they all finished saying grace everyone stood in line to fix their plate. Rita and Ed had outdone themselves. They had all of Smokey's favorite foods. Mosticolli, potato salad, seven-layered salad, baked beans, barbecue rib tips, pork steaks, hamburgers and hotdogs. Mina couldn't wait to dig in.

"Victor, have you ever had soul food before?" Nay asked.

"Yeah, my mother cooks like this all the time."

"Oh, really, so your mother is black?" Aunt Bernice questioned.

"Yes, ma'am."

"I thought I saw a little nigga in ya, boy," Uncle Chester added.

Damn near choking on her food, Mina tried her best not to crack up laughing. Victor, on the other hand, couldn't hold up and busted out laughing.

"I'm so sorry, baby," Mina mouthed to Victor. Leaning over, he whispered into her ear, "It's cool, Ma, I like your family."

"I love you."

"I love you, too."

"Sorry we're late," Mo said, entering the room with Delicious.

"I brought a fruit cake." Delicious beamed wearing a white, one strapped sequined top, ripped jeans with sequins going down each of the legs, and gold stiletto heels.

"Delicious, you look like a fruit cake in that get up." Mina let out a laugh.

"Whatever, I look good."

"What's up, Mo?" Victor spoke.

"Hey, Victor," Mo kissed his cheek.

"Watch it now," Mina joked.

Mo leaned down in her ear and said, "Girl fuck you."

"Hey, boo," Delicious said, getting ready to kiss Victor's cheek.

"Nah, dog, don't even try it." Victor shook his head, laughing.

"Just making sure."

"Mina, baby, before you leave, I want you to go upstairs in the attic," her mother replied.

"Why?"

"I saved some of your stuff from when you were a child."

"Like what?"

"Some of the blankets that your grandmother made for

212

you when you were a baby. They were so pretty that I didn't want to get rid of them."

* * *

"Mina, why you got me up in this dusty ass attic?" Delicious coughed, fanning away the dust that was in the air.

"Do you ever stop complaining?"

"No."

"I didn't think so. Look, the sooner we find this box the sooner we'll be downstairs eating Nana Marie's chocolate chocolate chip cake."

"Well, you look over there and I'll look over here."

Stepping around boxes and spider webs, Mina crouched down on the floor and started rummaging through some of the boxes. The first box contained some of Smokey's old toys and photos. Picking up one of the pictures, she laughed. It was the one with Smokey sitting on a wooden horse crying. Placing the photo back into the box, Mina put that one over to the side and begun to go through the next one.

"Ya'll need some help?" Nay asked, coming up the steps. Rolling her eyes, Mina knew she wanted to say no, but decided not to be mean.

"Sure, Nay, the more eyes the better."

"So, Nay. What's going on wit your baby daddy?" Delicious asked.

"Same ol' drama, different baby momma."

"Different baby momma? What you talkin' about?"

"Eric don' went and got the girl, Deja, from Northwoods pregnant, too."

"For real?" Mina asked, shocked.

"Yep, the bitch a month pregnant. Talkin' about if it's a girl, she gon' name the baby Erica." Nay rolled her eyes, picking at her nails.

"Does his wife know?"

"That dumb hoe is oblivious. She doesn't even know about me yet."

"Let me get this straight, Nay. Eric is married, sleeping with you *and* this other chick, Deja?" Delicious questioned.

"Yeah," Nay answered, looking at him like he was dumb.

"Girl, that nigga got AIDS." Delicious laughed.

"My man ain't got no damn AIDS," Nay snapped, hitting him in the arms.

"Yo', on the real, Nay, you need to get yourself together and stop fuckin' with that nigga," Mina said, trying to give her some advice.

"Well excuse me, Miss I-was-engaged-to-the-Mayor's-son-now-I'm-pregnant-and-engaged-to-a-drug-lord. Everybody can't have it like you."

"I don't know what you're talkin' about," Mina lied.

"You ain't got to lie, Mina. You ain't got to lie."

"Whatever, I ain't got time to argue wit you. I got to find these blankets."

"Hey, Mina, what's this?" Delicious called her over to him.

Holding up old newspaper and magazine clippings, he showed her pictures of the fashion designer, Meesa. There were articles done on her from *Essence, Jet, Sister 2 Sister*, and *XXL*. Some of the newspaper articles talked about the attack made on her life by a Daryl Jones. At the bottom of the box there was a small picture of a newborn baby girl.

"Ooh, Mina, you look so pretty," Delicious gushed.

"That's not me," she said, taking the photo from his hand.

"Uh oh," Nay said from behind.

Turning the picture over, Mina read the back. It read: *Daddy's little girl, Meesa Daniels.* Mina was confused. Why would her family have a picture of Meesa?

"Daddy's little girl? What the hell?" Delicious asked, confused as well.

"Don't ya'll get it? Evidently, Uncle Ed is that girl's daddy."

"You got to be out yo' fucking mind," Delicious waved her off.

"I'm tellin' you. Why else would he have a picture of her that said *Daddy's little girl*."

"Maybe she's right," Mina said, still in shock.

"Well, there's only one way to find out." Delicious said, grabbing Mina's arms and pulling her up. Leading her down the steps, they bypassed Smokey and Victor in the living room playing *Madden '05*, and headed into the kitchen. At the kitchen table eating cake and drinking coffee sat Rita, Ed, Uncle Chester, Aunt Bernice, Nana Marie and Mo.

"Why ya'll all in a rush?" Rita asked.

"I found this picture upstairs in the attic," Mina said, holding the photo of Meesa. As if on cue Aunt Bernice, Uncle Chester, Nana Marie got up and left. Mo's nosy behind stayed to find out what was going on. "Daddy, why do you have a picture of Meesa Daniels?"

"Honey, we were trying to figure out the right time to tell you," Ed started to explain.

"Tell me what!" Mina shrieked.

"Calm down, sweetheart."

"Don't fucking sweetheart me! What the hell is goin' on?"

"Now wait a goddamn minute! Don't you raise your voice at your father," Rita yelled.

"What's wrong, Ma?" Victor asked, coming into the kitchen.

"Mina, Meesa is your father's daughter."

"What?!" Mina, Mo and Delicious yelled.

"Right after we had you, your mother and I began to have problems. I met Ann, Meesa's mother, at a bar one night and from then on we began to see each other. I'm not saying it was right, but at that the time that's what I thought I needed. After two months of seeing Ann, your mother found out."

"And when I did, I went ballistic. I get mad just thinkin' about it. Honey, you don't even wanna know how I tore him up. I tore up everything in this house. I couldn't be in the same house as your father so I did the only thing I could do, I left. I packed us up and went to go live with your aunt," Rita added.

"When your momma left, I was distraught so I broke things off with Ann. A couple of weeks later your momma and you came back home and everything got back to normal after a while. Seventeen years passed and I get a phone call from Ann telling me she's dying from breast cancer and that we have a daughter together. I couldn't believe it. She told me that she was sorry, but after I left her and went back to your mother, she couldn't handle it. She told me that Meesa didn't know anything about me and that she led her to believe all of her life that I abandoned her." Ed began to cry.

"I didn't know what to do. Ann began to send me photos of Meesa and she began telling me different things about her, but I still couldn't build up enough courage to meet her. It just wasn't the right time. I took care of Meesa financially but I decided to devote my time here with you and your brother."

"I can't believe this. Didn't her mother die or something?" Mina said as Victor massaged her shoulders.

"Yes, she did. I tried calling Meesa but it was too late. The number was disconnected. The next thing I know is I'm reading the newspaper and on the front page there was Meesa. She had been attacked. I thought that finally I would be able to talk to her but she moved to New York."

"We should have told you and Smokey this a long time ago but we just didn't know how," Ed said with tears in his eyes.

"This is a hellava going away party." Smokey shook his head.

"I'm sorry, I really am."

"It's okay, Daddy. I just wish you would have told us earlier," Mina said as she hugged her father.

"Yeah, Pop, everything is cool," Smokey agreed.

Chapter Seventeen

Rewind

Victor Dean Jose Gonzalez, son of the deceased interna-
tional drug lord, Jesus Gonzalez, is set to wed Mina Elise
Matthews. Matthews was set to marry Andrew Wellington II on
August 1st but the engagement was called off for undisclosed
reasons. The couple is expecting their first child in February.

"I can't believe this!" Andrew yelled, slamming down the
newspaper.

"Do you know how bad this makes us look, son?"

"That bitch is making us look like fools!"

"We have to do something." Andrew began pacing the
floor.

"Sorry to interrupt Mr. Wellington, but Andrew, this just
arrived for you," Rosario said handing him a package.

"What is this?"

"I don't know. The UPS guy didn't say what it was. If you'll
excuse me I'll be getting back to my work now." Rosario
excused herself from the room.

"Open it up, son," Mr. Wellington urged, leaning back in his chair. Opening the large envelope, Andrew pulled a blank tape that read: *Play Me*. "Do you know who sent it to you?"

"No, there's no return address," Andrew responded, placing the tape into the VCR.

Instantly, the blood from Andrew's body rushed to his head, causing him to feel faint. He couldn't believe what he was seeing. His rendezvous with Stiletto from over the weekend was being played for all to see. Every sordid bit of their tryst had been caught on tape.

"What the hell is this?" Mr. Wellington shouted, rushing to close the door. For the first time in his life, Andrew was left without words. There was no way that he could talk his way out of this. "I'm not going to ask you again son! What is this?" Mr. Wellington said, shaking Andrew.

"I'm sorry, Dad. I didn't know how to tell you," Andrew cried. Suddenly a female voice came through the television. Focusing their attention back to the screen, the two men saw Mina sitting in a chair looking better then ever.

"Andrew, I'm truly sorry that things have come to this. You have hurt me too much for me to let you get away with everything that you have put me through. First, you beat me to the point where I could have died and then you took my shop away from me. I have never done anything to hurt you.

"All I have ever done was try to love you but that wasn't good enough. You are a sorry excuse for a man. I hate that I ever got into your car that day. I hate that I ever let you control my life. But most of all, I'm sorry that I ever let you abuse and degrade my body the way you did. But you know what? It's okay, because you will have to live the rest of your life knowing what you did to me.

"I pray that you never get a peaceful night's sleep. Nothing good will ever come to you until you do right by me. So give

me my shop back. Turn over all rights and ownership to me and this tape will never be shown again. If you don't I will give this tape to every news reporter and radio personality in St. Louis. Oh, yeah, I have copies of this tape all over St. Louis so don't try any slick shit. You have until the end of this week to turn over the shop to me or else."

"As of today, you are no longer my son. I want nothing else to do with you. Do you hear me?"

"Yes!"

"You are a disgrace. I didn't raise you to be some queer homosexual. What is wrong with you? Where did your mother and I go wrong?"

"I'm sorry." Andrew continued to cry.

"I will give you your trust fund money but I will no longer have anything to do with you, Andrew. I want that bitch taken care of. Do you hear me? You will not bring down the family name. Get rid of her!" Mr. Wellington breathed heavily into Andrew's face.

"Okay."

* * *

"But how long will you be gone?" Mina whined, sitting Indian-style on their king sized bed.

"I'll only be gone a week, Ma," Victor said, placing clothes into a suitcase.

"We just got back from Miami last week. Can't this wait until later? I need you here."

"Nah, this is business, shorty. I gotta take care of this." Looking into her hazel eyes and seeing her pout, Victor's tough demeanor weakened. "Look, Ma, I promise once I get back it's me and you. I just gotta square some business away and then I'll be good."

"Okay." She wrapped her arms around his neck and kissed his lips.

Sucking his bottom lip, Mina eased her hand down and began massaging his dick through his pants. Victor then kissed her hungrily while holding her face. Barely able to breathe, she ran her hands over his chiseled chest. Mina wanted to taste him, so she released her lips from his and placed them on his chest. Kissing him all over his chest she eased her way down. Seeing what she was about to do, Victor stopped her.

"Ma...what you doing to a nigga?"

"I'm giving you to a treat before you go." Mina unbuckled his shorts ready to please him.

"Let me take care of you."

Picking her up, Victor wrapped her legs around him as he carried her over to the bed. After laying her down, Victor pushed her legs apart. He rubbed her thighs, then placed loving kisses along her thigh. Victor made Mina scream out in ecstasy as he trailed kisses from her thighs down to her feet.

Taking her baby toe into his mouth, he probed and licked. Victor made sure that Mina was thoroughly satisfied by taking each of her toes into his mouth and giving them his undivided attention. Slowly, he eased his way back up her body, pulled her thong to the side and placed his mouth on her pussy. Jumping back Mina tried to contain her excitement. He held her thighs tightly to keep Mina's squirming body in place. After working his tongue all around her pussy lips, Victor found her clit and sucked. Mina felt herself coming to the brink of a climax, and she wanted to prolong her pleasure.

"Victor! Victor, stop, I can't breathe!"

Turning her over, he lifted Mina's skirt up and slapped her ass.

"Ahh!" She moaned in sheer delight.

Slap!

"Shit!" Mina cried.

Slap! Slap!

"Ooh," she squealed in pleasure.

Bending her over in the doggy style position, Victor licked each of her ass cheeks, then slapped each of them. Mina couldn't wait to feel him inside of her as she ran her tongue across her lips in anticipation. He playfully massaged his fingers between her thighs, making her scream. Mina pinched her nipples as she enjoyed Victor's fingers playing in her wetness.

She was just about to cum when his fingers stopped pleasuring her pussy. Before she could protest Victor slid down his pants and entered her. Stroking her slowly he relished every feeling and sensation. Pregnant pussy was the best pussy. Victor couldn't get enough of Mina since he found out she was pregnant. She was hot and wet, just how he liked it.

"You like that?" he moaned.

"Yes, baby, give me that big dick!"

"You love me?" He stroked harder.

"Oh, baby, yes!"

"You ready to cum?"

"Yes!" Pushing her legs back, Victor pumped faster. Fingers intertwined with each other's, they both exploded at the same time.

"That was the shit, Ma," Victor said, getting up.

"How am I supposed to go two weeks without that?" Mina pouted as she got up. After quickly showering together, they both redressed. An hour later, Victor was at the front door packed and ready to go.

"I love you."

"I love you, too," Mina whispered, ready to cry.

"What's with the water works?"

"I don't know. I guess it's just my hormones. The baby is going to miss you." Bending down, Victor whispered the words, "*I love you*" and kissed Mina's stomach.

"Daddy, can I go, too?" Lelah asked, coming down the steps.

"Not this time, baby. Come give Daddy a hug." Hugging her father tight, Lelah kissed his cheek. "I love you."

"I love you, too, Daddy."

"You be a big girl and take care of Mina and the baby," Victor said, pulling her nose.

"Okay," Lelah giggled.

"Sir, we have to get going," Armando informed.

"A'ight, man, here I come. Dro is going to be checking in on you and remember, don't go anywhere without Armando or one of the guards."

"Okay."

"You know I love you, right?"

"Yes," Mina nodded.

"Show me then." Victor took her into his arms.

Kissing him slowly, Mina tried her best to convey everything she felt inside. For some reason she felt as if this would be her last time seeing him. Shaking the thought out of her mind, she told herself that she was thinking nonsense. Not wanting to, but knowing she had to, Mina let go of Victor.

"Eww," Lelah said, pretending to gag.

"You got jokes," Victor laughed, tickling her stomach. "But check it, I'ma call you when I get there."

"Okay."

"Bye, Daddy," Lelah yelled behind him as he got into the car.

"Well, it looks like it's just me and you, toots." Mina looked down at Lelah while holding her hand.

"Let's play Barbies!"

"Barbies it is!"

* * *

"Andrew Wellington, please."

"This is Andrew. May I ask who's calling?"

"Let's just say I'm a person who has an interest in the same things you do."

"Who is this?" Andrew asked, becoming annoyed.

"Calm down, homey. Don't get so riled up. You want Mina and Victor gone just as much as I do."

"I'm going to ask one more time. Who is this?"

"Meet me at Forest Park tomorrow, in front of the Art Museum, at noon."

Click.

Chapter Eighteen

Program

"I'm bored, Mina. Can we go somewhere?" Lelah whined over breakfast.

"Where do you want to go Lelah?" Mina said, half listening,as she read the daily newspaper.

"Uhmm, let's go...to...Toys R Us!"

Placing the newspaper down, she looked at Lelah. "Now, what could you possibly want from there? You have every toy imaginable."

"The new Harry Potter book just came out and I want to get it. Pleaaaase!" Looking into her big brown eyes, Mina couldn't deny her.

"Okay-"

"Yeah!"

"But first, finish eating your cereal."

"Thank you, Mina."

"You're welcome, Lelah."

After breakfast, Mina searched the grounds of the house

for Dro. He became really withdrawn since the death of his father. Victor was gone for almost a week and Mina was missing him like crazy. They talked on the phone at least five times a day but nothing was like having him there in the flesh. Knocking on the door to the guest bedroom, which Dro was in, she waited for his reply.

"Yeah?"

"Dro, it's me, Mina. Can I come in?"

"Just a second." Leaning against the wall, she waited for him to open the door. She could tell that he was on the phone with someone, but she couldn't make out the conversation. Just when she was about to knock again, he opened the door.

"Yes."

"I just wanted to tell you that Lelah and I are going shopping."

"What else is new?" He smirked.

"Excuse me," she asked with an attitude.

"Nothing. We have a new driver so I'll be going with you."

"Where is Armando?" Mina questioned as they walked down the steps.

"He has the day off."

"Victor didn't say anything about him having a day off this week."

"He must have forgotten to tell you. Lelah!"

"Yes," she yelled running up to Dro.

"Let's go."

"Yeah! I'm going to get me a new Barbie and a new Brat doll!"

"I thought you said you wanted the new Harry Potter book," Mina arched her eyebrow, knowing she had been swindled by a seven year old.

"Oh yeah. That, too." Lelah grinned.

"Come on, you little devil." Mina took her hand and led

her out the door.

What was supposed to be a ten or fifteen minute run into Toys R Us turned into an hour and a half long shopping spree for Lelah and the baby. Since Mina didn't know the sex of the baby yet she purchased things that either a boy or a girl could use. She couldn't wait to show Victor all the things she bought.

Mina totally forgot about Dro even being there with them. He lagged behind the whole time talking on his cell phone. Mina figured he was on the phone with some chick, besides the less they talked, the better. Lelah was in toy heaven.

Not only did she get a Barbie and a Brat doll but she also got a miniature vanity and beauty salon set to go in her room. She and Mina had plans to spend the rest of the day playing beauty salon together. Finally, making it up to the check out line, their total came up to $1940.00. Mina didn't expect to spend so much money but it was for the kids. How could she not?

Standing in front of the store Mina watched as Dro and the driver Felix piled all of the bags into the trunk of the car. It was a bright and sunny September day. The sun was burning Mina's eyes so she unzipped her bag fishing around for her favorite Fendi glasses. Lelah was jumping up and down holding a balloon singing, *"Me want McDonalds, Me want McDonalds!"*

"Ohh, a fish sandwich does sound good right now." Mina's stomach rumbled as she rummaged through her purse.

"Mina, my balloon!" Lelah shrieked as her balloon flew in the air.

Just as Mina was about to reach for the balloon, an unknown rusted gray van came to a screeching halt right in front of them. Two masked men jumped out the back of the van wearing all black. Instantly, Mina's survival instincts switched into high gear. She screamed at the top of her lungs and grabbed Lelah's hand preparing to run.

"Run!" Dro yelled, pulling out a nickel plated 22.

But Dro was too slow. One of the masked men shot him in the leg, dropping him to the ground. Felix, the driver, was shot twice in the head and died instantly.

"Ahh!" Lelah screamed.

Frozen in place, Mina watched in fear as one of the masked men approached her. The closer he got to her the tighter Mina's esophagus got. Mina couldn't breathe, scream, or run. She could hear Lelah screaming for dear life. She even felt Lelah wailing her arms and kicking her feet but still Mina could do nothing. This was like something out of a bad dream.

It took Lelah to literally kick Mina in the leg for her to come out of her trance. Picking Lelah up, Mina ran for her life. She didn't even make it half way down the block when she felt someone's clothesline knock the shit out of her. Falling backwards she hit her head on the concrete ground and blacked out.

* * *

"Where is this girl at?"

"Who, Mina?" Rico asked Victor as he took a tote from the blunt. The two cousins sat on the deck getting blazed in the hot Miami sun.

"Yeah, I've been calling her all day and she ain't picked up the phone yet."

"Did you try the house?"

"Yeah, Julisa said that she, Lelah and Dro had went shopping earlier, but they still weren't back yet."

"Try Dro's phone then."

"I did. That nigga ain't answering either. Yo', something ain't right, man." Victor said with concern written all over his face. He could feel it in his soul that Mina needed him.

"Everything's cool. Just calm down, she'll call soon," Rico

reassured.

"Yeah, you better hope so, or all hell is gonna break loose." Victor took the blunt from his cousin and inhaled.

* * *

"Ahh!" Mina screamed as she inhaled the smelling salts that was placed under her nose. Searching the room with her eyes, she tried to remember what happened but she couldn't see a thing. She was blind-folded. "Where am I? Where's Lelah? Is she all right?"

"Mmm!"Mina recognized the voice as Lelah's.

The kidnappers placed tape over her mouth. Four hours passed and Lelah screamed and cried the entire time. Wanting to feel her stomach, Mina tried to move her hands but they were tied. Trying to kick her feet, she realized that they, too, were tied.

The room was quiet except for the sound of a leaky pipe. Every time she moved she could hear the sound of broken glass underneath her feet. The feel of cold air brushing against her skin made Mina shiver. Suddenly she heard something scatter across the floor. Frozen, Mina tried her best to decipher what the sound could be. Feeling something run across her feet Mina jumped.

"Where are we...I know you hear me...Please just tell me what you want...Answer me Goddamnit!"

"Shut up before I put tape over your mouth, too," one of the kidnappers shouted.

"Let me cater to you...cause, baby, this is your day...do anything for my man...baby, you blow me away..." Mina's cell phone rang.

"Look, that's my fiancé. He's rich. He'll give you anything you want. Just let us go!" Mina begged.

"Shut up!" the man became more and more irritated.

"Please, just let us go!"

"I said shut the fuck up!" he yelled, back-handing her face causing blood to fly out of her mouth.

* * *

"Something's up!" Victor yelled, pacing the floor with his cell phone in hand. It was one o'clock in the morning and he still hadn't heard from Mina or Dro.

"She might be over her ol' bird's house. Try over there?" Rico added.

"You're right, I ain't even think of that." Just as Victor was about to dial Rita's number his cell phone rang. "Yo' this her right here. Hello?"

"Wake up, nigga. I got yo' bitch."

"Who the fuck is this?"

"Who I am is not important. What's important is that yo' bitch and yo' daughter return home safely. Say hi to your fiancé."

"Victor!" Mina cried into the phone. Clinching the phone tight, Victor gritted his teeth and tried his best not to scream. Suddenly it was 1999 all over again.

"Yo' whoever this is, I swear to God when I find you I'm gon' kill you!"

"Yeah, yeah. I'll contact you tomorrow at nine. If you want your bitch back you'll have yo' cell phone on nigga."

Click.

"Yo' Vic you a'ight," Rico questioned. Ignoring his cousin, Victor immediately dialed his home number.

"Hello, Gonzalez residence."

"Julissa, is Mina there?"

"*Oh, Mr. Gonzalez*, I'm so sorry," Julissa cried.

"Tell me it's all a lie, Julissa."

"I'm so sorry. Mr. Gonzalez." Julissa continued to cry.

"Just spit it out, Julissa! Tell me what's up!"

"Mina and Lelah have been kidnapped."

How could this be happening again? No, this can't be happening again. This is some kind of sick joke, Victor thought.

"Vic, what the fuck is going on dog?" Rico barked becoming worried.

"Mr. Gonzalez, are you still there," Julissa cried.

"Yeah, I'm here. Tell me everything that happened, Julissa. Don't leave anything out," Victor instructed.

"This morning, Lelah wanted to go the store, so she asked Mina if they could go. Mina said yes, so she, Lelah and Dro went to Toys R Us."

"Did Armando go?"

"No sir, he had the day off." Not remembering whether or not he gave Armando the day off, Victor bypassed that part of the information.

"Okay, go on."

"The police say that a couple of witnesses saw a gray van pull up while Dro and the driver were putting the bags into the trunk. Two men, dressed in all black, jumped out. Apparently Dro tried to shoot one of them but got shot in the leg. Mina and Lelah tried to run but one of the men pushed her to the ground then snatched her and Lelah."

"She fell? What the fuck? Oh my God!" Victor continued to pace, enraged.

"The nurse at the hospital said that Dro is in surgery but he should be fine."

"Julissa, call the airport and book me a flight. I'm coming home." Victor slammed his phone shut.

"What happened?" Rico asked.

"Mina and Lelah have been kidnapped!"

"What?"

"I can't believe this shit is happening again! She begged me stay home but I didn't!"

"How could you have known that this was gonna happen

Vic? Don't go blaming yourself dog."

"Nah this is my fault! Once again, I let business come before my family, and look what happened!"

"Here, hit the blunt and calm down. I'll let Hope and them know what's up," Rico said getting up to leave.

"No, don't tell them anything. They've been through enough as it is. I will handle this by myself."

"A'ight. Well, at least let me get your shit together for you."

"Thanks Rico."

"No problem."

Five hours later, Victor sat in the back of his Rolls Royce staring out the window pondering life and what it all meant. Since as far back as he could remember his entire life was about business. Nothing else in life mattered. That's all he knew. Even when he met Samia, he loved her, but business always came first. But all that changed when he met Mina. She was his world, his everything.

Victor couldn't fathom living his life without her. She was the love of his life, his soulmate. He knew this the first time he laid eyes on her. He was finally ready to put the cartel, and that part of his life, to the side and concentrate solely on Mina and Lelah. Just the thought of his daughter caused his eyes to sting with tears. She was the spitting image of her mother and Victor vowed to Samia at her grave that he would keep her safe. Yet once again he let her down.

If Victor lost either one of his girls, he would surely go crazy. Pulling up to the house he jumped out and ran into the house. Before he left Miami he put the word out about the kidnapping. He figured that the same person behind Emilio's murder was behind the kidnapping.However the kidnapper, in Victor's eyes, was already dead.

Chapter Nineteen

Search

Almost twenty-four hours into the search for Mina and Lelah, Victor finally broke down and told Mina's parents what happened. He dreaded telling them that their only daughter was kidnapped and could possibly be dead. No parent wants to hear anything like that so Victor put off telling them as long as possible. In less than an hour, Victor's home was filled with members of Mina's family.

Rita and Ed sat on the couch holding each other. Bernice paced the floor smoking her second pack of Virginia Slims Menthol. Uncle Chester and Nana Marie sat and watched the news while Nay cleaned up after her three kids. Smokey was on his way down from school. He attended Mizzou which was only an hour and a half drive away.

Mo, Delicious, Janiya, Tiffany and Neosha sat on the floor, hoping for the best. Jodie, on the other hand, was sitting alone in the corner of the room reading her Bible, praying for Mina's safe return. Since Dro only had minor surgery, he would be released from the hospital any day. Victor didn't want to cooperate with the police, so they left and told him when they had any more news, they would contact him.

Ring...

Everyone in the room froze. No one moved a muscle. It was exactly nine o 'clock. Picking up his cell phone, he saw that the kidnappers were calling from Mina's phone again.

"Hello?" Victor said.

"I see you take directions well," the kidnapper laughed.

"Just tell me what the fuck you want!" Victor snapped.

"You know patience is a virtue my friend."

"Fuck all the pleasantries and tell me what's up!"

"Since you insist, I want a million dollars in cash."

"I can't come with that kind of money just like that."

"Come on, Victor, you and I both know you're caked up. You got money coming out your ass. I guess your fiancé and child don't mean that much to you after all."

"How do I even know Mina and Lelah are still alive? Put them on the phone!"

"Say hi."

"Daddy!" Lelah screamed. Hearing his daughter's voice started a steady stream of tears that ran down his face. These were tears of joy, just knowing his daughter was alive.

"You happy now."

"I didn't hear, Mina! Where is Mina?"

"You know, Victor, your fiancé is quite beautiful. You must be a very happy man. Tell me how many times a week do you wax that ass," the kidnapper teased.

"If you lay one hand on her, I swear to God-"

"Now, now Victor calm down. I'm simply stating that Mina is a nice piece of ass and I would like very much if you let me get a taste."

"Fuck you, you sick bastard! You'll have your money,"

Victor barked.

"You know my man here likes her ass but I like her mouth. Yo', Mina, let me put my dick in yo' mouth!" The kidnapper laughed in a maniacal tone.

"You better not touch me!" Mina yelled.

"You better tell her to calm down Vic 'cause in a minute yo' bitch is about to get a pearl necklace."

"Nigga, yo' dick wouldn't go past her two front teeth."

"Oh, this nigga got jokes! This nigga a jokester! Let's see how funny you are when I fuck yo' daughter in the ass! Now make a joke about that nigga!""Fuck you!" Victor yelled.

Click.

"Hello? Hello?" Victor said into the phone. Nothing. The kidnapper hung up.

"What happened?" Rita asked.

"They want a million dollars in cash."

"Did you talk to Mina?"

"No, they only put Lelah on the phone this time."

"Oh, my God, what if she's dead! Oh, Ed, what I'm gon' do without my baby!" Rita cried.

"I'm so sorry, Mrs. Matthews. This is all my fault," Victor apologized.

"You damn right this is your fault! I don't know why my niece got involved wit you in the first place! You ain't no good you just like that old pompous ass nigga Andrew," Bernice shouted.

"Now that's enough Bernice," Uncle Chester warned.

"No it's not! My niece has been kidnapped because of him and his family! Yeah I know all about yo' drug dealing family! Your uncle was killed because of what you do and now Mina is suffering, too!He ain't no good, Rita! He ain't no good!"

"I ain't got time for this," Victor said as he left and went outside. Mo and Delicious followed behind him.

"Victor, wait up," Mo yelled after him.

"What, you wanna go off on me too?"

"No we have something we need to tell you."

"What?"

"About two weeks ago me, Mina, Delicious and the girls set up Andrew."

"What? I told Mina to stay away from him!"

"We know you did, but Mina thought that setting him up was the only way to get rid of him and to get her shop back."

"What did ya'll do?"

"We taped him having sex with another man and then we threatened to expose him with it."

"We should have told you earlier but the thought didn't even cross our minds until Bernice mentioned his name," Delicious added.

"So you all think that Andrew had something to do with this?" Victor questioned.

"Yeah, his father is running for Governor of St. Louis. If this tape got out it would ruin Mayor Wellington's career as well as Andrew's."

"We're so sorry Victor. We should've talked Mina out of it," Delicious cried.

"It's cool. The most important thing right now to me is getting Mina and Lelahback.

* * *

"I'm hungry," Lelah whined.

"Bitch, shut the fuck up!"

"Don't talk to her like that! She's just a child," Mina yelled, taking up for Lelah.

"You shut up, too! I'm getting sick of both you bitches!"

"I'll be glad when this shit is over so I can off this bitch," the other kidnapper replied.

"I promise, I won't say another thing, just take the blindfold off of our eyes please. It's starting to hurt."

"Fine, anything to shut you the fuck up!"

It took Mina a couple of minutes to get her vision back but once she did, she focused all of her attention on the kidnappers. They were still dressed in all black and their faces were still covered with black masks. The room was sparse except for two chairs, a couch and a television. Mina couldn't quite figure out where she was being held.

It looked like she was in an unfinished basement. Looking up at the ceiling, she noticed that a pipe was leaking, plaster was falling from the walls, the insulation was coming out the wall and an old piss-stained mattress sat in the corner of the room. In front of her sat a large brown couch. Feeling the baby move around in her stomach, Mina knew that the baby was hungry. She hadn't eaten since the prior day at breakfast. Mina didn't know how much more of this she could take.

* * *

Back at the house, Victor was on the Internet, feverishly trying to locate Mina's whereabouts. He had totally forgotten that Mina's Nextel cell phone had a tracking device in it. In less than five minutes, without the police's help, Victor had Mina pin-pointed. The map indicated that she was at 4354 Thrush Street. Victor couldn't have been happier. He had one up on the kidnappers. *Stupid muthafucker,* he thought. Plus, Dro knew the area well.

"Excuse me, Mr. Gonzalez. Dro has arrived."

"Thank you, Julissa," Victor said, quickly writing down the address. Running down the steps he greeted his cousin with a hug. "Everyone, this is my cousin, Dro."

"Hello," everyone said except for Bernice. She simply rolled her eyes and looked in the other direction.

"What's her problem?" Dro asked.

"Don't mind her. Come on, I need to talk to you."

Sparking up a blunt Victor sat across from Dro. Inhaling slowly, he let the smoke fill his lungs before he released it through his nose. Victor thought carefully before he spoke. He didn't know if he could trust Dro or not. At that moment he honestly couldn't tell whether or not Dro was his ally or enemy. Victor wanted to divulge the information he learned with him but something in his soul was telling him to be careful and to trust no one, including Dro. Looking at Dro once again Victor knew he couldn't let what happened to Samia happen to Mina. Going with his instincts he kept Mina and Lelah's whereabouts to himself.

"So what's up? What them muthafuckers say?" Dro asked.

"They said they want a mill or Mina and Lelah are dead."

"That's all? You got that in the safe downstairs."

"Yo', what you doing at seven?"

"Ain't too much I can do with a fucked-up leg."

"I need you take a ride wit me."

"What's up? You got something you need to tell me?"

"Nah, just ride wit me."

"I got you. Whenever you're ready, just let me know," Dro replied getting up.

"Thanks, man."

"No problem. I got you."

Victor felt kind of bad lying to his cousin. The two were close their entire lives but there was no way he was going to jeopardize Mina and Lelah's safe return home. He needed to keep the fact that he knew their whereabouts to himself. Dro was his cousin, but Mina was carrying his child and Lelah was his own flesh and blood. Living without them wasn't a factor. He would do whatever he had to do to have them back in his arms where they belonged.

* * *

Seven o'clock and the sun was sitting high upon the St.

Louis skyline. Bumping 50 Cent's "I'm Supposed to Die Tonight" Victor navigated his all black '05 Hummer through the streets while smoking a blunt. Never in a million years did he expect to be in the same position of having to save the woman he loved and his daughter again. Checking his rearview mirror he saw that Dro was right behind him.

Concentrating back on the road he knew that a blood bath was about to go down. Victor was prepared to kill everyone that was involved with the kidnapping. He knew that there was a chance that he might not make it out alive but that was a risk he was willing to take as long as Mina and Lelah were unharmed.Seeing the street, Victor made a quick left onto Thrush. Parking on the corner, he placed his burner into the waist of his pants and got out.

"Yo', why we stop?" Dro asked, getting out.

"You see that house right there?" Victor questioned, pointing down the street.

"Yeah."

"That's where Mina and Lelah are being held."

"I thought you ain't have nothing to tell me?"

Ignoring him, Victor turned his back to him, and headed down the street. He took the clip out of his pocket, then loaded it into the .380. When he reached the house, he looked behind him to find Dro lagging behind.

"Come on, nigga. We ain't got all day," Victor snapped.

"Here I come."

Shaking his head, Victor continued up the steps. The all white house was fairly large. Two huge windows sat on each side of the front door. The screen door was bent and barely hanging onto the hinges. A condemned notice was placed on the front of the door and the smell of urine mixed with spoiled milk caused Victor to almost throw up. Placing his hand on the knob, Victor checked to see if it was unlocked; it was.

"Ay it's unlocked." Victor signaled to Dro.

With the door unlocked they both crept throughout the house with their guns out, ready to shoot anything moving. As they checked each room for Mina and Lelah, they found nothing. Suddenly they saw that there was a door that led to the basement. Victor signaled to Dro to come on. Hearing someone coming up the steps, Victor stood silently on the other side of the door, ready to shoot.

The guy never knew what was coming. As soon as he hit the top step and opened the door, the barrel of Victor's .380 was pointed at his face. Smiling, Victor grabbed him by the neck and pointed the gun into his back. The kidnapper couldn't even put up a fight. He was caught. Creeping down the steps with the man in front of him, and Dro behind him, Victor found the other guy sitting in front of a television while Mina and Lelah sat back-to-back tied to a chair, behind a couch.

"Wake up, nigga, I got yo' bitch!"

Startled, the other guy went to reach for his gun, but it was too late. Victor already had his gun pointed at his head.

"Baby!" Mina screamed happy to see her man.

"Give me a minute baby. Now which one of ya'll niggas was talkin' that gangsta shit over the phone?" Victor questioned the two men.

"Fuck you, nigga! Either kill me or shut the fuck up!" the guy that Victor was holding yelled.

"It must have been you 'cause you still talkin' shit! Nigga, I'm Victor Gonzalez! Did you really think that you were going to get away with kidnapping my girl and my daughter?"

"We did get away with it," Dro laughed.

"What did you say?" Victor asked, stepping to the side to get a good view of Dro and the guy sitting down.

"It was me. I did it. I put this all together," he continued to laugh with his gun pointed at Victor's head.

"Dro?" Mina said confused.

"Bitch, shut up!" Dro yelled. Turning his attention back to Victor, he said, "I didn't expect it to go down this way but just to see the look on your face is priceless."

"You kidnapped my girl and my daughter?" Victor said in disbelief.

"This whole thing was a set up and yo' dumb ass fell for it! I took a bullet in the leg that's how bad I want you dead! Nigga, I've been in yo' shadow for years and I'm sick of it!" Dro snapped, getting serious. "I should have been the one running the family business not you! But, nah, Father never saw it that way! It was always Victor this, Victor that! He never loved me!"

"Don't tell me you were the one that killed Uncle Emilio, Dro."

"How else was I going to lead this family if you two were still alive? I overheard your little conversation in Miami! Ya'll muthafuckers was gonna let Rico run the business! What about me?"

"What about you? Uncle Emilio was right! You have no business running the cartel!"

"Fuck you, you half breed muthafucker!" Dro inched closer to Victor.

"Oh God, please no," Mina cried.

"Daddy!" Lelah shrieked.

"Nineteen ninety-nine ring a bell to you?" Dro questioned Victor.

"What the fuck you talkin' about does Nineteen ninety-nine ring a bell to me? That was the year Samia and Lelah were kidnapped." Out of the corner of his eye, Victor sensed the other kidnapper reaching for his gun. "Don't even try it," he snapped pointing the gun in his direction.

"Guess what, nigga? I was the one that killed yo' bitch," Dro sneered with a sinister look in his eyes.

"You killed Samia?"

"Yeah, right after I fucked her one good time."

"You crazy son of a bitch! You know you're not leaving out of here alive," Victor barked, enraged.

"Yeah, a'ight. We'll see about that." Pulling the trigger back Dro let two tears fall from his eyes. "Say goodnight, cousin, but first I want you see firsthand what real pain feels like." Turning the gun from Victor to Mina, Dro aimed at her head, ready to shoot.

"NO!" Mina screamed, closing her eyes preparing to die.

POW! POW! POW! POW! Shots flew everywhere. Dro fired off a shot trying to shoot Mina in the head but missed. Aiming his gun at Dro, Victor fired his gun, only to miss. Falling down on the ground, Dro ducked for cover. Seeing his opportunity to get away, the kidnapper that Victor was holding elbowed him in the stomach, but Victor was still too fast for him.

In a quick move, Victor put the gun to the back of the kidnapper's head, pulled the trigger and killed him instantly. The man's blood and membranes splattered all over Victor's face. Using him as a human shield, Victor pointed his gun at the other kidnapper who was already aiming his gun at him. Shooting twice, Victor hit the kidnapper in the head and in the heart. Not needing the kidnapper's body as a shield anymore Victor threw him to the ground.

"Mina, baby, you all right?" he asked, seeing that she was behind the couch and he couldn't get to her.

"Yes," she trembled, frightened out of her mind.

"I told you you weren't leaving here alive, didn't I?" Victor barked at Dro. Both men had their guns out, aimed at one another.

"One of us gon' die tonight and it ain't gon' be me, part-na!" Dro barked back.

"DAMN, Dro?" Victor began to cry. "I can't believe you put me in this position dog? I knew you was a snake mutha-fucker, but damn! How am I going to explain to Alita that I killed her son? We blood, man. It didn't have to end this way?"

"Fuck you, nigga, we ain't family! Never have been never will be!"

"What the hell is going on here?" Andrew yelled, coming down the steps.

"Andrew?" Mina yelled surprised. Seeing the two men with their guns out, Andrew pulled his out too, aiming it at Victor.

"So we finally meet in person. It's a shame we had to meet under these circumstances," Andrew said to Victor.

"Muthafucker, you better shoot me because in a minute you about to be dead, too!" Victor snapped.

"Andrew, you were in on this?" Mina asked.

"You tried to ruin my life with that sex tape! I wasn't gonna let you get away with that!"

"Fuck all this bullshit, somebody about to die!" Dro yelled pulling back on the trigger.

Just as he was about to shoot Victor, Lelah hopped out of the chair and ran around the couch. She had gotten loose. Running over to her father, she shouted, "DADDY!" Looking back and forth between Andrew, Dro and Lelah, he knew he had no choice but to keep his daughter safe. Taking his daughter into his arms, Victor fell to the ground shielding his daughter from any harm. A shot was fired, hitting Victor in the back. Right then and there he knew that his life was over. Hearing two more shots Victor knew that they were meant for him. A minute passed and he didn't feel or hear anything. Then suddenly a hand touched his shoulder.

"Mr. Gonzalez, are you all right?" Armando asked, turning

him over.

"Bout time you got here," Victor smiled.

Chapter Twenty

Fast Forward

Mina couldn't wait to be home surrounded by her family and friends, but memories of the shoot out between Victor and Dro continuously replayed in her mind. When Lelah broke loose, Mina feared the worst. She just knew that Lelah and her father would be killed. When Victor was shot in the back her worst fear came true.

Then suddenly out of nowhere, Armando appeared and shot Dro in the head twice. Seeing someone being killed right in front of him took what little toughness he had out of Andrew. He immediately dropped his gun and begged for his life. Mina couldn't believe her eyes. Blood was everywhere. As Armando turned Victor over, she prayed silently to God that he was still alive.

"Mr. Gonzalez, are you all right?" Armando asked turning him over.

"Bout time you got here," Victor smiled.

"Daddy, get off of me you're heavy," Lelah said, pretending like she couldn't breathe. Standing up, Victor ripped off his tee shirt revealing a bulletproof vest.

"Baby, I thought you were dead!" Mina shouted from across the room. She was still tied up.

"There is nothing in this world that could take me away from you," he replied as he untied her hands and feet.

Despite the pain she felt in her arms and legs, Mina couldn't wait to jump into her man's arms. Grabbing her face, Victor kissed her lips slowly, all the while whispering, "I love you." Not wanting to, but knowing he had to, Victor let go of Mina and picked up his daughter. He held her tight and promised to never let her leave his sight. Victor thanked God over and over for keeping her safe and for letting her return to him unharmed.

"Did they touch you, sweetheart?"

"No, they just put tape over my mouth for a while."

Placing Lelah down onto the floor, Victor slowly approached his deceased cousin. Despite all that had gone down he still loved him. As he bent down, Victor said a silent prayer to God to heal Dro's soul. Taking his hand, Victor closed Dro's still open eyes.

"What are we gonna do about him, boss?" Armando questioned Victor while holding a gun to Andrew's head.

"The police are on their way, they'll take care of him."

"Are you sure? Because I can off this piece of trash right now if you want."

"Yeah, I'm sure, 'cause not only is he going to confess to beating Mina half to death he's going to admit to kidnapping her as well."

"Please, just kill me. I can't live the rest of my life behind bars," Andrew cried.

"I am gonna make sure you pay for every horrible thing you did to me!" Mina spat, slapping him in the face.

Letting Mina get that off, Victor walked over to her. "That's enough, baby. It's time for us to go home. Armando, keep an eye on him until the police come."

* * *

"MINA!" the entire family yelled as she entered through the door.

Running, she fell into her mother's arms. Mina didn't know if she would ever see her family again. Tears ran down her face at lighting speed. At that moment she realized the true meaning of family. Releasing her from her arms Rita kissed her baby girl's forehead. Wrapping her arms around her father, Mina told him how much she loved him.

Just the feel of having her father's big arms wrapped around her brought back memories of her childhood. Mina could vividly remember her father tucking her into bed at night and him reading her bedtime stories. Mina was truly Daddy's little girl. One after another, she was blessed with endless hugs and kisses.

"Girl, what are we gonna do about this head of yours?" Delicious teased.

"I missed you, too, Delicious."

"You make sure you come see me as soon as possible so I fix your wig."

"Trust me, I will," she laughed.

After showering and changing her clothes, the rest of the night consisted of Mina crying and talking to her family. She was so happy to be around people she loved. Rita made sure that she ate until she couldn't eat anymore. No one left the house until the wee hours in the morning.

Nobody wanted to say goodbye. When the last person left Mina realized she hadn't seen Victor since they returned home. Needing to be by her man's side she headed up the steps to their bedroom. Not finding him there she went down the hall to Lelah's room. Quietly opening the door she found them both curled up in bed together. The sight brought tears to Mina's eyes. Walking over to the bed, she kissed them both on the cheek, and climbed into bed with them.

* * *

The next morning Mina awoke to find herself alone in Lelah's Barbie decorated bed. Rubbing her stomach, she thanked God, once again, that she and her baby were alive and well. Wondering where Victor was, she headed to their bedroom. His back was to her as she entered the room.

"Baby, I'm so glad to be home." She smiled as she wrapped her arms around his waist.

"I'm glad you're home too, Ma."

"Where is Lelah?"

"I sent her back to Miami until things blow over, but look, I got something for you," he said, turning around. He handed her a set of keys.

"What this? You didn't buy the baby a new car already did you?" she laughed.

"Nah."

"Well, what is this for then?"

"This here is yours. I changed the locks. I figured if you wanted me to have a key you would give me one. No pressure, it's up to you."

"What do you mean this is mine?"

"I got me a lil' spot downtown."

"*Okay*," Mina asked, still confused.

"Come on, Ma, don't play dumb! I'm up! I don't wanna be with you no more!"

"Victor, don't play wit me," Mina laughed, waving him off.

"Do I look like I'm Martin Lawrence? Do I look like I'm on Def Comedy Jam? This ain't no fuckin' joke! It's over!"

"What do you mean it's over?!"

"Are you fuckin' retarded? It's over! You can have the crib! I'ma take care of my seed, but you and me, we ain't together no more! What the fuck about that don't you understand?!"

"You don't wanna be wit me no more? Nigga, have you lost your fuckin' mind? I'm pregnant with your baby! I just came home from being kidnapped and you're telling me that it's over! Nigga, you got me fucked up!"

"Look, I don't know what else to tell you!" Victor shrugged, walking away. Thinking the worst, Mina quickly assumed that Victor was leaving her for another woman.

"Oh, wait a minute. I know what this is about! You got another bitch!"

"What the fuck are you talkin' about?" he yelled, turning around.

"You mean to tell me you were fuckin' another bitch while I was gone? How could you do that to me?"

"You need to chill 'cause you're talkin' out the side of your neck right now! Don't you know that I love you? I would never cheat on you!"

"Fuck you, Victor, 'cause you're lying! Go and be with the bitch! I can't believe I fell for this shit again! I thought you fuckin' loved me!"

"I do!"

"No, you don't, but it's all good 'cause have no fear there are a million niggas waiting to take your spot! And if you leave this house don't think I'm gon' let you see this baby!" Mina shot, trying to hurt him as much as he was hurting her.

"Yo', I...will...fuckin'...kill you! Don't you ever come out your mouth like that to me again!"

"I hate you!"

"What? Say that again? You hate me? After all I've done for you?"

"Nah, nigga, after all I've done for you! I left everything I had to be with you! I'm living with you, carrying your baby, taking care of your daughter and you want to up and leave me for another bitch! I stayed wit your ass through it all! Even when you neglected to tell me about your child and dead wife I stayed wit you! But you know what, like I said, fuck you 'cause the next nigga will pick up where you left off!"

"I swear to God if you weren't pregnant with my baby I would beat the shit outta you for talkin' that shit to me!"

"Me getting beat ain't nothing new! Whatever! Like I said, leave!"

"Continue to talk that silly shit! I'm out!"

Seeing that he was really leaving, and never coming back, Mina instantly became insane with anger.

"So you're really gonna just leave me like this? You lied! You said you would never leave me! How could you do this to me?" Trying his best to ignore her cries for him, Victor headed down the steps. Right behind him, Mina followed. "I hate you!" she yelled repeatedly, hitting him in the back.

"Stop before you hurt yourself!" Victorheld her hands, trying to restrain her.

"I hate you! I hope you fuckin' die! You stupid bastard!"

"Look, Ma. Don't stress yourself. You've been through enough as it is."

"I have sacrificed my life for you! I could never just up and leave you like this!" Mina cried, holding onto his arm. "Why are you doing this to me?"

"Ma, you killing me here!"

"I'm killing you? You're killing me! I have never loved anybody the way I love you!"

"I gotta go." Victor shook his head, with tears welling in his eyes.

"What about the baby?"

"You know I'm gon' take care of mines."

"You ready, sir?" Armando asked.

"Yeah," Victor said, trying to leave again.

"I can't believe you are doing this to me! Why did you even fuckin' save me if you were just gonna leave me? You should've just left me there!" she continued to yell as Victor walked out the door. "It's that easy for you to leave me? Well, fuck you then! Leave!"

"Just remember this before you get with the next nigga. I'm not leaving you because I don't love you. I'm leaving you because I never want to put you or my child's life in danger again. So see if the next man you're wit is gonna care enough about you to do something like that," Victor said as he slammed the door behind him. Sliding down the door, Mina placed her head into her hands and cried until she couldn't cry anymore.

* * *

Two days passed by and Mina hadn't seen or heard from Victor. Being without him was worse than being kidnapped. At least then she still had him in her life. *How could this be happening to me?* she asked herself. Brandy's "It's Not Worth It" was on repeat.

You came into my life…And it's so funny…how you made everything right…And know your saying to me…Something ain't right…What did I do…Did I hurt you…Baby can you tell me…How to dry your eyes…But let me say…I never meant to make you cry…If anything I meant to…Be right by your side…How did I go wrong…When my love was strong…And all it ever wanted was you… Mina sang as she sat in bed, eating a bowl of Edys chocolate ice cream.

She picked up the phone for the umpteenth time that day and dialed Victor's cell phone. Letting it ring five times, she hung up once his voicemail kicked in. She couldn't believe he was doing her like that. Victor promised to never hurt or leave her and in one day he had done just that.

The more and more Mina thought about him leaving her, the madder she became. This was a time for celebration. She returned home safely and they were expecting their first child together. Instead she was laid up in bed alone, crying and feeling sorry for herself. It wasn't like she didn't understand his reason for leaving but everything he mentioned they could work through.

Ring...

Picking up the phone without looking at the caller ID, Mina prayed for it to be Victor.

"Hello?"

"Girl, what are you doing? We haven't heard from you since you got home," Mo asked.

"Victor left me," Mina cried into the phone.

"He did what?"

"He...left...me."

"Girl, stop crying we're on our way." Less than twenty minutes later, Mo and Delicious were on Mina's bed, consoling her. "Mina he's just confused right now, he'll be back," Mo assured.

"But I haven't talked to him since he left."

"Girl, you gotta give that man some time. Think about it. This is the second time this shit has happened to him. That would drive any man crazy to have his first wife be kidnapped and killed and then to turn around a couple of years later and have the same thing happen to his new woman. Girl, please, I would've left you too," Delicious retorted.

"Have you tried calling him?" Mo asked.

"Yes, but he won't pick up the phone."

"Didn't you say that Armando dropped him off where ever he's at?"

"Yes," Mina nodded.

"Ask him where he's at."

"Armando's not going to tell me anything. Whatever Victor says he does."

"Sounds like my kinda guy." Delicious snapped his fingers.

"There's got to be a way to find out where this nigga at," Mo replied thinking outloud. "By George, I think I got it!"

"What?" Mina and Delicious both questioned.

"You know Victor found out where you were being held by using the tracking device in your phone."

"No, I didn't know that."

"Yeah, he simply went on the Internet and tracked yo' ass down by locating where your phone was at."

"Hell naw ain't that some shit," Delicious shook his head.

Using the Internet, Mina found that Victor was at the Renaissance hotel in downtown St. Louis. Since Delicious was there, she had him to style her hair in her usually spiked hairstyle. After showering, applying her makeup and putting on a white spaghetti strapped Pea in a Pod maternity dress Mina was ready to reclaim her man. Thirty minutes later, she was at the hotel. Standing at the front desk, she asked for Victor's room number. He was in one of the presidential suites. Stepping off the elevator Mina was determined that she would be returning home with Victor. She placed her finger over the peephole and knocked twice.

"Who is it?"

"Room service," Mina replied, disguising her voice.

"I didn't order any room service," Victor said as he opened the door.

Shocked to find Mina on the other side of the door, Victor stood there not saying a word. Mina, too, couldn't find the words to speak. There he was, the man she was set to marry, wet, in nothing but a towel.

"I was right! You are fucking another bitch!"

"Is that what you came here for, to argue with me. Ain't no bitch up in here."

Looking past him, Mina saw that he was telling the truth. Focusing her attention back on him a jolt of electricity shot through her body as she eyed him. She couldn't figure out what she found most attractive, his arms, chest, or six pack. Each area seemed to be calling her name. If she didn't know any better she would have sworn that she had a mini orgasm. It had been far too long since she saw him naked. Finally he said, "What you doing here shorty?"

"I came to take you home."

"See you hard headed! What I tell you? It's over!"

"Whatever! It's not over until I say it's over," Mina yelled, bogarding her way into the room.

"I ain't got time for this, Ma! A nigga tired I ain't got no sleep! Just go home!"

"So you've been just as sick as I have?"

"I ain't gon' even front. I've been missing you like crazy."

"See."

"See nothing. You and me just ain't meant to be."

"How can you say that? We have loved each other since we were kids! We lost each other to find each other again! How many people can say that?"

"Don't you think I've thought about that? I think about that every day! But I will not, and I repeat will not, put you and my unborn child's life in danger! I love you but if keeping you safe means leaving you alone, then that's what I gotta do Ma!"

"Victor, I understand what you're saying but baby we can work this out." Mina gazed into his eyes taking his hand into hers.

"Look, Ma, I need some rest. Can we talk about this later?"

Victor took his hand away from her.

"No, we cannot talk about this later! I love you and you love me! That's all that matters! Yeah, I take the blame 'cause part of me getting kidnapped was my fault and I'm sorry! I'm sorry for making you worry! I'm sorry for making you cry! I'm sorry for everything! What more can I say besides I love you!" Mina yelled as tears fell from her eyes.

"Stop. You know I hate to see you cry. Just a give a nigga some time," Victor said as he wiped her eyes.

"I wish I could but I can't do that. I need you home with me and I'm not going to take no for an answer."

Not able to argue with that, Victor dropped his towel and walked past her, naked. Another jolt of electricity ripped through Mina as his tight, muscular body walked by. Victor's ten-inch dick swung from left to right, hitting his thigh with every strut. Not able to control herself, she grabbed him again before he could get dressed.

"I know you missed me as much as I missed you." She held onto his waist and whispered into his ear.

"Come on, Ma, I gotta get dressed," Victor groaned, staring at the ceiling.

"Look at me," Mina demanded. Staring down into her hazel brown eyes, Victor knew he couldn't fight it anymore. "I love you," she said.

"I love you, too," he said, taking a hold of her ass and lifting her up. Kissing each other passionately, Victor placed Mina onto the dresser. He lifted up her dress, pushed her moist thong to the side and played with her clit.

"Oh, baby, I missed you," Mina moaned.

Easing his way down, he pushed her thighs up and apart.He began to lightly circle his tongue across her clit. Victor watched as it twitched. He loved how her body responded to his every touch. Mina was in sheer heaven. The feel of Victor's tongue running across her clit caused her to cum immediately. Sucking her pussy, until every last drop of cum was in his mouth, Victor got up and carried her over to the bed.

Laying her body down, Victor massaged her thighs as he inserted his thick, hard, dick inside of her. The emptiness Mina had been feeling the past two days was instantly gone. It felt like Victor's dick reached all the way to her soul. Rotating his hips he pumped in and out of her while saying her name over and over again.

"Mina…. Shit…Damn, I love you…Mina…Mina."

Victor couldn't get enough of her. He pulled Mina down to the edge of the bed, then turned her over. This is what Mina had been waiting for. She loved it when he hit it from the back. Spreading her legs apart she leaned down onto the bed and arched her back. Gently inserting himself back into her, Victor held onto the sides of her waist while pumping hard but slow. He wanted to feel every stroke.

Mina bit her bottom lip, closed her eyes and relished the feel of his dick. In her eyes, nothing was better than make up sex. Digging in deep, Victor found her spot. Suddenly Mina started screaming and hollering talking about she was cumming.

"Bebe, Voy a cum!" (Baby, I'm gonna cum.)

"Vas a cum para mi?" (You gonna cum for me?)

"Yes Poppi!"

"Oh, Ma, don't call me Poppi."

"Poppi!"

"FUCK! I'm about to cum!"

"Yo tambien, bebe!" (Me, too, baby.)

Screaming each other's name, they both came at the same time. Exhausted beyond belief, Mina climbed up into the bed and laid down. Tired too, Victor climbed into bed and the couple spooned in each other's arms.

Holding her close to him, Victor whispered into Mina's ear, "I'm sorry. I promise I'll never leave you again."

"You better not."

"I promise I won't."

Epilogue

June 2, 2006, the day of Mina and Victor's wedding, finally arrived. In less than an hour Mina was about to walk down the aisle. The day couldn't have come soon enough. Mina's life couldn't have been better. Victor was still in the head of the cartel but there was nothing she could do about that. She was about to marry her childhood sweetheart, her son was born alive and healthy, and she had her shop back. What more could she ask for?

Andrew was in jail on kidnapping and abuse charges. Once the public found out about Andrew, Carol Leverly beat Mr. Wellington with a landslide vote for Governor of Missouri. Shortly after voting day, Mr. Wellington suffered a nervous breakdown. With Mr. Wellington in a mental hospital and her only child in jail, Mrs. Wellington sunk into a deep depression, causing her alcohol problem to spiral further out of control.

But Mina could care less about the Wellingtons. Today was to be the happiest day of her life. Everyone she loved was there to show their support. Her entire family, as well as Victor's, were in attendance. It was a beautiful June day and Mina couldn't have been happier. Gaining a lot of weight she postponed the wedding until she regained her old figure.

Standing in front of a full-length mirror, in a light robe, Mina watched as Delicious fingered her hair. Unlike most brides, Mina opted to wear her hair short with no veil. Her makeup was immaculate and her nails and feet were perfectly done. Hearing her baby cry, she stopped to go and calm him down.

"Hey, Momma's baby," Mina cooed as she took her four-month-old son, Jose, from the nanny MaKayla's arms. Jose looked just like his father. He possessed the same olive skin, jet black hair and piercing eyes. The only resemblance to Mina was his hazel brown eyes. Rocking him back in forth in her arms until his little eyes closed shut, Mina put him down.

"Girl, you better come on here or you're going to be late for your own wedding," Mo warned.

"Okay, here I come." Mina hated being away from her son.

He was her pride and joy. Taking one last look at him, she handed him back to the nanny. Stepping into her $10,000 ivory, v-necked, sleeveless, satin Vera Wang dress, tears filled Mina's eyes. It was really happening; she was going to marry the man of her dreams. Zipped up and fully dressed, everyone stood and stared at her. Mina was absolutely beautiful.

"It's time," Smokey said, poking his head through the door.

The wedding was held at Victor and Mina's house. It made no sense for them to have it anywhere else. Their backyard was the size of a baseball field and they had one of the prettiest gardens on the block.Hundreds of golden tulips and white roses filled the yard.

A hundred chairs with white satin covers were aligned in

place. Baby's Breath flowers and vines decorated the arch under which Mina and Victor would recite their vows. The guests piled in, took their seats and awaited Mina's big entrance. Looking over her bridesmaids, who consisted of Mo, Tiffany, Janiya, Neosha, Jodie and Nay, she smiled. They all looked so beautiful. Each of them wore bronze colored, dropped waist, satin dresses and their bouquets were made up of golden calla lilies. Even Rita and Bernice looked nice. They, too, were dressed in bronze colored dresses.

Peeking outside, Mina could see Victor, Rico, Victor's cousin Hector, Uncle Chester, Smokey and Delicious. Fixing Lelah's dress, Mina kissed her on the forehead and led her to the door. She looked so cute in her flower girl dress. Hugging the girls one last time, she watched as they all descended down the steps. Locking arms with her father Mina tried her best to fight back the tears. Hearing the orchestra cue the wedding march, Mina kissed her father on the cheek.

"You ready?" Ed asked Mina as he held her arm in his.

"As ready as I'll ever be." Mina gushed.

"I love you, Mina, and even though I don't approve of what Victor does for a living, I still love you and give you my blessing."

"Thanks, Daddy. I love you, too. I promise you have nothing to worry about. He's gonna take good care of me."

Before leaving out, Mina applied one more coat of lip gloss. She smiled in the mirror. She knew she looked fabulous.

Mina could hardly wait to make the trek down to the altar. Seeing Mina walk down the steps in her gown caused Victor to break down. She had never looked more beautiful. Once they reached the arch that was in the middle of the yard, the preacher asked, "Who giveth this woman to marry this man?"

"I do," Ed smiled, hugging his baby girl one last time.

"And I do, too," Rita added.

The ceremony lasted about fifteen minutes. When the preacher said, "You may now kiss your bride," Victor took Mina into his arms and kissed her for what seemed like an eternity. After taking pictures in the garden and under the arch they danced their first dance, which was to Faith Evans "Tru Love" as a married couple on the custom made dance floor Victor had built just for the occasion.

"It's true love...When you say you need me like I need you...And you can't be without me...Like I can't be without you...It's true love...When we spend time talking on the phone...'Cause when we're not around each other...We don't want to be alone...It's true love, love, love, love...Don't you know that it's good to be in love, love, love, love...Just believe me truthfully cause...Love...Is never ever making you cry...Before I tell you a lie...I'll give my life...'Cause that's true love," Mina sang into Victor's ear as they swayed together on the dance floor.

As they sat at the head table together, holding hands, they gazed into each other's eyes. They had a wishing well wedding so throughout the reception, people were coming up to them with congratulations and giving them envelopes filled with money.

Suddenly a baritone voice spoke up that Mina didn't recognize. "I know twenty g's is like chump change to a nigga like you, but here you go anyway. Congratulations, homey!"

"I know that ain't my nigga Black!" Victor stood up, giving him dap.

"You know I had to come support my man."

"Good looking out, dog. Yo', this my wife, Mina. Mina, this is my boy Black. "Nice to meet you," Mina spoke with her eyes fixated on the girl with him. Except for the height and weight difference they looked just alike. The girl was caramel, with hazel-green eyes and long black hair flowed down her back.

"Nice to meet you too, Ma."

"So, baby, how do you two know each other?" Mina questioned Victor.

"I use to be Black's connect."

"Yeah, those were the good ol' days," Black laughed. Suddenly the girl with him playfully hit him in the chest. "What? I'm just playing," he continued to laugh. "Before she kills me, this is my wife, Meesa."

"Hello," Meesa greeted the newlyweds, all the while eyeing Mina up and down.

"Is it just me, or do they look just like alike?" Black raised his eyebrow in a quizzical manner.

"It ain't just you. I'm peepin' the same thing," Victor agreed.

"Is it really you?" Mina questioned.

"I'm sorry. I don't know what you mean." Meesa sounded confused.

"I can't believe you're here."

"Is she all right?" Meesa asked Victor.

"Baby, what's wrong with you? You're scaring the damn girl."

"You don't remember?"

"Remember what?"

"The picture."

"Oh shit!"

"What picture?" Meesa asked, becoming annoyed.

"My father Ed has a picture of you. Meesa, I don't know how to tell you this but...you're my sister."

ORDER FORM

Triple Crown Publications
2959 Stelzer Rd.
Columbus, Oh 43219

Name: _____

Address: _____

City/State: _____

Zip: _____

TITLES	PRICES
Dime Piece	$15.00
Gangsta	$15.00
Let That Be The Reason	$15.00
A Hustler's Wife	$15.00
The Game	$15.00
Black	$15.00
Dollar Bill	$15.00
A Project Chick	$15.00
Road Dawgz	$15.00
Blinded	$15.00
Diva	$15.00
Sheisty	$15.00
Grimey	$15.00
Me & My Boyfriend	$15.00
Larceny	$15.00
Rage Times Fury	$15.00
A Hood Legend	$15.00
Flipside of The Game	$15.00
Menage's Way	$15.00

SHIPPING/HANDLING (Via U.S. Media Mail)   **$3.95**

TOTAL   **$_____**

FORMS OF ACCEPTED PAYMENTS:
Postage Stamps, Institutional Checks & Money Orders, all mail in orders take 5-7
Business days to be delivered.

ORDER FORM

Triple Crown Publications
2959 Stelzer Rd.
Columbus, Oh 43219

Name: _____

Address: _____

City/State: _____

Zip: _____

	TITLES	PRICES
	Still Sheisty	$15.00
	Chyna Black	$15.00
	Game Over	$15.00
	Cash Money	$15.00
	Crack Head	$15.00
	For The Strength of You	$15.00
	Down Chick	$15.00
	Dirty South	$15.00
	Cream	$15.00
	Hoodwinked	$15.00
	Bitch	$15.00
	Stacy	$15.00
	Life	$15.00
	Keisha	$15.00
	Mina's Joint	$15.00
	How To Succeed in The Publishing Game	$20.00

SHIPPING/HANDLING (Via U.S. Media Mail)   **$3.95**

TOTAL $_____

FORMS OF ACCEPTED PAYMENTS:
Postage Stamps, Institutional Checks & Money Orders, all mail in orders take 5-7
Business days to be delivered